MY MIND IS NOT YOURS

Welcome to Tarot Tori City

ELIOT D. ESPARZA

Book Nebula

ISBN: 979-8-9852329-2-9

My Mind Is Not Yours

Welcome to Tarot Tori City

CONTENTS

ACKNOWLEDGMENTS

Thank you to my brother Victor for all the background support he gave me during my time writing.

Thank you, Willowbarq, for the commissioned illustrations on pages 61, 143, 213, and 277.
All other Illustrations were drawn by Eliot D. Esparza.
All rights reserved.

Many thanks to Bianca Orellana. I cannot thank her enough for proofreading my manuscript. Her feedback and encouragement were the words I needed to hear.

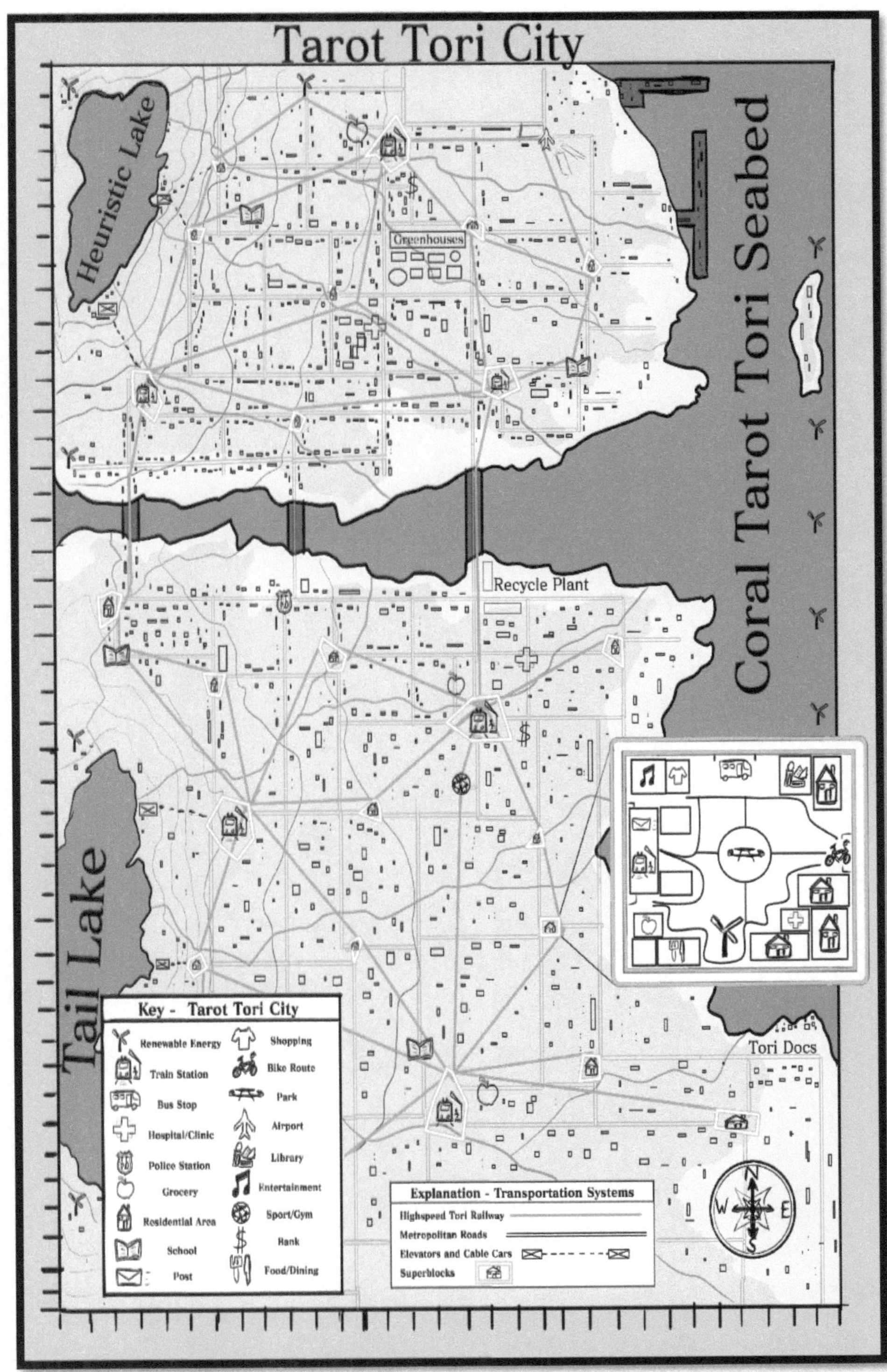
Tarot Tori City
Heuristic Lake
Greenhouses
Coral Tarot Tori Seabed
Recycle Plant
Tail Lake
Tori Docs
Key - Tarot Tori City
Renewable Energy
Shopping
Train Station
Bike Route
Bus Stop
Park
Hospital/Clinic
Airport
Police Station
Library
Grocery
Entertainment
Residential Area
Sport/Gym
School
Bank
Post
Food/Dining
Explanation - Transportation Systems
Highspeed Tori Railway
Metropolitan Roads
Elevators and Cable Cars
Superblocks
N
W
E
S

ACT 1
TAROT TORI GATE

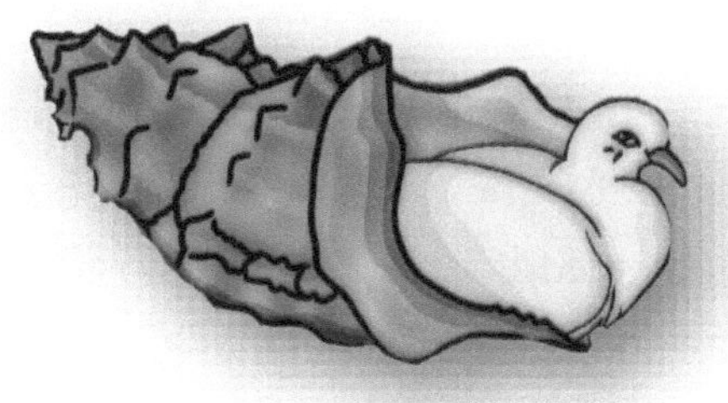

ONE
THE TRADE

EMERGENCY ROOM
JUNE 3ᴿᴰ X281

The old man quietly died in his seat. The only one who noticed was a seven-year-old girl named Florian Lilly Cobblestone.

An hour earlier, Florian and her family had rushed to the hospital. She sat in the back seat of the car with her mother as her father drove quickly. Her mother was writhing in pain. A dog, an iguana, and a teddy bear sat in the passenger seat, stressed all the same.

Florian was a short kid with black hair, a faded pink jacket, and tattered jeans.

"The lizard is laying an egg!" Florian said.

"Not now!" her father said.

Florian realized the severity of the situation from her father's expression. She adjusted her glasses and leaned her head against her mother's shoulder. The iguana and the dog stared.

Arriving at the emergency room, Florian froze. Nurses opened the car door with arms covered in veins, stone, and talons, grasping Florian's mother and placing her in a wheelchair. Standing tall at the nurses' sides were creatures at the ready, stained with blood. One covered in rubble and debris pushed the wheelchair. The other beast had hair falling out—its thin skin and veins were visible. It coiled its meaty arms around Florian's mother, embracing her head and stomach.

"Wait. . ." Florian could barely utter the words as her heart sank at the sight of the monstrosities. She scurried out of the car, clutching her teddy bear. She could only watch as they escorted her mother away.

The iguana hopped out of the car, eager to follow its owner.

"No, not you too? Please don't go," Florian said.

The iguana looked back at Florian. It nodded, almost as if reassuring her.

The nurses moved efficiently, admitting her mother into the hospital. The iguana followed, not too far behind the wheelchair.

Florian turned to her father. "Dad, don't let them take Mom."

"Mom will be just fine. They will take good care of her."

Florian, at eye level with her father's dog, noticed its tail wag calmly. Florian's gut told her to trust her father's words. The two held hands as they entered the hospital.

The emergency room was filled with a murky haze, chock full of people who were sick or injured. Patients, each next to beasts, were waiting in turn, coughing, snarling, bleeding, bruised, moaning, or gasping.

The air made Florian quiver as she clung to her father.

"Dad, what're those?" Florian asked.

"Those are patients, Flo. Let's find a seat, shall we?"

"You can't see them?" But Florian was talking only to herself.

Mangled beasts moaned in pain. A hunched camel covered in embers and ash lay alongside a woman facing the floor. A bird was missing one of its wings. A pig with an exposed bone stood next to a man in a wheelchair. By the entrance, a glaring wolf guarded the door. Slipping through the walls was a large bony tail swaying from one side of the room to the other. A haze spewed from the head of a dried-out horned eel lying motionless on the floor. Dying slowly, the animals cried in agony. Florian couldn't avoid the internal screams. She'd never seen this many gathered in one place. So many, they bled through the walls. So many, she couldn't identify which belonged to whom.

Except for one pair sitting alone. An old man, sound asleep, bundled up in layers of dirty old tattered clothing. He had a gray beard, eyes tucked in his skull, and was foul-smelling. Next to him was a giant conch with claws that drooped out from inside. Slime spewed outward from its cracking shell, crumbling slowly, as if no longer safe for what was inside.

Florian and her father sat a few rows in front of him. The dog sat beside them.

Florian didn't utter a word as she stared at the beasts. She wrapped herself in her jacket and tucked her head away. Peeking every now and then, she checked on her father.

"Flo, what's the matter?" her father asked as they were surrounded by ghouls.

Florian remained silent. She just stared at her father with his peaceful smile.

"What's wrong? You can tell me." He hugged his pink jacket-wrapped burrito daughter.

Florian let out a slight groan. She peeked through the jacket to see her father and all the other creatures staring back. Shrouded, they scurried around. They silently crept closer with concern. She pulled away from her father's grip and huddled in the corner of the emergency room.

Her father didn't say anything. The dog followed Florian and curled up next to her, never leaving her side.

The creatures soon loomed about once again, following the patients and nurses around the hospital.

Florian closed her eyes and clutched her teddy bear. She could hear a faint whisper from the sleeping old man.

"I'm a citizen of Tarot Tori City." The old man shivered.

Florian opened her eyes and turned to the old man sitting a dozen seats away.

"I'm a citizen of Tarot Tori City," he whispered again, eyes closed, talking in his sleep.

The five-foot conch next to him shook and trembled. The bony claws fell to the floor, detached from what was inside, and started evaporating.

"I'm a citizen of Tarot Tori City." The last of his words leaked out as he became stiff. The conch cracked in two and evaporated.

The old man quietly died in his seat. No one noticed, except for Florian, witnessing his final words.

Florian ran to her father. She covered her head with her jacket and trembled. Her father and the dog reassured her everything was fine.

A few hours passed.

"Wake up, Flo. We can see Mom now. Come on," Florian's father said.

The old man behind them, along with the conch split in two, was no longer there.

Florian was half-asleep as she followed her father. His dog was a step ahead of them, almost as if leading the way.

Fangs protruded from the floor and ceiling. Jowls engulfed the entire hallway. The walls salivated and parasitically pulsated against each person walking through. An unwelcome territory.

Florian stopped before entering the salivating corridor. Already deep inside, her father and his dog led the way without hesitation. Anxious not to get left behind, Florian stepped over the rows of teeth. She splashed through the puddles of drool and ran to her father.

"There is nothing to be afraid of," he said.

As Florian walked down the hallway with her father, she witnessed many people and creatures. She passed rooms with silent patients, hollering patients, and sleeping patients. She covered her ears and marched along with her father.

Florian cautiously headed toward her mother's room, descending deeper in the bowel full of monsters.

She walked past a blood-covered possum, a stern doctor, a hissing shark, a bandaged horse, a man with crutches, and a padded beaver.

They stopped at a giant jellyfish engulfing an elevator. Inside, a nurse was holding the door for the family to board.

Her father entered the jellyfish and pressed the elevator button. Florian stopped in her tracks.

"Come on. What's the matter?"

Florian wanted to see her mother, no matter what. She stared at the wall of jelly and slowly stepped forward. Closing her eyes, Florian jumped to her father.

She didn't open her eyes until they exited the elevator.

☎೮ಚ

They arrived at her mother's room.

"See, Mom is just fine."

Florian's mother was in bed, holding something. Florian stepped closer.

At that moment, everything else didn't matter.

"What's wrong? Surprised? Will you help me protect her forever?" Florian's mother asked.

It was a baby—a little sister. She was tiny, delicate, silent, and heavenly. She was wrapped in a blanket, cradled in her mother's arms.

"Her name is Hope," her mother said.

A faint chirping sound came from the baby. Florian inspected the baby, and within its small grasp was an egg slowly cracking open. A pure white dove poked its head out from the egg. The eggshell split in two, sprinkling out of the baby's hand, disappearing as it fell. Wings sprouted, transparent, flapping and stretching. Its beak opened wide calmly, innocently, and it held a gentle gaze.

Florian hesitated for a moment. On its tail was a seashell. The seashell was giant enough for the dove to take refuge, much like the old man with the conch shell who had died in the waiting room.

The baby didn't cry. It remained sound asleep.

First, there was an iguana, a dog, and now a seashell dove.

That day, Florian lost her teddy bear but found her little sister.

☯☊☋

Meanwhile, at the Tarot Tori City Airport, the mayor of Tarot Tori City, William Rite Banquet, opened the airport security room door with a bright, exciting smile.

"Oh, sorry about detaining you. It won't happen again."

In his early thirties, Mayor Banquet, blond and tall with a slim build, wore a green suit with not a single wrinkle. He walked with confidence, and his smile was welcoming yet somewhat stoic.

"You see, when I heard you were arriving in Tarot Tori City, I just had to meet you in person. Believe it or not, I'm a huge fan of your work."

Mayor Banquet shook the hand of the mysterious detainee. Smirking yet somewhat smug.

"Just kidding. Oh, don't worry; I'm honored you have taken an interest in this peaceful sanctuary for ghosts. Of course, haha, speaking figuratively."

The detainee was not amused and remained silent.

"Jokes aside, this city is definitely a humble one. Please allow me. I, as mayor, welcome you to Tarot Tori City. You might think that's Territory City, but it's spelled T-a-r-o-t, like the deck of cards, and T-o-r-i, which holds many architectural and botanical meanings. It also means bird in another language. This city is growing, soaring to new heights if you will."

The mayor's bravado didn't falter. It, in fact, intensified with every hand gesture. Mayor Banquet bowed slightly.

"Please enjoy the lovely sights of the most efficient city in the world. In less than two generations, we minimized its ecological footprint and maximized its efficiency. This city is leading the world in every category of infrastructure, economy, optimized power sources, transportation, education, and health care. Also, who could forget the low crime rate? Haha."

Mayor Banquet paused and checked his phone. Only news like this would break this man's speech.

"It's a shame. We just lost one of our oldest beloved citizens this afternoon. He'll be missed. I'll pay my respects properly when I get the chance."

The detainee didn't utter a word.

The mayor rechecked his phone. "On a brighter note, it seems we have a new resident besides you. The hospital reported another healthy newborn. Isn't it just great! So many new citizens in one day!"

The detainee stood up.

Security immediately rushed into the room, barking orders.

"Now, now, everyone. Settle down."

The detainee only glared at the mayor with his deep demonic eyes.

"What's that? How did I know you weren't just a sightseer? I'm the mayor, after all. I love this city. A little too much."

The detainee slowly sat back down. Security exited the room soon after.

"I have just one rule before you are free to go. Not a single soul. If I lose a single citizen connected to you in any way, I'll get distracted." Mayor Banquet clapped his hands just once. "Now that's settled, have fun. I'm so excited. Don't forget to play nice with your new neighbors."

Mayor Banquet left with a brighter smile than he had brought with him.

TWO
MOTHERING HEN

COBBLESTONE HOUSEHOLD
JUNE 24TH X281

The baby's cry made the house silent.

Florian Lilly Cobblestone was now an older sister to Hope Cobblestone. Hope was healthy; however, not a single peep could be heard when she let out a cry. She had been born mute.

Her parents were unsure what to do at first but were busier than ever. After consulting specialists, many changes had to happen fast.

Since the infant did not have a voice to let out a cry, the Cobblestone family had to concentrate on the baby's body language. That meant someone had to monitor Hope constantly to make sure her needs were being met. If Hope was hungry, she could not cry. If she needed a diaper change, the smell was the only identifier. If she woke up while everyone else was asleep, no one would even notice.

Florian had an easier time understanding Hope. It was as if she could see things others couldn't.

However, seeing Hope and her seashell dove reminded Florian of the old man with the conch crab and all the other creatures. She couldn't get it out of her mind. All this time, she had thought the animals at everyone's sides were pets. What she saw at the hospital went beyond pets.

The conch crab next to the old man faded right before her eyes, and not a single person reacted to the monsters roaming about. Even her own father thought she just had an overactive imagination.

Florian found comfort in writing down the event. She drew as many of the creatures as she could since no two were alike. It was fun for her and calming. She understood the animals better after drawing them. She drew many pictures of Hope as well. She analyzed her sister every day.

Naturally, Florian's parents kept checking on her. They didn't know what to say; Florian drew strange things.

School for Florian felt different. As usual, Florian's classmates had their pets. However, Florian's body began to feel numb. Everyone's regular activities made Florian dizzy. Overwhelmed, she soon put her head on the desk and shut everyone out. Lost in thought.

One of the other kids next to Florian called out to her. "Florian? What's wrong?"

"She's tired. Leave her alone."

"Flori, you can call me a bat girl like you always do."

"Yeah, Flori, the teacher will get angry with you. Wake up."

"Leave Florian alone, monkey boy. She's tired."

"Really? See what you did, Flori. Your stupid nicknames are sticking."

"What's with the nicknames anyway, and why am I bore boy?" a boy with a boar said.

Florian never cared to remember names. She just named people based on their pets. She could only tell people apart by the creature beside them.

"That is just what Flori does." The children accepted this but not so much the adults.

As the teacher passed out sheets of paper, the class settled down.

"Good morning, class. Today we will be doing something rather different. Last week we looked at photos of animals and wrote down what words best described them and what they were doing. Today, we are going to decide which animal best represents you."

One of Florian's classmates raised his hand. "Like a spirit animal?"

"Yes, exactly, like a spirit animal." The teacher nodded.

This caught Florian's attention. She sprang up and, without waiting to be called on, asked, "What is a spirit animal?"

"Excellent question. A spirit animal is an animal that best represents you. Like a symbol that best shares what kind of person you are."

"Like a pet?" another student asked.

"It can be any animal. A pet, like a dog, or not a pet like a lion, or even an extinct dinosaur. What do you want your inner self to be? Start with thinking about your favorite animal. What does the animal do, and how does it do it? Are you like this animal or any of the descriptions we listed?" The teacher showed the class the activity they had done last week and the lists of words they had gathered.

Florian felt wide awake at that point. She realized what she was actually seeing.

Florian looked around and observed all the animals among her classmates.

The monkey boy, boar boy, and bat girl sitting at her table were calm and collected along with their corresponding pet. Every classmate was deep in thought, along with their animal. As if they were connected.

"What is your spirit animal?" bat girl asked the teacher.

"My spirit animal is a swan. I love lakes, and I want to fly with beauty and elegance." The teacher presented herself as a ballerina.

"No way, your spirit animal is most likely a bookworm," monkey boy said, causing the class to burst out with laughter.

"All right, trouble table, that's enough. Everyone! Let's get back to choosing your spirit animals, and we will share them with the class." The teacher steered everyone back on track.

Florian gazed at what was right in front of her. *A swan . . . My teacher said she wanted to have a swan as her spirit animal. She wasn't too far off.*

As the teacher assisted the class, her pet extended its wings and spread its feathers over the kids one at a time. The span of its wings could cover a whole desk. A few of its brown feathers floated around the classroom, nesting themselves on each kid's head. Florian's head too.

Florian tried to touch the feather, but it was stuck to her hair. She was getting frustrated. She tugged and pulled relentlessly. Florian rushed to the closest pair of scissors and snipped away.

The monkey boy and his monkey just stared at Florian with their jaws dropped as Florian struggled for a bit. The teacher promptly confiscated the scissors from Florian.

"Don't do anything that might hurt you, okay." The teacher pecked Florian on the cheek, and so did the teacher's pet, leaving another feather stuck to Florian's head.

Her pet was not an elegant swan but was, in fact, a chicken. A motherly brown hen, teaching her chicks.

The other kids kept working, laughing and talking about each other's choices. Everyone else couldn't see the chicken or any of the other animals. All this time, Florian had thought they were pets.

Now she realized all the animals she could see were actually spirit animals. She couldn't touch them but clearly remembered petting a few of them. Maybe some real pets had been mixed in, like the neighbor's cat and the dogs at the park.

Florian pulled out her personal journal and flipped to a new page.

"Flori. What did you choose for a spirit animal?" the bat girl asked. "I chose a butterfly."

Florian looked the bat girl in the eyes and then at the top of her head. The bat was still sleeping in her hair. "I think your spirit animal should be a bat," Florian said.

"A-a-a bat? I'm scared of bats; I don't like them." Bat girl's eyes watered. The bat in her hair squeaked.

"Sorry, I didn't mean it," Florian said. *Why doesn't she like bats? Her spirit animal in her hair is literally a bat.*

"It's okay. Batgirl isn't afraid of bats. Batgirl isn't afraid of bats. Batgirl isn't afraid of bats," bat girl mumbled.

"Flori! I chose the best animal in the world. The lion. What's yours?" the monkey boy asked.

The monkey boy had also gotten it wrong.

Florian stared at her open journal. *What about mine? What is my spirit animal?*

Florian couldn't think of anything else because all she could think about was why she couldn't see her own spirit animal. She would always beg her parents for a pet when everyone else had one. Now she questioned why she didn't have a spirit animal.

Florian realized she had a lot of work to do. She started a new page in her journal, writing "Test 1" as the title.

If she could see spirit animals, how did that explain what she had seen at the hospital? She had a mission to investigate what she was actually seeing.

THREE
TRIAL & ERROR

WEST TORI PARK
JUNE 26TH X281

Florian prepared to conduct her experiments. She was ready with her list of tests and tasks compiled in her journal.

Each day she planned every experiment carefully to solve all of her questions.

Are these really spirits?

What do these spirit animals do?

What do they mean?

Are they really connected in some way to their owner?

How can I distinguish between real animals and spirit animals?

What happened to the old man and his spirit at the hospital?

Day one. The first test.

Florian grabbed a fist full of rocks and chucked them at the first animal in her sights.

"Florian, stop throwing rocks or else we are going home!" her mother yelled, ending the first test altogether.

Florian moved on to test number two: observe every move the animals make.

She examined her parents' spirit animals.

Her father had a dog that sat upright most of the time. Whenever Florian upset her father, the dog's ears would dart back and forth and it would stand on its hind legs as if it were looking for her. Its fur would change color slightly, and its tail would stop wagging whenever he spoke to her mother.

Florian noticed the kids didn't have animals that could change color. Would her spirit animal look like her father's spirit animal?

They both had black hair and brown eyes. They both liked pizza and always made her mother worry.

She took notes and drew the spirit animal of her father in her journal.

The spirit animal of Florian's mother was an iguana with a mane of fur around its neck. The iguana would sometimes even purr whenever Florian's father was nearby.

Florian stared intensely at the iguana. Florian's mother stared back. The iguana's eyes darted back and forth as its tongue wiped its eyes clean. When Florian's mother talked to other people, the lizard's mouth would expand and bloat up.

Florian wondered if her spirit animal was anything like her mother's.

☮☯

Day two. Test number three: touch the bat on bat girl's head.

If I can't feel it, then it really is a spirit animal.

Florian tailed the bat girl all over the park. When bat girl finally sat down, Florian snuck up on her. The bat was sound asleep, clinging to the top of her head. It was small, but its ears were massive compared to its head.

The frail bat squeaked as if it were yawning. Florian quickly regretted choosing bat girl, thinking the bat was too gross to touch. She grabbed a stick and tried poking it.

The bat girl fled to her parents.

಩ಳ

Day three. Test number four.

"Don't move, monkey boy," Florian said.

"Do you even know my real name?"

Florian threw a ball at the monkey standing right beside the boy. With this test, she could figure out if the monkey was real or not. *If I throw something at a spirit, it should go right through it.*

The boy instinctively moved away from the ball. The monkey followed suit.

"Where were you aiming? That was nowhere near me. You're not that good at dodgeball, are you?" the monkey boy said.

"I wasn't aiming for you," Florian said.

"Yeah, right, Flori. No one else is playing."

"I told you not to move."

"Now it's my turn." He picked up the ball.

"Wait. . ." *This wasn't part of my plan.*

The monkey boy pushed up his sleeve. The boy's monkey also wound up its arm. The monkey threw something toward Florian. She ducked, but the object the monkey threw went right through her head. She didn't feel a thing. The ball smacked her right in the face.

"Are you all right? The ball is soft, so it shouldn't hurt too much," monkey boy said.

The monkey had thrown something at Florian right where the ball had hit her. Directly where the monkey boy was aiming. They were connected. Some of their actions mirrored each other. Or rather, the spirit animal did the actions slightly earlier. Florian had never witnessed anything like it or at least never noticed it until that moment.

"What're you doing? I'm bored." The monkey boy turned around and walked in the direction of the other kids. However, the monkey spirit animal stayed behind and stared at Florian.

Now it was the opposite. This time the monkey wasn't copying what the monkey boy was doing. Florian couldn't wrap her head around it.

"Hey, aren't you coming?" The monkey boy turned around and waved his hand. The monkey approached Florian, and she got a closer look at it. The monkey was not brown but light tan. Its face was expressive, and it grinned brightly. It looked concerned as it looked up at Florian.

Florian reached her hand out to pet it, but her fingers passed right through it.

"Monkey boy," Florian called out to him.

"Are you done talking to your imaginary friend?" he asked.

"What's your name?"

"Are you going to remember it this time, Flori?"

"I'm Florian Lilly Cobblestone. What is your name?"

"For the millionth time, I am Alex. Alexander Rodriguez . . . and I know you are going to forget it."

"Alex, do you have any pets?" Florian asked.

"I have a hamster at my dad's house," Alex said.

"The guy with the elephant with the small ears is your father, right? And your mother is the lady with the octopus hair, right?"

"Okay, now I know you're making fun of me," Alex said.

Florian ran off to the other kids. "Bat girl," Florian called out. "What's your name?"

"My name? You can still call me Batgirl. I don't mind."

"I want to know your real name."

"Oh, it's Amalia Simmers." She smiled.

"Do you have any pets, Amalia?"

"No, I don't have any," Amalia said as the bat on her head squeaked.

Florian continued asking for names. She forgot some along the way, but she asked again and again. If she asked them if they had any pets and they said "it's right here," the animal was genuine and not a spirit animal.

Everyone has a spirit animal but me. The words echoed in the back of Florian's mind.

Almost every animal with a person was a spirit animal. A few dogs and squirrels got in the mix, but Florian recognized the grown-ups had strange animals. The adult spirit animals had abnormalities that felt utterly random.

"Alex's dad? Do you have any pets?"

"Hello, Florian. Are you having fun with my kids? They have soccer practice, so we'll be leaving soon," he said.

"Do you have any pets!? Do you have any pets!? Do you have any pets!?"

"What?! I can't really hear that well. Can you speak up?" The elephant with the small ears. Florian started to get it.

"Florian, stop yelling at people, and stop asking people if they have any pets! It doesn't matter how many people you ask. We won't get you any pets if you keep acting this way!" Florian's mother hollered.

"What's she doing this time?" Amalia asked.

"Who knows? She always wanders off to do her own thing," Alex said as they were making some observations of their own.

☙❧

Day four. Test number five.

Florian pieced things together using her own terms throughout her journal. Most in crayons and doodles. She concluded these were definitely spirits. The spirit animals were part of the person they accompanied. Their spirit was a physical manifestation of a person's true self, and their actions could somewhat mirror their owner. To distinguish between real animals and spirit animals, most spirit animals had abnormalities or just straight didn't belong in a city. In Florian's eyes, all of the animals and creatures were spirits. But she could ask, "Do you have any pets?" Any answer would identify what was in Florian's vision.

The last question. What happened to the old man and his spirit at the hospital?

Sometimes the adult spirit animals tended to hide until they interacted with someone, but the kid spirits never disappeared. Grown-ups spirits tended to show themselves when the adults were speaking to someone.

The old man's soul, the conch crab, didn't just disappear but cracked and crumbled to pieces. If a person dies . . . then their spirit would also die.

She remembered the slime leaking out of the conch crab and its limbs falling off. *So the old man really did die.*

Florian noticed a spirit missing a limb was following a man jogging along the waterway. She was worried. The man's spirit was not an animal. It looked almost human. The creature had long bony limbs. Its skull had a swirling spike pointing straight up. No eyes, mouth, or face, yet it tilted its head upward toward the sky as if looking at the clouds passing by. It made muffled screaming noises as it ran with the jogger.

What animal is it? Is it even an animal? Can spirits take the form of something other than an animal? Like the other adults. Some souls had jumbled limbs or weird changes.

She was scared, yet a far greater fear was consuming her. The spirit was missing a leg and was making painful noises in agony. She was more worried about the jogger. *Is the man going to die too?*

Florian took a deep breath and approached the jogging man. He turned toward her and made eye contact.

A frail arm took shape from the back of the jogger. As if in a struggle, the arm squirmed and pulled itself against the ground. Clawing at the pavement, the spirit stood up, taller than the six-foot jogger.

It stood straight up facing the sky and let out a muffled scream.

22

My Mind Is Not Yours: Welcome to Tarot Tori City

FOUR
TIRED SOLDIER

WEST TORI PARK
JUNE 29TH X281

Wake up.
Warm-up.

05:00 Jog
06:00 Breakfast, hygiene, suit up
08:00 Mon–Fri Work shift
08:00 Sat/Sun Clinic appointment
11:30 Mon–Fri Lunch (Sat/Sun) Light jog, lunch in park

Every day since his first deployment, Sergeant Nowell followed his routine systematically without question. Manners, cleanliness, and order were drilled into his life and body. Buzzcut dark gray hair, a stern face at every angle, tan skin, and a trimmed gray beard were all notable features. As of that day, he was a veteran at the age of thirty-nine.

Or at least he tried to. Tarot Tori City had changed entirely during the time he was deployed. The roads had changed, the buildings had changed, even the people had changed. He had been abroad for fourteen years, and his hometown had become the fastest developed city in the world.

ॐ

About six months ago, when the sergeant finally came home, he checked his saved-up earnings from active duty.

"A hundred sixty-eight thousand flex spending? What's this?" Sergeant Nowell asked the bank teller.

"That is your flex spending balance that will expire in thirty days. Since you've been abroad for fourteen years for military service, your monthly one thousand dollar flex spending balance stacked every cycle until the day you returned. Don't worry; that's separate from your savings and checking account," the teller said.

"Hold on, what? I get a thousand dollars a month?"

"It's flex spending. Credit that can be used on anything in Tarot Tori City. However, it refreshes to a balance of one thousand every thirty days."

"So I get paid to stay in this city?"

"Incorrect. If you visit the Tarot Tori City medical center once a month and are a resident of this city, you will get the one thousand dollar credit. Since active-duty soldiers are required to keep up with their physical health, you were exempt from the required monthly medical center visits. Schedule a check-up every month to guarantee your balance refreshes to one thousand the following month."

"What the—? Do I need to sign my soul to the medical center or something?"

"Nope, all medical visits are absolutely free unless severe medical treatment is required. My uncle even used his flex spending on the surgery he needed. I just use mine on food expenses."

"So Tarot Tori City is paying me to stay here and be healthy?"

"I never thought of it that way, but yeah, that's basically it."

"A hundred sixty-eight thousand to spend in one month?"

Sergeant Nowell felt conflicted as he made an appointment at the medical center. Nowell thought this was all a dream. Yet he used the money on a condo within the city limits. He had never dreamed of owning his own place.

The same day Sergeant Nowell moved in, he received a housewarming gift with a handwritten note attached.

Thank you for your service, and welcome to your new home.

Sincerely,

Mayor William Rite Banquet

The gift included a brochure that introduced new residents to the city. Mayor Banquet's face was plastered right on the front.

Flipping through it, Nowell noticed it strangely included job listings and minimum wage prices. He crumpled up the brochure and chuckled. He batted the basket of gifts to the floor and stomped the handwritten note. His laugh turned into a sob. His fist turned into a tissue.

"Are you kidding me? Are you making fun of me?" Sergeant Nowell clutched his right leg. "Do you know what I've been through? I sacrificed everything. You rebuilt my home. I devoted my life, and you shove this in my face. Are you telling me my sacrifices were for nothing? Are you nudging me to quit the armed service? Why is the minimum wage double my salary in this city?"

∞

Sergeant Nowell tried to jog the same path he did when he was younger. He used to follow the creek that strayed right through the city. Now it was a clean aqueduct, with tiny water mill generators every few blocks. He continued, reaching the Tarot Tori Central Park.

Not much farther. Hooah. This reasonably new habit Sergeant Nowell had implemented gave him the rare opportunity to process his thoughts.

The water is still flowing east toward the pier. They say even the most insignificant streams connect to the vast oceans. It reminded him of how big the world was. Lost in thought, he used his collar to wipe his sweat.

Things have definitely changed. This area was engraved in his memory. What was once a small town was now a grand city.

Nowell checked his watch. *Not seeing any improvements here; I guess this is my limit.* Nowell sat down and stared blankly at the aqueduct that had once been a dirty creek, lost in thought. Like a typhoon roaring within him, voices flooded his mind, those of his friends and family. Most of them were long dead. He couldn't stop feeling despair for what he had lost.

Among his raining thoughts, a spotlight took him by surprise. A kid from the playground close by approached Sergeant Nowell.

"Gloria—" Sergeant Nowell stopped himself, mistaking the kid as his daughter.

Unknown to the sergeant, it was Florian Lilly Cobblestone. She wore simple clothing under a bright, colorful jacket that was difficult for the sergeant to look at directly. What kept Nowell's attention was the look on her face. The strange kid staggered closer to Nowell, shaking and flustered. She avoided eye contact but stopped about six feet in front of Nowell.

"Are you lost?" Sergeant Nowell asked, nostalgic at the look thrown at him. It reminded him of the first day he met his daughter. She was around the same age too.

Florian, in plain view, ducked and slugged her way toward the sergeant.

"Is that the new dance the kids are doing nowadays?" Nowell joked.

She kept a careful yet concerned look, an expression on a child that Sergeant Nowell hadn't seen in a very long time. The war-torn children plagued with diseases and famine used to stare at him the same way. Children covered in dirt, malnourished, murderous, covered in rashes, or dead; all carried the same face. Absolute turmoil.

Nowell could feel the burning sensation radiating from his old wound, moving up to his heart.

"Hello." She gasped.

"Can I help you, kid?" Nowell asked.

"Um, do you have any pets?" she asked.

"I did, but not anymore." The blinding pink jacket was not the issue; she was trembling.

"Okay. You are not going to hurt anyone, are you?" she asked.

"Why would you think that, Glor— I mean, kid? Am I scary? I never met anyone who thinks I'm scary." Nowell jumped up out of his seat.

"Is your leg okay?" Florian asked. She jolted backward and fell. Kicking, she squirmed, pushing herself away in a panic.

Nowell's heart ached. His right leg screamed in pain. He rubbed his prosthetic, but the pain would not go away.

It was as if they both saw a ghost.

"Flo, what's wrong? What happened?" Florian's dad rushed over, picking her up.

Nowell recomposed himself. "Hello, you must be this kid's guardian. I'm Sergeant Honest Nowell, and I think my prosthetic leg scared your daughter. It must have gone stiff on me when I stood up, is all."

"No, I'm the one that needs to apologize. Flo is always up to something. She sees something weird, and she gets curious," Mr. Cobblestone said.

"Yeah, I'm used to it. So, this little one's name is Flo?" Nowell asked.

"That's what I call her; her name is Florian. I am David Cobblestone, her father."

"Nice to meet you, Mr. Cobblestone, and it is a pleasure to meet you, Florian Cobblestone," Sergeant Nowell said.

"Say hello, Flo."

"Hello." Florian seemed to calm down as the conversation continued.

"See, Sergeant Nowell has a prosthetic leg. He lost his leg, so the doctors fixed him up," Mr. Cobblestone said.

"So that's why you were giving me strange looks. Do you want to hold it? Here." Sergeant Nowell sat down and plucked his leg right off. "You see, I have to make sure I take care of it. Otherwise, it will get stuck like before. This leg does not heal. If you scrape your knee, you will heal. This one won't."

Florian inspected the leg calmly and then Sergeant Nowell.

"I guess your daughter was worried about me," Sergeant Nowell said.

"Please don't die, okay," Florian said.

Her words hit Nowell like an ocean wave. Crushing him and washing him out to sea.

"Well, I better get going. I have a schedule to keep," Nowell said.

"Yes, we better get going too. Take care. Say goodbye, Flo."

Florian waved silently as her father carried her away.

Sergeant Honest Nowell was thirty-nine, a veteran, and a survivor.

13:00 Mon–Fri Finish shift.

19:00 Dinner.

22:00 Lights out.

FIVE
ADOPTED APPRENTICE

WEST TORI PARK
JUNE 29TH X281

Florian remained silent as she looked over her father's shoulder. Her eyes were affixed to the sergeant and his soul. The demonic soul standing on one leg bent to its knee. It crunched to a running start position—the stub where its leg should have been branched out maliciously. Then one single bone punctured out from its insides. It formed a peg for itself to stand upon.

Florian trembled at the sight.

This wasn't going unnoticed by her father. "Flo, it's not polite to stare. That man sacrificed so much so we all can live at ease." Mr. Cobblestone patted his daughter on the back.

Florian recorded everything in her journal as soon as she got home, writing down how she approached the sergeant with the slender spike spirit. She wrote about how the spirit reached out blindly as the sergeant spoke. Florian could only concentrate on the spirit's swaying arms that branched toward her.

When her father's spirit animal rushed over and barked, the slender spike spirit retracted its arms. As Mr. Cobblestone spoke to the sergeant, it was as if the two spirits could see one another.

Sergeant Nowell, missing a leg but still standing tall. Polite, even though he squinted sternly. She was worried whether the sergeant was going to hurt someone or get hurt himself. The sergeant seemed nice, yet Florian couldn't understand why his soul was so different. She kept drawing in her journal, getting her personal thoughts in order. Trying to understand the sergeant and the old man who had died in the hospital.

☙❧

A few days later, the Cobblestone family was invited to the school to discuss Florian's misbehavior in class.

The principal of the school listed Florian's class disruptions, incomplete assignments, and classmate harassment. Florian had given everyone insulting nicknames like boar boy and rat lady.

"Throughout the entire school year, your daughter has not learned a single person's name. She drifts off in a daze and loses her concentration almost immediately. She even started cutting her own hair in Mrs. Jones's class," the principal said.

This was after Florian had finally resolved to start learning names.

"Lately, we've noticed weird mood swings," Mrs. Cobblestone said. "She throws rocks at animals. She was chased by a dog the other day because of it. She wants a pet so badly, yet she shows she's incapable of caring for one. Ever since her sister was born, she has been acting very strangely."

Florian sank in her chair. She stayed quiet, unsure of what to say.

"I see, violence toward animals—new sibling entering the family. Sudden changes can cause her to feel neglected. If that is the case, I think it would be best to go see a professional for help," the principal said.

"You mean a doctor? A specialist? Will that be covered by the Tarot Tori City medical center? The accommodations with Hope, our newborn, are eating up our expenses right now," Mrs. Cobblestone said.

"It is a facility that has remained open since before Tarot Tori City. Recently, it joined under the umbrella of the medical center coverage. It's the S. Brook Counseling & Therapy Clinic, Dr. Steinsbrook," the principal said.

⚭

The S. Brook Counseling & Therapy Clinic was small but was tucked in between shopping centers. To get to it, you had to take an elevator along a cliffside. The elevator was entirely powered by the aqueduct system from the waterfall beside it.

The door to the clinic chimed open.

"Dr. Steinsbrook? Is Dr. Steinsbrook in?" It was the chief of the Tarot Tori City Police Department. A little heavyset, gray mustache, wearing a TTCPD cap.

A young man answered. "Sorry, he isn't here. How can I help you, officer?" He had black hair with a couple strands of gray, styled back confidently. The man wore glasses, a button shirt with a vest without a tie, and khaki pants.

"Do you know when Dr. Steinsbrook will return?" the chief asked.

"To tell the truth, I don't know. Dr. Steinsbrook left abruptly about two years ago. I tried many times to get a hold of him, with no luck."

"Pity, and you are?" the chief said.

"I'm his apprentice, sir. Dr. Ronaldo Von Nirvanas. He taught me everything I know."

"Really? Well then, I don't see why I can't ask you. Dr. Steinsbrook worked with us numerous times before. Can you help us with a psychological profile? Of course, compensation for your assistance is negotiable."

"Sorry . . . well, I thought about it during my studies . . . but. . ."

I don't specialize in criminal psychology.

"Well, think about it. . . Tarot Tori City's crime rate is low, but the few crimes that do take place tend to be more extreme. Maybe true sociopaths come out of hiding when peace is at its extreme?"

The chief shook Dr. Ronaldo's hand, gave his contact info with a respectful nod, and departed.

Dr. Ronaldo thought about the chief's sociopath comment.

That's not quite right; it's the other way around. During times of peace, we have more time to help the sociopaths.

The door chimed again. This time it was Florian Lilly Cobblestone entering the clinic.

Dr. Ronaldo's life was about to change forever.

Florian's parents spoke with Dr. Ronaldo, briefing him on the situation. They firmly decided that no matter what, they were going to work together to make things right.

Dr. Ronaldo approached and crouched down so he was eye level with Florian. "It's a pleasure to meet you. What's your name?"

"Florian Lilly Cobblestone." She responded without any issues.

"I'm eighteen years old. How old are you?" Ronaldo asked. He already knew her age but wanted her to respond in her own words.

"I'm seven years old," Florian said.

Dr. Ronaldo analyzed every word and gesture Florian used. *Nothing out of the ordinary.*

Florian's eyes darted around the room, as if she were looking for something.

She must want to explore the clinic. Her eyes sure are full of curiosity. "Let's get started; we'll work here in the lobby. By all means, parents, sit anywhere you can observe. My office is a mess. We're moving some things out. I just got excited about having a new patient and decided to renovate a bit. Most of it is my mentor's stuff being hauled off to storage."

The lobby had a large antique coffee table at its center. A dozen or so chairs were spaced out accordingly. Florian's parents sat one seat apart from her. Ronaldo interpreted it as the family giving their daughter space for the session but remaining close enough to protect her. Ronaldo could tell they truly cared for Florian.

"You seem rather young to be a therapist?" Mr. Cobblestone said.

"Oh, I get that a lot. I'm eighteen, but I have studied under Dr. Steinsbrook for many years. As his protégé, I inherited his clinic. But I refused to officially take over until I finished my degree and got my license a little over a year ago."

When the family sat down, he grabbed a notepad and pen. "You can call me Ron for short. What would you like me to call you?"

Florian didn't answer.

"Shoot, I don't think I have the right notepad." Ronaldo opened it up, revealing a pop-up book. "Nope, that isn't it. Where is it?"

Florian let out a chuckle.

Ronaldo reached under the coffee table and grabbed a small whiteboard. "Here it is."

Florian just stared at him.

Ronaldo looked at Florian. "I heard you like to draw. Can you draw me?" He handed Florian the whiteboard.

Florian started drawing Dr. Ronaldo.

"I'm here to listen to you, Florian. If anything is bothering you, you can ask me without anyone getting mad at you. If not, we can talk about whatever you want."

Dr. Ronaldo explained to Florian's parents that his first goal was to build up her self-esteem, followed by improving her social skills. Later, he would help her understand her emotions and situation. Then expand her vocabulary to strengthen her communication skills.

Florian handed Dr. Ronaldo the drawing.

"Oh, how nice. You drew my glasses and vest really big. I love it. You even drew the sun behind me. Very good."

"That isn't the sun," Florian said.

"What is it?" Ronaldo asked.

"I don't know," Florian responded.

"If you don't want to tell me, that is completely fine. I am still happy you drew me. Thank you, Florian," Dr. Ronaldo Von Nirvanas said gleefully.

Dr. Ronaldo had no idea Florian was seeing a creature looming over him, a giant spiky ball floating around the room. Pitch dark needles protruded from its center, slowly moving and shivering back and forth.

It was a two-foot urchin crawling through the air aimlessly.

SIX
NEW FRIENDS

S. BROOK COUNSELING & THERAPY CLINIC
JULY 7ᵀᴴ X281

The clinic door chimed again, interrupting the Cobblestone family session.

A woman stumbled in with a giant parasol and a worried look. When she turned around, she jumped in terror at the sight of everyone in the lobby. She clammed up and fidgeted her hands in front of her face.

"Am I early? Oh no. Did I mix up my appointment dates again? I'm so sorry," the parasol woman said.

"No, Miss Fumblehouse, you're right on time." Dr. Ronaldo waved.

When Miss Garcia Fumblehouse closed her parasol, she seemed to shrink. She wore a long dress that touched her toes and had long, partially braided hair that sprang outward on both sides. Her dress had puffy shoulder pads and a massive, elegant yellow bow on her blouse. She was in her mid-twenties.

Florian smiled when she noticed Miss Fumblehouse holding a turtle. Florian jumped out of her seat and approached her.

"Hello, I'm Florian Lilly Cobblestone. Can I please pet your turtle?"

Miss Fumblehouse hesitated for a moment. "Ah, sure. His name is Sir Polyester Press Cotton the Third. Paul Three for short."

"Hello, Pauly," Florian said.

"Pauly's fine," Miss Fumblehouse said.

Florian examined the turtle. It was a box turtle with a spiral pattern on its back, taking refuge in its shell.

Miss Fumblehouse started to quiver. "Would you like to hold him?"

"Sure."

Miss Fumblehouse plopped the turtle in Florian's hands and tiptoed to a seat next to Dr. Ronaldo. The adults introduced themselves and conversed.

The turtle changed. Florian held a plush turtle. It had rainbow yarn stitching and soft green layers of padding. It had button eyes and detailed pockets that allowed it to tuck in its limbs.

It wasn't a real pet turtle but a plush turtle, and it was also Miss Fumblehouse's spirit animal. Its shape encompassed the plush. Florian had thought it was a real animal because Miss Fumblehouse was holding it. Spirits can't be touched by people as they just pass right through them. In reality, Miss Fumblehouse had been holding a doll.

A plush turtle that turns into a real turtle when Miss Fumblehouse is holding it. What does that mean? Is there something special about the doll?

Florian shoulders slumped and she frowned slightly as she paused in thought. Her eyes met Dr. Ronaldo's. She turned away.

The clinic door chimed open one last time.

"I know you. You're that girl from the park."

It was Sergeant Honest Nowell. He walked in with his slender spike spirit right behind him.

Florian retreated back to her seat and returned the plush turtle to Miss Fumblehouse.

"Oh, you know each other? Wait, the girl from the park? The one you told me about?" Dr. Ronaldo asked.

"Florian, was it?" Sergeant Nowell, standing six feet tall, saluted and bowed his head to Florian. "I wanted to thank you for your kind words the other day. I just really needed to hear them; I never expected them to come from you, but the weight was still the same, if not stronger. Thank you!"

The slender spike spirit jolted upward, shaking its bony structure, and bowed alongside the sergeant.

Dr. Ronaldo commended Sergeant Nowell.

The sergeant introduced himself properly to the Cobblestone family.

"Both Miss Fumblehouse and Sergeant Nowell visited this clinic before this town became Tarot Tori City. We first met when Dr. Steinsbrook adopted me when I was four. They're like family to me," Dr. Ronaldo said.

"Now that we're all here, how about we play a card game? It is one of the best ways to get to know one another," Dr. Ronaldo said.

"Wha? M-me too? I-I don't think you would like it. I might ruin your game," Miss Fumblehouse said.

"Don't be ridiculous. It'll be fun. You can sit beside Honest," Dr. Ronaldo said.

Miss Fumblehouse glowed bright red as she moved her seat closer to the card table.

"Sorry if I scared you the other day. You seemed rather concerned, and I wanted to reassure you I was fine by showing you my prosthetic," Sergeant Honest Nowell said.

Florian silently observed everyone.

There were four players: Dr. Ronaldo, Miss Fumblehouse, Sergeant Honest Nowell, and Florian.

Each spirit animal was behind or next to its corresponding partner.

The plush turtle spirit was on Miss Fumblehouse's lap.

The slender spike spirit sat behind Sergeant Nowell, dangling its long arms over the table.

Finally, the dark urchin spirit scuttled on the ceiling and halted right above Dr. Ronaldo.

Their souls interacted calmly with each other. The plush turtle was friendly and supportive of the slender spike. The dark urchin's quills vibrated, releasing six threads. They dangled from the ceiling and drifted above each spirit.

"We're all friends here. Let's have fun. We'll play Old Maid," Dr. Ronaldo said.

Dr. Ronaldo dealt the deck of cards while explaining the rules to Florian. She took a liking to the game and understood quickly.

The game was relatively easy for Florian. Their souls revealed everything. The most valuable card was always guarded by their soul. The plush turtle nodded at the joker card whenever it was in Miss Fumblehouse's hand. The dark urchin's threads wrapped around the joker card whenever Dr. Ronaldo found out who had it. It would unravel whenever he lost track. The slender spike spirit's fingers counted the cards on one hand as the other hand constantly pointed at the joker card's location.

All Florian had to do was not take the joker from Sergeant Nowell.

"You won again, Flo? Wow. You're so good at cards," Florian's father said.

"One more round. This time we will change up the order." Sergeant Honest Nowell said, his eyes moving to track the cards.

Round after round went by. Florian didn't grab the card the sergeant needed from Fumblehouse's hand.

Florian won the game.

"One more round, reverse order. I'll deal the cards this time," Sergeant Nowell said.

He sat next to Florian, and she noticed he gave himself the joker, perhaps hoping whenever it was Florian's turn, she would have a probability of grabbing the joker from his hand.

Florian's hand hovered over the joker card, but every time she grabbed something else.

She won that game as well.

"Wow, remind me to never play poker with you. Ever. You are going to grow up to be a nightmare for gamblers," Sergeant Honest Nowell said.

"That's the spirit; you were really trying to win that one, weren't you, Honest?" Dr. Ronaldo said.

"Come on, Ron, I was just playing around. I'm not mad. I'm amazed," Sergeant Nowell said.

"No, I'm happy you got more involved. In my opinion, this group session was very successful. Don't you agree, Florian?" Dr. Ronaldo said.

"Yeah," Florian said.

"Would you like to stop by again?" Dr. Ronaldo asked.

"Sure." Florian nodded.

"That's great. I could learn a few things from you, Little Liter," Sergeant Nowell said, high fiving Florian.

"Little Leader." Florian had misheard Sergeant Honest Nowell. She was honored to receive such a high rank from a sergeant.

"Yay!" Miss Fumblehouse cheered. "Little Leader will stop by again. Does that make us friends?" she asked Florian.

"Yep!" Florian said.

"Hurray! Little Leader," Miss Fumblehouse chanted.

"Little Liter," Sergeant Honest Nowell chanted.

"You really like Sergeant Nowell? Are you two married?" Florian asked Miss Fumblehouse.

"W-w-w-what!? Where did you get that idea from? Honest, it's not like that, I swear. Kids these days just say whatever pops up in their head." Miss Fumblehouse was beyond flustered. Her plush turtle spirit tucked away in its shell.

Sergeant Nowell cleared his throat. Dr. Ronaldo and Florian's parents chuckled.

"You are very observant and clever. I am truly impressed," Dr. Ronaldo said.

"I could tell just by looking," Florian said.

The two adjusted their glasses at the same time.

"See, we are team glasses. That means we are automatically friends," Ronaldo said.

Florian couldn't stop grinning.

"I look forward to speaking with you again, Florian Lilly Cobblestone," Dr. Ronaldo said sincerely.

The Cobblestone family left the clinic satisfied. They all felt better about their situation and knew this was just the first step in their new lives.

From then on, Florian would meet with Dr. Ronaldo every week.

SEVEN
PARTY GAMES

TAROT ELEMENTARY WEST
JULY 23RD X281

Florian was lost in thought walking down the hallway of her school. Her classmate Alexander was having some trouble reaching for something in his locker. The locker was an utter mess. His monkey soul hopped off his head and ran up his arm, leaping into it. It tapped a book as if trying to knock it down.

Florian subconsciously assisted the boy.

"Whoa. Thank you," Alex said.

Florian shrugged. "You're welcome."

"How did you know I needed this book? I have like thirty books stuffed up there," Alex said.

"I could tell just by looking." Florian walked away, thinking about other more important things.

"Hey, Flori. What's with you? You've been acting strange," Amalia, the bat girl, said.

"Yeah, she's acting more grown-up. I don't like it," Alex said.

"Yeah, Flori, we like your normal self," Amalia said.

"I am my normal self," Florian said.

Florian was thinking about what Dr. Ronaldo had asked of her. He had tasked her to write down any goals she wanted to achieve.

"Big goals, small goals, and any in between. Whatever you want. It doesn't matter if you can't complete them. All that matters is writing down as many as possible," Ronaldo had said.

Florian was already doing that with her Spirit Journal. Even if the tasks were exclusively spirit-related, she thought that wasn't what the doctor was asking for. Florian thought the doctor was asking for more normal goals. Maybe, just maybe . . . she could ask about the old man in the hospital.

"Flori, my birthday party's tomorrow. Don't bring anything weird this time, okay," Alex said.

"That's it!" Florian shouted. Alex's monkey spirit shot up through the ceiling.

Florian wrote down to get a gift, go to a party, eat cake, and have fun. She remembered Alex had an older sister, only a year older than him. Florian could get some advice from Alex's sister about being an older sister.

☯

Alex's birthday party was held at his father's house this year. However, Alex was not there yet.

Florian had gotten Alex a pair of boxing gloves and wrapped them herself. She couldn't wait for the look on Alex's spirit's face.

She bet the monkey would smile and spring about like an out-of-control bouncy ball.

Alex's father was hard at work, ensuring everyone was entertained, trying to stall until the birthday boy arrived. His spirit was a three-foot elephant with small ears. It extended its trunk as it was trying to assist him in handing out party favors.

The party went silent when a motor revved from outside. It got louder and louder as if a vehicle was approaching the home at an incredible speed. The sound of the engine got so loud everyone rushed outside.

A parked motorcycle roared at full blast. The motor sound was loud, clean, and pleasant to the ear. Its blue paint shimmered without a single smudge or dent.

Three passengers were nested on the bike, wearing tight leather suits and tinted helmets. Based on their builds, they were two adult females and one child. The kid was tightly squeezed in between the driver and handlebars.

A giant cat was panting next to the motorcycle. A five-foot cheetah, bulky, covered in scars and bloodstains. It stood on all fours without fear.

The kid hopped off the bike and removed his helmet; it was Alex, the birthday boy. The monkey spirit peeked its head out from inside Alex's leather suit.

The female driver stayed on the bike without removing her helmet.

"Thank you for the present." Alex blushed as he fist-bumped the female driver he had been squeezed up against.

"S dnyom rozhdeniya, kid. Happy birthday," the driver said.

The woman on the rear hopped off too. It was Alex's mom. She swayed her long hair free from the biker helmet, revealing her elegant face. Her hourglass figure was enhanced by the biker suit, and she carried herself with utmost confidence and pride.

She kissed her son on the cheek. "Happy birthday, Alex. Call if you need anything."

"Knock it off, Mom. Embarrassing me," Alex said.

Alex's mother had an octopus gently nestled behind her head concealed within her hair. It wrapped its many arms around Alex and the monkey, squeezing them tightly. Both were calm and collected. They shared a deep bond, that was certain.

The mother waved goodbye and hopped back on the bike. The two women drove off as quickly as they had come.

Alex went upstairs to change, and his sister came down.

"Finally! I finished it!" she shouted. She had been writing a song for her brother.

Her name was Sera Rodriguez. She was one year older than Alex, and she adored music. She was always wearing some kind of hat, usually with something cat-related on it. Her spirit was an orange goldfish that grew twice its size every year.

She turned on the TV and connected her phone to it. She started singing the lyrics to the song without warning anyone. Her brother wasn't even there to hear it.

Whenever she sang, her goldfish soul would swim around her and the audience. Her music captivated the other spirit animals.

"Oops, Alex isn't here yet. Guess I'll sing it again!" Sera said, laughing maniacally.

Florian waited for the right moment to ask her about being an older sister. She wondered if all older sisters acted the way Sera did.

Alex came down and opened his presents.

"Boxing gloves? Whatever," Alex said. He tossed Florian's gift aside.

Florian's jaw dropped, shocked that Alex didn't like the gift.

"I would rather take another ride on the motorcycle with Mom's hottie friend," Alex said. His monkey spirit rubbed its face in delight.

"What did you say?" Florian picked up the boxing gloves Alex had tossed aside and put them on. She furiously approached him.

"That was your gift, Flori?" Alex said. He took off running.

"You forgot your gift!" Florian shrieked as she chased Alex around the house.

"Hold it right there, Flori," Sera said. She had boxing gloves of her own. "That's my little brother. I can't have you terrorizing him on his birthday."

"I don't want to fight you," Florian said.

"Any fight involving my brother is my fight too. That's what it means to be an older sister," Sera said.

"He said he would rather ride motorcycles with hotties instead of getting our gifts," Florian said.

"Yeah!" "How dare he!" "Teach him a lesson!" Amalia and the other friends said.

"Is that true? Alex!?" Sera glared and hissed at Alex. Her goldfish spirit swam aggressively through Alex's face.

"Uh oh." Alex started running again.

After some time, they caught the birthday boy.

Sera announced to the party, "It's unfair to beat him up like this. It's time for a boxing tournament. We'll see who's the strongest, and that person gets to face him in the final round."

It was a three-round ring-out tournament with six boys and two girls. The only girls confident enough to face the boys were Florian and Sera. The goal was to make the opponent step out of bounds.

Each round went by quickly. Sera was the oldest, so she made short work of her first bout.

Florian took her time observing her opponents. The first boy was shorter than her. He had a small penguin spirit animal that charged at Florian two seconds before the boy did. She could predict what he was going to do. He ended up running out of the ring on his own.

Her second opponent had some boxing experience from a local kid's gym. He had a skunk spirit animal that wagged its tail as he swung his punches. Once Florian got his rhythm, the boy's arms could no longer reach her. She was able to dodge every swing. Florian punched the kid right on the head. The soft glove padded the blow, but it scared the boy so much he tripped and fell out of bounds.

Sera had one more match to get to the final round. She was facing a boy who was taking karate classes. Sera was taller, but the boy planted his feet into the ground. He took a low stance that made it difficult for anyone to move him. Sera had no luck. The boy found an opening and tripped her out of bounds.

"Yes, I'm one step closer to facing Alex. How dare he ride such a cool motorcycle with two hotties," the boy said.

"Gross! One of them was my mom!" Alex said.

"Florian, you must win. Our pride of being older sisters is at stake," Sera said as she dramatically closed her eyes.

The final round. No matter who won, Alex was going down.

The karate boy grounded his stance again. His kangaroo spirit mirrored him. Florian tried copying the boy too. She lowered her posture and crept closer to him. The kangaroo waved its paws wildly as the boy flailed his arms. Florian closed her eyes and flailed her arms too. They weren't hitting each other.

"I didn't want to use real karate moves, but since these boxing gloves are soft, I guess it won't hurt too much," the boy said.

He pulled his right arm inward and shot his left arm outward in perfect unison.

Florian had observed the kangaroo's paw jutting outward a second earlier.

The boy's punch was fast and hit its target. But Florian had blocked his blow. The boy staggered.

Florian punched the boy in the face, ringing him out.

Florian was the winner.

Alex was no match for Florian in the final round.

The party settled down, and Florian had a chance to ask Sera about being an older sister.

Sera said, "There's nothing to it. I just do my best and have fun."

Florian remembered to write about her day in her journal. She'd had a blast.

✿

After the party, the karate boy approached Florian and her parents.

"Hello, my name is Samuel, and I wanted to ask if you take karate lessons," he said, stumbling a few times.

"No, I don't," Florian said.

"What!? No way. I must ask you to join our gym. I think you would do really well. When I first started, there was no way I could have blocked or dodged a fist. Please consider joining karate lessons. I'm sure you would be great at it." The karate boy with his kangaroo spirit left with his parents.

EIGHT
HAUNTING THOUGHTS

S. BROOK COUNSELING & THERAPY CLINIC
AUGUST 28ᵀᴴ X281

Hope Cobblestone was three months old.

Even though the baby had been born mute, her soul was flourishing. Florian could easily understand her. Whenever she was hungry, her seashell dove would stick its head outside its seashell and open its beak wide. Florian could tell just by looking.

The Cobblestone family had to bring Hope to check-ups regularly to see if there were any other impairments as she developed. The family also had no other choice but to hire two nurses to monitor the baby—one for the day and one for the night.

Thanks to the Tarot Tori City People Priority Policy, the medical center visits were completely free. The two parents also had two thousand dollars a month thanks to the residential flex spending. This covered a quarter of the salary for the nurses.

When Hope Cobblestone turned three months old, the Cobblestone family received a package from the mayor himself. It had fruit, wine, a few documents, and a handwritten note.

Dear Hope Cobblestone,
Welcome to Tarot Tori City.

With much deliberation, we have concluded to waive the age requirement for the Residential Flex Spending exclusively for you, Hope Cobblestone.

I'm genuinely heartbroken that we may never have the chance to speak to one another.

Condolences,

Mayor William Rite Banquet

It was an odd letter, but good news nonetheless. From then on, Hope had access to a renewable one thousand dollars every month. It went straight to the medical costs, significantly decreasing the financial burden on her parents.

The Cobblestones would have lost many opportunities if it weren't for all of this. However, they weren't out of the woods yet. The whole family needed to learn sign language. It would be the baseline for communicating with Hope, and exposure at an early age would allow Hope to pick up on it quickly.

Each family member took lessons whenever possible. They were told to use the hand signs as they spoke so Hope could memorize and mimic gestures as she grew up. The language relied heavily on facial expressions and interpreting them. It was very engaging for the Cobblestone family to be more expressive and open to one another.

ॐ

Florian's mind would wander as the spirit animals interested her more than learning sign language.

She had trouble sitting still in general. Her grades were subpar, but her attitude started to mature as she visited her counselor, Dr. Ronaldo Von Nirvanas.

"Your drawings are so beautiful, Florian. Where do you come up with such unique creatures?" Dr. Ronaldo asked.

Florian drew many spirit animals during her sessions with Dr. Ronaldo.

Dr. Ronaldo didn't suspect anything from the drawings. He only saw a girl with a fantastic imagination expressing herself with therapeutic art. Florian was calmer when she drew her art. Whatever was bothering her, drawing helped her understand it.

Dr. Ronaldo interpreted her drawings. Florian's drawing of Sergeant Nowell had a tall shadow behind him; it must have meant Florian thought the sergeant was tall. Miss Fumblehouse's drawing had her plush turtle included with her giant parasol, nothing strange about it. Drawings of her family showed an imaginary iguana and dog. Her friends also had animals beside them, all peaceful. She drew many pictures of her sister, and Ronaldo sensed a lot of effort was put into them. Florian included a dove inside a seashell in every one.

"Do you love your baby sister?" he asked.

"Yes, I love her a lot," Florian said.

Dr. Ronaldo already knew the answer. He was allowing her to say it herself.

Still, he was missing something big—the actual reason Florian seemed distracted. Florian wasn't telling him something. As a counselor, all he could do was wait until Florian was ready to talk about it.

"Florian? How is everything going with Hope at home?"

"Great, I'm learning sign language now."

"That's great. Can you teach me a few words?"

"Yeah, this one means baby sister." She cradled her hands. "This one means old man." She squinted her face and made a wrinkled expression.

"Like this?" Ronaldo followed suit.

"No, like this." Florian squinted harder.

The two laughed.

Florian paused for a moment. "The day my sister was born, I saw an old man. He was wearing a bunch of clothes that smelled. I don't know what happened to him, but I think he died so my sister could be born."

Dr. Ronaldo suspected this was what he was waiting for. "Died? Why do you think he died?"

"Because he disappeared. When I fell asleep, he was there; when I woke up, he was gone."

"I'm sure the doctors called his name, and they treated him."

"No, he disappeared. His conch crab disappeared too."

"Conch crab? I'm sure the old man is alive and well. Why do you think your sister is here because this old man might have died?"

"Because Hope also has a shell."

Dr. Ronaldo remembered the seashell dove. "So on the day your sister was born, you think you saw a man die, correct?"

"Yeah," Florian said.

"How do you feel about the old man?"

"I don't know," Florian said.

Dr. Ronaldo reassured her and asked her for more information. Florian did not mention anything about the other creatures in the hospital or anything about the spirits.

"I see," Dr. Ronaldo said. "I'll do some research on my end. I'll do my best to get answers about this individual. I'm sure the old man is alive and well."

Florian's eyes widened. She acted like her chair was about to eject her into the air. This was the first time Ronaldo had seen Florian so excited. His words must have meant a lot to her.

Ronaldo scheduled Florian to come back the next day. He was confident he could get answers quickly. He was incredibly excited as things were getting interesting.

Florian nodded, wide eyes affixed above Dr. Ronaldo.

"What's the matter, Florian?"

"I trust you," she said.

After the session, Dr. Ronaldo thought the old man might have been the underlying factor weighing Florian down.

Florian was just a kid, yet she was worried about the well-being of a stranger. Ronaldo knew her intentions were honest and sincere, but. . .

Childhood was the most influential part of an individual's life, and this stranger was eating away at hers.

Ronaldo started investigating to see what closure he could bring to Florian.

NINE
THE HERMIT

S. BROOK COUNSELING & THERAPY CLINIC
AUGUST 28TH X281

It was around 8 p.m., and Dr. Ronaldo was at his office investigating Florian's predicament.

Dr. Ronaldo checked the Tarot Tori City obituaries for persons who passed away on November 16th, the day Hope Cobblestone was born.

He found only one, an individual by the name of Zachary Venmont.

Florian was right. Someone really did die the day her sister was born.

He passed away at the Tarot Tori City medical center due to underlying health issues at the age of eighty-six.

Ronaldo wanted more information. He called the Tarot Tori City medical center, using his clinic's clearance to access the archives. He obtained a detailed medical record for Zachary Venmont.

He didn't have an address listed, meaning he had been homeless. He visited the hospital regularly as the visits were free. His exams showed he had lung cancer.

Dr. Ronaldo's phone rang. It was the chief of the Tarot Tori City Police Department.

"Hey, Dr. Ronaldo. A little birdie told me you looked up some medical records of a Zachary Venmont? Can I ask for the reason?" the chief asked.

"Oh, it's for a patient of mine. I can't say more than that."

"I see. Does this patient of yours seem suspicious in any way?" the chief asked.

"My patient is only seven years old. Was there foul play in the death of Zachary Venmont?" Ronaldo asked.

"We are just following procedures. I can share what we have if I get your verbal consent for. . ." The chief listed several legal and ongoing investigation disclosures.

"I accept," Dr. Ronaldo said.

"It wasn't much, but after an autopsy, we discovered he had swallowed a little bit of rat poison. We suspected he may have eaten some discarded food and ate some rat trap by mistake—poor bastard. I knew him too. He was a smart man. He was visiting the medical center regularly but couldn't pay for any cancer treatments. Since he wasn't a resident, he didn't qualify for the Tarot Tori City monthly flex spending. That would have paid for the treatments for sure."

"That's awful."

"Yeah, but things in this city are a lot better than they were before, I'll tell ya," the chief said.

"Thanks for telling me," Ronaldo said.

"I called you as soon as I saw your name in the alert system we cooked up. Don't worry, Doctor, you aren't a suspect. The real reason I called was to see if this talk would spark an interest in helping us out in the future. We could really use your help," the chief said.

"I thought the crime rate was low?" Ronaldo said.

"Exactly, low, not zero. The penitentiary is also in desperate need of a new counselor. Your mentor Dr. Steinsbrook would—"

"I know; he used to work with correction facilities," Ronaldo said.

"I will send the case file to your office. It should arrive tomorrow morning," the chief said.

"Thank you." Dr. Ronaldo hung up the phone.

That night, Dr. Ronaldo thought about the offer but was more worried this sad news might not be what Florian was looking for.

∞⚬∞

The following day, the case file arrived. After looking it over, Dr. Ronaldo canceled Florian's appointment. He sat silently in the lobby of his clinic. Alone.

Later that day, something outside the window caught Ronaldo's eye. It was Florian sprinting on the opposite side of the aqueduct. She ran across the bridge, over the aqueduct, and back around the walkway. The clinic door chimed open.

Out of breath, she said, "You found something! Didn't you?" She must have run all the way there from the bus stop.

"What? I didn't," Dr. Ronaldo said. He adjusted his glasses and wiped his vest. "I canceled our appointment. Why are you here?"

"You're lying!" Florian said.

"I didn't find anything," Ronaldo said.

"I can tell just by looking! You can't hide from me!" she said.

"Do your parents know you are here? Go home."

"No! I'm not leaving until you tell me what you found out!" Florian pouted, arms crossed. She sat down in the lobby.

Ronaldo called her parents.

Florian didn't move an inch. She sat and gave Dr. Ronaldo a piercing glare.

Dr. Ronaldo sighed and went back to boxing documents to move to storage.

Florian followed Dr. Ronaldo around as he went from room to room.

"You're not going to follow me to the bathroom, are you?" Dr. Ronaldo said.

"If you do that, I'll block the door so you can't get out," Florian said.

"Please just wait until your parents get here."

"I won't leave," Florian said.

He was astonished.

"If my parents take me away. I'll be back tomorrow, and the next, and the next. You can't avoid me forever."

"You aren't old enough to understand what happened to Zachary Venmont," Dr. Ronaldo said.

"Zachary Venmont? That's the name of the old man, isn't it?"

"No, no more. I'm not saying another word."

"You say I'm not old enough, but you'll have to tell me eventually. You can tell me now and get it over with or wait and make me feel like an idiot."

"Why do you want to hear about this stranger so badly? You don't need to know about him to live your life."

"I want to look at my sister without crying," Florian said.

Dr. Ronaldo went silent. He berated himself for not realizing sooner how Florian was feeling. Zachary Venmont was haunting her mind, and she was reminded of him every time she looked at her sister. It would be cruel to make her suffer any longer.

Ronaldo sat down and told her about Zachary Venmont. He told her how the old man in the hospital waiting room had died. He did not leave a single thing out.

Florian started to cry.

"It's all right . . . Mr. Venmont lived a long life of eighty-six years."

"It's not that," Florian cried.

"It's okay to cry. Fear, sadness, depression, no emotion is a bad thing. Emotions show we care about something so much our bodies can't contain it, and that's a miracle."

Florian laughed. "Thank you. I'm so happy I met you, Sergeant Nowell, Miss Fumblehouse, and Mr. Venmont. I'm not alone," she said.

Florian was relieved, content, and happier. Her tearful smile was genuine and inspiring. Dr. Ronaldo gave Florian a hug as her parents escorted her home.

⁊⁓

As soon as Florian got home, she embraced her baby sister for what felt like the first time.

⁊⁓

That night Dr. Ronaldo found himself flipping through his mentor's notes. He began studying once again. Florian inspired him to work harder. He had so much more to learn and big shoes to fill compared to the achievements of Dr. Steinsbrook.

⁊⁓

Dr. Ronaldo turned on the TV to catch the news. The mayor of Tarot Tori City, William Rite Banquet, was on screen. His fine blond hair, tall slim build, and pressed dark blue suit took up the whole

59

screen. His smile gleamed brighter with the flashing cameras as he announced the grand opening of the city's newest homeless shelter.

Ronaldo thought it was just another PR stunt.

"This three hundred bed shelter will be named after a very close friend of mine, Zachary Venmont."

Ronaldo spat out his drink.

"Tragically, he passed away a little over three months ago. He was unable to pay for his medical treatments and thus succumbed to his cancer." Mayor Banquet's smile turned into a concerned frown.

Dr. Ronaldo turned up the volume.

"So, as of today, thanks to this shelter, the word homeless will no longer be in Tarot Tori City's dictionary. You heard right; this shelter shall be an official residential address for the currently homeless in this city." The press all stood up and asked questions right in the middle of the speech.

Mayor Banquet's narcissistic smile returned as he didn't stop. "That means, starting tomorrow at noon, these new residents of Tarot Tori City will be eligible to apply for the monthly flex spending following the guidelines, the same as everyone else. They'll have a warm bed to sleep in. They'll be given the opportunity to start a new chapter in their lives. They'll even have funds to pay for major medical procedures. Oh, and who could forget that they'll be eligible to vote!"

This was Mayor William Rite Banquet. Thirty-two years old. The protégé of the previous mayor. It was his first year as mayor, and he knew damn well what he was doing. He had founded Tarot Tori City alongside his mentor, three generations in the planning, fourteen years and counting to institute.

ACT 2

FLOURISHING

64

TEN
IDENTITY THEFT

LANGUAGE SPECIALISTS WING
SEPTEMBER 8TH X288

Florian Lilly Cobblestone was fourteen. She still had short black hair and sported rectangular glasses, a brown hoodie, and denim shorts.

Her demeanor was confident, and her intuition was genuine as she added years of understanding to her ability.

She leaped out of the high school bus, heading to pick up her sister, Hope Cobblestone, from her tutors.

Hope was seven years old. Her black hair was tied in a ponytail, and she wore a white T-shirt paired with a yellow skirt. Most importantly, she had a whiteboard strapped around her shoulders at all times.

Hope's seashell dove spirit was nesting on the top of her head. It looked almost like a hat or an accessory.

Hope had an easy time learning sign language basics, thanks to Florian and their parents' consistency. However, solving one problem led to another. Ordinary school teachers had difficulty understanding Hope when she used sign language in school. She had to rely on her whiteboard most of the time. Thus, the after-school tutors. Hope had to pay extra attention during her lessons, which required her to hear new words, learn their spelling, and memorize the hand sign counterpart. Any seven-year-old would find these additional steps challenging.

This was the new normal for Florian. She attended the last hour of Hope's lessons to review what she'd learned. That way, Florian could encourage using Hope's new words at home.

It was an average day for Florian. She arrived at the tutoring lab and waited in the lobby to be called in to review the day's lesson.

She was browsing on her phone when she heard a young girl's voice.

"Hello, is Hope Cobblestone still here?"

A short girl at the front desk seemed around the same age as Hope. She was blonde with twin ponytails, a pink dress, a flashy purse, a golden locket, and a long frilly skirt.

"I'm her sister, and I'm here to pick her up," the short girl said.

-POP-

Florian stood up, making sure she had heard correctly. *No way. Who the hell does she think she is? She's impersonating me.*

The blonde brat turned her nose up at the lady at the front desk.

Florian calmed down for a moment. The front desk lady wouldn't let this kid in.

-POP-

"Sit down, and we will call your name when Hope is ready."

They let her in anyway?! It struck Florian's nerves.

The girl strutted in with a smirk.

Florian was ready to teach this identity theft kid a lesson when she noticed bubbles drifted aimlessly around the girl. They hovered around the entire waiting room. When Florian swatted a few out of her face, they wouldn't pop. In fact, they went right through her hand.

Behind the blonde brat was a small white dog with brown spots. It was a Jack Russell Terrier but had a strange stream of bubbles as a tail, which waved erratically.

The bubbles were coming out of the butt of the spirit animal. Florian was disgusted that the butt bubbles were in her face and she could do nothing to get rid of them.

The brat found a seat in the middle of the room.

Florian cleaned her glasses and approached the girl pretending to be her. Florian grabbed the chair and loomed over the blonde brat.

"Hello, I am Florian Lilly Cobblestone. Do you have any pets?"

"Pets? What are you talking about? Who are you?" the blonde brat asked.

Florian towered over the girl. "Don't you get it? I am the only sister of Hope Cobblestone. Who are you?"

The girl was flustered, but only for a moment. "I see, so you have uncovered my clever plan. You are correct; I am not Hope's sister."

"Who are you? Where are your parents?"

"Fine, I'll talk. My name is Blythe. I wanted to surprise Hope. Please don't call my parents."

Blythe's spirit animal was also cowering. The bubble-tailed dog spirit whimpered softly.

"So you are friends with Hope?"

"Yeah, I wanted to play with Hope after school, but she wrote that she had after-school tutoring. I followed her here a few days ago but couldn't stay for long. After a few preparations, I decided to surprise her today."

Florian took a deep breath and sighed. This girl had gone through some effort to see Hope. She must have really wanted to be friends with her.

"Blythe, was it? You can stay. Just never impersonate anyone again."

"Okay. I promise." Blythe smirked.

-POP-

One of the bubbles popped in Florian's face.

Florian was called to come back to review the lesson. Blythe was about to be left alone in the waiting room.

Florian turned around and called to Blythe, "You can come too. Just sit quietly and wait until we are done."

Blythe hopped up and followed Florian, her bubble-tailed dog not far behind.

Florian and Hope waved to each other joyously. When Hope noticed Blythe, she jumped out of her seat and hugged her.

Florian was happy to know Hope had no trouble making friends. She was also relieved that this impersonator actually was telling some truth.

"All right, let me and Hope finish the review, and we can hang out for a while, okay."

They reviewed the lesson, and Blythe watched, sometimes imitating the hand signs.

"Is Blythe a good friend?" Florian used sign language so Blythe couldn't understand them.

"Yes, she is an okay friend," Hope signed.

"Okay? She is not a good friend?" Florian signed.

"She likes to say things." Hope signed a peculiar sign Florian didn't quite understand. Hope shook her head and rolled her eyes.

Florian didn't recognize the new gesture. "What was that?" Florian mimicked the gesture.

"She likes to exaggerate," the tutor said out loud.

Florian signed to the tutor to stop speaking out loud. Luckily Blythe had no idea they were hand signing about her.

After the meeting, the three girls decided to walk to the nearest restaurant.

Hope paraded around with Blythe, window shopping and sightseeing. Hope even used her whiteboard to teach Blythe a few sign language gestures.

"Blythe, what time do you have to be home? Do you want me to call your parents and let them know you are hanging out with us?"

Blythe's bubble dog spirit wagged its tail in excitement. Its bubbles floated toward Hope and Florian.

"I can stay with you two for as long as I want. Even sleepovers. My parents already know, and they said all clear!"

-POP-

All of the bubbles popped around Hope, who was happy Blythe might be able to hang out longer. However, Florian knew this was a complete lie. The bubbles around Florian didn't burst; they accumulated around her head.

"Where do you live? We can take you home after dinner, okay?"

"I live a few blocks down. Don't worry about it. Let's go!"

More bubbles dispersed from the tail of the bubble dog spirit. They drifted around Florian's head.

Florian tried to swat them away, but her attempts were meaningless since they were part of a spirit.

In confusion, Florian noticed another spirit from the corner of her eye. She turned around fully, and it disappeared.

Florian thought it was strange but ignored it and went on her way.

"Florian, do you have a boyfriend?" Blythe asked.

"What!? Where did that come from?"

"Well, do you?"

"I do not. I don't have time for a boyfriend."

"Hehe, I have three," Blythe said. She smirked and giggled as her bubble dog spirit waved more bubbles into the air.

Hope blushed.

-POP-

Hope believed the lie. New bubbles joined the others on Florian's head and were not going away. These bubbles were Blythe's lies. Florian realized if they popped around an individual, that person believed the lie. If the individual didn't fall for the lie, the bubbles accumulated and didn't disappear.

Florian was surprised such a complex spirit belonged to a young kid. She wondered what would cause Blythe's spirit animal to take on such a form.

Florian felt a chill down her spine and turned around.

ELEVEN
WANDERING GHOST

SNIPES TRAIL ST.
SEPTEMBER 8TH X288

Florian caught a glimpse of it as it scrambled into an alleyway. The spirit took the form of a lizard waddling on its hind legs. It had a leathery mane that bowled around its neck and collected its overflowing drool dripping from its salivating tongue.

Florian was worried. The spirit's owner was nowhere in sight, and it was following the three of them.

Florian has never seen a soul without an owner before. But she didn't have a spirit of her own, so a soul without an owner might be plausible.

"Can we eat here?"

The restaurant was almost empty. Florian felt it would be safer to eat some place more crowded.

"Let's try somewhere else."

The three girls continued. Florian kept an eye on the drooling lizard spirit going in and out of hiding. She couldn't spot the owner.

She thought it was some wandering spirit haunting them.

The spirit swept its tail on the ground like a broom. It was as if it was wiping away its tracks.

Florian led the girls to an open plaza to get a better look at this spirit. The drooling lizard spirit just sat at a corner staring at the girls.

Hope was teaching Blythe the hand sign for the fountain but looked up at her sister's strange behavior. Before Hope could even hand sign anything to Florian, she reassured her sister that everything was okay.

She could tell just by looking that her sister was starting to worry. Hope's seashell dove spirit would stick its head out of the seashell and in the air whenever Hope was concerned about something.

"Everything is all right," Florian signed.

Blythe and Hope followed Florian. The drooling lizard wheezed and gargled as it tailed the group. Its movements got more agile. It sank itself lower on all fours and slithered. When it stood up, it was almost three feet tall. When on all fours, from snout to tail, it appeared about seven feet long.

Florian's observations confirmed her suspicion. It wasn't a solitary spirit; a person was stalking them. The soul displayed a process of warming up.

Florian had observed the same process before. Dr. Ronaldo suggested she find some outlet for her stress, recommending a sport or a hobby. Florian chose martial arts since a classmate wouldn't stop bugging her about joining. When stretching and warming up, she noticed the individual spirits would follow suit. It resulted in the souls becoming quicker, confident, and more intimidating.

Florian turned a corner with the group and immediately ran into a store. Hope and Blythe followed, not far behind as if thinking this was a game.

Florian remained near the entrance and waited as the other two browsed the store.

Florian waited, yet the lizard didn't pass by the front of the store. *Did we lose it?*

Florian crept below the display window and peeked through it. She couldn't see it.

"Florian, I got to use the bathroom," Blythe said.

Her bubble dog spirit whimpered. Not a single bubble floated away from its tail, so Blythe was telling the truth.

Florian didn't want to split up the group. "Let's all go together."

"I can go by myself," Blythe said.

"I don't need to go," Hope signed.

"We are all going together!"

Florian waited outside the restroom, keeping an eye on the front door. She saw no sign of the drooling lizard or their stalker.

Florian suspected either the stalker had lost them or her eyes were playing tricks on her. The bubbles from Blythe's spirit animal were still bothering Florian. Thinking back, she still had no idea why Blythe had lied about telling her parents where she was.

Florian knew they would have to leave the store.

When they did, the drooling lizard reappeared behind them. Florian shivered at the sight.

When the girls entered a densely populated shopping district, countless spirits were roaming about with their owners. The sheer number of souls would usually distract Florian. She took a deep breath and composed herself.

"It doesn't matter why. At this moment, I have to protect Hope and her friend!" Florian knew they were safer in a crowded place.

"Concentrate, Florian! Concentrate!" She pushed herself to drown out the overwhelming crowd of people with their unique souls.

She ignored the tusks, the gills, the appendages, the eyes, and parasites.

She disregarded the furs, the feathers, the giants, and the scales.

Florian focused her sights on the drooling lizard, Hope, and Blythe.

When they entered the crowd, their stalker would have three options.

The first option would be to give up and leave them alone.

The second would be to wait until they were out of the crowd and pursue them once again.

The third would be to continue to follow them in the crowd, revealing their identity.

Your move, creep. Make your move! What are you going to do?

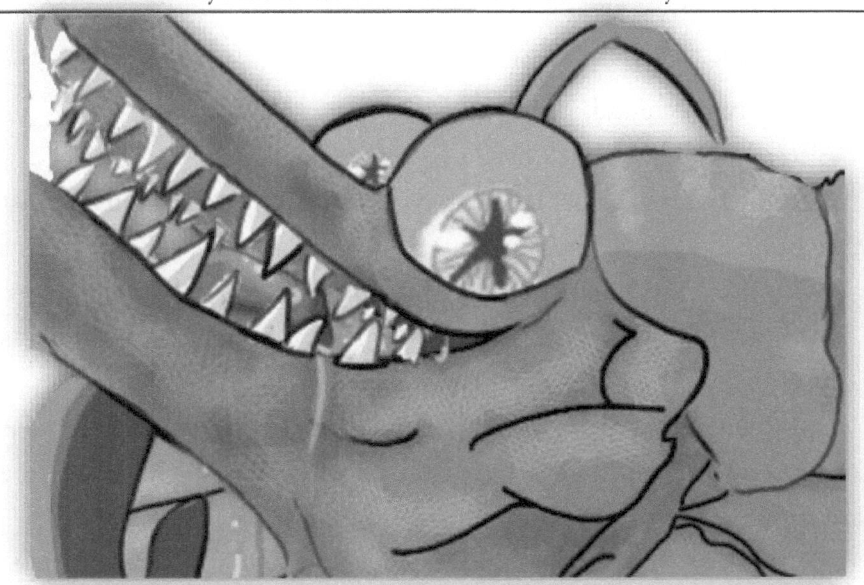

TWELVE
STAR SHOOTING COWBOY

MERCH MARCH PLAZA
SEPTEMBER 8TH X288

Out of all the bounties, CIA, MI6, and militias I have hunted down, I've never seen anything like this.

The stalker answered his phone. "I'm afraid Wit Law can't take your call right now. Please leave a message after I hang up."

"Knock it off, Travis. What's taking so long?"

"Gahaha, hey, Juke. How's it going?"

"You were supposed to be back an hour ago."

"There has been a minor setback. I should be back in about forty minutes."

"This isn't like you. Don't tell me the police—"

"Don't worry. It's got nothing to do with the police."

"Then what's the holdup?"

"One kid."

"Wha?"

"You said one kid, not three."

"Really? That's what's holding you up."

"I only got two arms! If I grab two of them, the third kid will just run away and yell for help."

"We just need the one in the photo."

"I know, but this teenager is sharp. I have no idea how she does it, but it's like she has x-ray vision or someth—"

"A teenager with x-ray vision is giving you trouble? Is that supposed to be another one of your jokes? Just grab the target; we are running out of time."

"Oh, shit." The stalker hid from Florian's sight. "This girl is insane. I can't take a single step without her noticing."

"Don't tell me you need backup? For a teenage girl? If you mess this up, I won't bail you out this time."

"When have I ever failed to catch a bounty?"

"That time at the archipelago, the casino, and who could forget the international wa—"

"You keep bringing those up. Those were team slip-ups; they don't count. When working on my own, I always get the job done."

"Just hurry up."

Travis Wit Law hung up. He concealed his face with his hood, a hygiene mask, and a pair of sunglasses. His target was the blonde brat, Blythe.

This chick with the glasses wasn't in any of our intel. Why is she guarding this Blythe kid?

When Florian's group entered the crowd of people, Travis whipped out a pack of cigarettes. He leaned back into the alleyway, pulled off his mask, and lit one.

That intense stare she throws around is scary. She's not pretending she didn't notice me, and that's proof she's just an amateur. But through a freaking wall? Is she baiting me somehow? Nah, not likely. She moved my mark to a more public area too. That's her definitely saying, "go ahead and try something in this crowd, coward." Unfortunately for you, kid, you're gambling with the star of this show.

Travis Wit Law covered his face and merged with the crowd.

☙ဎ❧

Florian couldn't tell who the owner of the drooling lizard spirit was in the crowd. All she knew was that the lizard continued its pursuit as if it were hunting prey.

She directed her group to a busy family restaurant, Party Pancakes. She chose a booth that faced the only entrance. The restaurant had portrait windows on three sides, allowing Florian to monitor the outside. If the drooling lizard spirit entered the establishment with a human being, that would identify the stalker.

☙ဎ❧

Unfortunately, the windows also allowed the stalker, Travis Wit Law, to observe them from the outside.

She keeps glancing at her phone. She must be ready to call the authorities if she sees anything suspicious. Is she starting to panic? Whatever this chick is planning, this is checkmate. I can easily get all of them out of there. It's a double-edged sword but very efficient.

Travis counted all the security cameras. He found his escape route and his scapegoats.

Too bad, kid. I have no idea who you are, but I have a job to finish. It was fun, but now I have to get serious.

Travis swiped two boxes of small fireworks from a store nearby and approached his scapegoats. He placed one package on a bench in the plaza.

ಐಐಐ

Florian's group ordered food.

"Hope, if anything happens, I want you and Blythe to stick together no matter what," Florian signed to Hope.

Hope nodded with a determined look. Her seashell dove darted its head back and forth on high alert.

ಐಐಐ

"Now for the final piece."

Travis blocked the employee exit and tossed a few lit fireworks in the back window of the restaurant.

Avoiding all the security cameras in the vicinity, Travis found a seat to watch the show. *This is an all-time classic "smoke em out."*

The restaurant's fire alarm rang and started a panic.

Now they have no other option but to exit the restaurant.

Travis had to act quickly. It would take fifteen minutes for firefighters and police to show up. Among the chaos, he planned to grab Blythe and disappear through the escape route he'd secured.

About twenty people stormed out of the restaurant. Cooks, waiters, and customers all ran to safety. The restaurant filled with smoke.

Where are they?

There was no sign of Florian's group.

Don't tell me those girls are still inside the building. You're kidding me?

He waited another minute.

ಐಐಐ

Inside the smokey restaurant, Blythe was crying under a table. Her bubble dog spirit was curled up beside her, whimpering.

Florian tried pulling Blythe out, but she resisted. "Come on, Blythe, we have to get out of here."

Hope bravely pulled Blythe's arm trying to help her. Her seashell dove flapped its tiny wings in a frenzy, terrified.

☜☞

Travis ran through the crowd and rushed toward the entrance. He entered the smoke-filled building. "Is there anyone else here? I'm here to help!" Travis called out.

Florian saw the drooling lizard spirit. It accompanied a man covered in a hood, a medical mask, and shades.

She immediately knew that was their stalker.

Florian grabbed Hope, covered Blythe's mouth, and hid under the table.

"Make a sound if you can hear me?"

Blythe struggled to break free.

"Quiet, Blythe. We can't trust him," Florian whispered.

Blythe continued to struggle, kicking and squirming, as her bubble dog spirit growled at Florian.

Travis searched thoroughly, kicking over tables and chairs. His drooling lizard scurried on top of the tables, eyes open, sniffing the air.

The deafening alarm and smoke helped hide Florian's group, but not for long.

"There you are!" Travis and his spirit rushed to Florian's group. "Come on! The fire will spread quickly. We gotta move!"

The drooling lizard beside him stood straight and stared at the group. It snarled as saliva spewed from its mouth.

"Stay away!" Florian yelled.

Travis lifted the table and tossed it aside.

Florian stood up and took a stance. "Hope. Take Blythe and run!"

Florian thrust her fist toward the stalker in self-defense. He was taller than Florian, about five-foot-eight. So she targeted his stomach.

The drooling lizard spirit wrapped around Florian's fist as Travis effortlessly blocked her arm with one hand.

Florian pulled back her fist and continued with a strike toward his legs.

In self-defense, Florian had learned, opponents taller than you have a longer arms' reach than yours. When fighting someone taller, the best option was to use your legs and aim for the opponent's legs. Limit their mobility by injuring or at least bruising their limbs.

Florian targeted the attacker's right shin with a low kick.

The drooling lizard spirit hopped up into the air. That must have meant the man was also going to leap and dodge the low kick.

In mid swing, Florian adjusted her kick slightly higher. Travis did leap slightly, and Florian followed through with her kick, landing a solid blow.

"No freaking way. You know martial arts too? Girl. That's awesome!" Travis said.

"Leave now, and nobody gets hurt," Florian said.

"If you were dealing with anyone else, I'm sure that would work. Unfortunately for you, I'm not one of those nobodies."

Travis was unharmed. He tucked in his body and lunged toward Florian, throwing punch after punch.

Florian could see his moves before he made them; his spirit shot its tail in the path of his punches. It sprang toward Florian like an accordion. She weaved and avoided each one of his jabs. It was still difficult for her; she could not counter his volley.

Under his mask, Travis had a smile on his face the entire time. Blow per blow, he laughed. "Nice footwork. It must have taken you years to master, but you are still too green to dodge this one!"

Travis readied himself. His spirit's cheeks inflated.

Florian knew something was coming. Whatever it was, she stepped inward toward Travis to close the gap.

The drooling lizard's eyes grew wide as it shuffled backward. It then clawed the floor with a confused glare.

Did I catch him off guard? Or is this what he wants?

Travis reached behind his back, making Florian stop in place. "Who are you, kid? You're all over the place. I can't tell if you're a pro or a novice. You're making moves that don't make any sense," Travis said.

Hope grabbed Blythe's hand and made a beeline for the door.

"I didn't forget about you."

Travis's spirit shot its long tongue toward Blythe. His arm shot toward Blythe, picking her up with one hand. Hope did not let go of Blythe's hand and silently hit Travis with her tiny fist.

"Let her go!" Florian said.

She grabbed a knife off one of the tables and lunged toward Travis. He effortlessly grabbed her arm and twisted it with his free hand, making Florian cringe in pain.

Travis tossed Blythe over his left shoulder and pinned Florian's arm with his right hand.

"Let go of me!" Blythe squirmed. "Do you know who my dad is? He is the strongest man in the world, and he will not forgive you if you don't put me down."

Blythe's bubble dog spirit barked endlessly and dispersed countless bubbles toward Travis.

"Haha, your father? Yeah right. He would never do something like that."

"Then my uncle will pulverize you! He is a police officer, and he will lock you awa—"

Blythe's bubble dog continued to shoot bubbles at Travis with no effect.

Hope's spirit chirped as Hope dangled from Blythe's hand, not letting go.

Florian grabbed a plate with her free arm and swung it wildly. Blythe kicked and screamed. Hope trembled as she clung to Blythe's hand. Travis kept Florian's arm locked in position, limiting her movements.

"Nice try, kid, but it will take more than that to beat me," Travis said.

"I would let them go if I were you."

Travis turned around to a six-foot-tall muscular man. He grabbed Blythe and Hope and knocked Travis across the room.

"You all right, Little Liter?"

It was Sergeant Honest Nowell. Behind him stood his tall slender spike spirit, exhaling, with its fists clenched tight.

THIRTEEN
BURNING BRAWL

PARTY PANCAKES
SEPTEMBER 8ᵀᴴ X288

Travis keeled over as he collided with dining tables and furniture. He rolled through the leftover food and drinks, off the tables, and into cover in one fluid motion. The drooling lizard spirit squirmed as it tumbled across the floor.

"You got my text!" Florian said.

"Get out of here, Little Liter."

"But it's two against one! We can catch him and turn him in."

"He's got a gun."

Florian froze for a moment. She knew firearms were strictly prohibited in Tarot Tori City. The entire time, the kidnapper had a gun. It freaked Florian out.

"Are you sure?"

"I know a gun holster when I see one. Get you and your sister out of here!"

"I wouldn't do that, kid. Unless you can outrun bullets too." The kidnapper, hands tucked in his pockets, blocked the exit. He maneuvered his way behind all the obstacles and smoke, catching Florian's group off guard.

"Judging by your attire, you are military. Let me guess, infantry?" The kidnapper had not drawn his gun yet. His spirit inflated its cheeks as it swept the floor with its tail.

"Not anymore. I'm more of a pencil pusher these days." Sergeant Honest Nowell tried to deescalate the situation while his slender spike spirit crouched in a running start position.

"Those must be some big pencils. No matter how many are a part of that fitness program of yours, I can still smell the blood on your hands from here."

Their spirits gurgled, each locked on to one another. Muffled sounds came from the faceless slender spike spirit as it twitched. The scales of the drooling lizard recoiled as its gaping mouth slathered its body with its tongue.

Florian shielded Hope and Blythe. She knew to escape as soon as she saw an opening.

Flames spread from the kitchen.

Honest hurled a chair toward the hooded man, weaving behind it. His spirit sprinted not a second slower.

The kidnapper swatted the chair out of the air with a kick. He kept his hands free to draw the gun at any moment. His lizard spirit spat saliva at the slender spirit.

Sergeant Nowell did not hesitate; he closed the distance and swung his fist. Travis chuckled as he backflipped over a table, dodging the blow.

The slender spike spirit swung its long arms, reaching for the drooling lizard spirit. It dodged every attempt, springing its tail like a backboard, leaping the same as its owner.

Honest tossed the table that was in his way, throwing it toward Travis.

Travis caught and held the table as Sergeant Nowell continued his combination of punches. Honest's first punch pierced right through the wooden table. The slender spike's arms passed through the furniture with each of Honest's strikes. A second, then a third hit shattered the table into pieces.

Travis whistled as if impressed. He stepped back with his footwork, luring Honest closer. The sergeant did not hesitate, diving straight into Travis's feint. The drooling lizard squeaked with a smile as the slender spike speared forward with both arms pointed out like an arrowhead.

"Honest! Watch out!" Florian said.

Travis flipped his whole body upward, landing a high kick to Sergeant Nowell's neck. Honest staggered but was still standing. The slender spike spirit stood straight and hovered its arm over the kidnapper. Honest attempted to grab Travis by his neck, but Travis followed up with a low sweep, trying to trip Honest. Travis's shin landed directly on the sergeant's metal prosthetic leg, concealed by his baggy pants and boot.

The lizard cried out and squirmed on the floor while Travis concealed his pain, hopping backward with his good leg.

"What the hell was that? First a magical girl and now a tin soldier?" Travis said.

Sergeant Honest continued his onslaught chasing Travis, throwing tables and chairs when the distance widened.

"You're so concerned about my gun. Great judgment on your part," Travis said.

Honest tackled Travis and shoved him into a table and then another.

Travis regained his footing when Honest's prosthetic tripped over a glass and leftover pancakes. Travis grabbed a couple of knives and forks lying on the floor. He stabbed them in Honest's back, but it wasn't enough to make the sergeant flinch.

Florian saw their souls grappling with one another. The lizard's drool splashed about as it sprang and slithered around Honest. The slender spike soul struggled, the same as Honest, its arms flailing about, finally grabbing the kidnapper.

Travis kept struggling, but Honest wouldn't budge.

"You're kidding," the kidnapper said.

Honest flipped Travis over his shoulders and body slammed him into another table. Shards of glass stuck out of Travis's back. Without letting go, Honest was on top of Travis, pinning him down with all his weight.

"Go! Little Liter!"

Florian forced Hope and Blythe through the flames and smoke toward the exit.

In the corner of Florian's eye, she noticed the lizard spirit was still moving; Honest's soul did not pin it down. The lizard's cheeks inflated as it wound up its tail.

"Watch out!" Florian said.

Travis arched his back and his legs, shifting Sergeant Nowell's body weight, rolling him over. Travis was able to break free from the pin and retreated a few tables back. Forks and shards of glass were sticking out from his back.

Their souls glared at one another: each roaring, teething, and taunting. The drooling lizard wound up its tongue and squished in its neck. Florian knew it was coming.

She grabbed Hope and Blythe and pulled them to the floor.

Travis reached for his gun with his left hand. Honest concentrated on the weapon, diving straight for it, leaving himself wide open. Travis slammed Honest's ear with a right jab. The light concussion caused Honest to lose his balance. Travis had merely pretended to draw his gun, luring for an opening.

"What's wrong, big guy? Did you finally realize you were dealing with the real deal?"

"A sucker punch won't work a second time," Honest said.

"Are you sure? I'm an excellent actor." Travis drew his pistol, pointing it at the girls ducking in cover.

Florian stared directly into the eyes of the drooling lizard. Its cheeks grinned, and its neck was tucked in, ready to fire its tongue.

Honest and his slender spike spirit dove in front of Florian and the girls, shielding them.

The gun's hammer snapped as the lizard shot its tongue, licking through the slender spike spirit. Outside, the gunshot was mistaken for the fire burning, breaking the building apart.

"See. Too easy." Travis laughed.

When Florian opened her eyes, the kidnapper had vanished. The fire had spread further, almost reaching the exit. Florian rushed over to the sergeant.

"Honest! Are you all right?"

"Yeah."

"Did you get shot?"

"No. I'm fine," Honest said, with utensils sticking out of his back.

Honest stood up, lifted Hope and Blythe, and carried them out of the burning Party Pancakes restaurant. Honest, Florian, Hope, and Blythe exited the restaurant safely from the front door.

Soon after, firefighters, ambulances, and police officers arrived on the scene.

"Honest, did you see how the kidnapper escaped?" Florian asked.

"It doesn't matter; all that matters is that you are safe now," Honest said.

Blythe and Hope were a little shaken but relieved they were safe.

ಜಿ

Travis escaped without a single witness. He went through the alley window, where he had tossed in the fireworks. Then he left through the escape route that he had secured in advance, ditching his mask and hood when he was in a secure location, and met up with his getaway driver.

"You're late, Travis. Vere's the girl?"

"Yeah, I botched the job. Big time."

"You vill not hear the end of it from Juke."

"It's my first failed solo job. What's the worst that could happen?"

"Dat vasn't you on the police scanner vas it? Setting fire to a restaurant?"

"Gahaha, that restaurant was terrible. I did the public a favor."

ಜಿ

In front of the burning Party Pancakes, it was near dusk. Florian's party sat a safe distance from the building alongside the onlookers. All four were covered from head to toe in soot and debris.

"I can't believe it—a real superhero. You saved us! Florian was like, kapow and bam! Then the sergeant came and threw the bad guy all over the place! Wham!" Blythe said, reenacting the scene.

Her bubble dog spirit squirted out a few tiny bubbles as she exaggerated a bit.

"Are you all right, Little Liter?" Honest asked Florian.

"Yeah. Are you all right? Those forks sticking out of your back can't be good."

"Yeah, don't take them out. Leave it for the EMT," Honest said. It was as if he didn't feel any pain whatsoever.

"Who was that guy?"

"I don't know, but he was the real deal. If he had used live rounds, I would have been a goner," Honest said.

"I thought he missed and ran away?" Blythe said.

"They were blanks. The kidnapper's gun, his tactics, his attitude, he was playing us the entire time," Sergeant Nowell said.

His slender spike spirit sat beside him, grunting and fidgeting in frustration.

Florian felt indebted to Honest. She had witnessed him jumping in front of the gun, shielding them with his body.

"Thank you for your heroic work! Now! Florian. Introduce me to our heroic gentlemen!" Blythe's bubble tail dog spirit wagged its tail and woofed with joy.

You little brat. Florian knew she was innocently acting the way she usually did.

The slender spike petted the bubble tail dog.

Honest Nowell bowed his debris-covered head and introduced himself to Blythe, wholly composed and respectfully.

Medics arrived and patched up the sergeant.

With them was a slim, blond, lightly tanned police officer accompanied by a red fox with a finely groomed cloak.

"Well, well, well. So you four were the last to leave the burning restaurant? Three kids and a military man. You do know the military are not the first responders. We are. If anything, you are the last responders."

He wore a standard Tarot Tori City Police Department uniform; it included handcuffs, a baton, a taser, a radio, a bodycam, and a badge. The only thing missing was a gun.

In Tarot Tori City, police were issued guns with careful deliberation and when the situation met specific conditions. They did have guns in their vaults and at their practice shooting ranges. But this emergency didn't call for weapons of that nature.

The officer's hair was combed back flat underneath his cap. He had a broad smile with sassy squinted eyes. He approached them with a laid-back saunter, tipping his hat with a wink. Beside him, the red fox sniffed every person in Florian's group, analyzing meticulously, looking for evidence. Florian confirmed the fox was the officer's spirit animal as no one batted an eye at it, examining everyone.

"I'm Officer Keen. I'll be asking you a few questions. Is that all right with you?"

The restaurant was ablaze behind Officer Keen as he questioned Florian's party. They explained to Officer Keen the events that unfolded from their perspective.

"So you're saying you fought a guy concealing his face, armed with a gun, who was stalking these three girls. Conveniently, all the identifiable features are clothing he could easily remove or change. Are you sure it wasn't a cap gun since it did not fire?" Keen asked.

"I'm sure. It was a magnum, silver, with a wooden grip," Honest said.

The fox spirit examined Honest, sniffing and snorting at the injuries. It quickly spotted his prosthetic leg. For a moment, the fox growled at the slender spike spirit as it swatted the fox away from the prosthetic. Florian believed this meant Honest Nowell was self-conscious about his prosthetic.

Officer Keen was only concerned with finding clues, making sure everything was consistent. He continued. "Let me get your names."

"Sergeant Honest Nowell."

"Florian Lilly Cobblestone."

"And you?" Keen said, pointing toward Hope.

Hope signed her name as her seashell dove flapped its wings, imitating the hands used in the gestures.

"Sorry, she is mute. She's my sister, Hope Cobblestone," Florian said.

"I see. Thank you. And you?" Keen asked.

"Blythe Banquet. The princess saved by my knights in shining armor, the—"

"Wait, Banquet? Blythe Banquet?" Keen said. The fur on the red fox spirit stood on end, puffing into a ball.

"Y-yes, what's wrong?" Florian asked, remembering the name from somewhere before.

"How did you get here?" Keen asked Blythe.

"I was hanging out with my friends, and they said they would take me home after dinner . . . and. . ." The bubble tail dog stopped wagging its tail. Worry appeared on Blythe's face.

"Wait here for just a moment." Officer Keen left to speak with his senior officer and soon contacted their chief.

They checked their database and returned to Florian's group with handcuffs.

"Sergeant Honest Nowell, under the suspicion of kidnapping, you are under arrest. We will question you further at the station. Anything you say may be used against you."

Florian thought she misheard him. "What!? Sergeant Honest saved us. There has to be some kind of mistake."

"Don't worry, kid. We are just following procedures. Of course Honest Nowell is innocent until proven guilty. We will review all evidence and investigate further," Officer Keen said with a smug smirk. His fox spirit was wagging its tail calmly, infuriating Florian further.

"Why are you so calm? Were you even listening? I told you the real culprit is still out there! Honest is not a kidnapper. I texted him to meet us at the restaurant because someone was stalking us," Florian said.

"Little Liter, it's fine. I'll be fine," Honest said with the monotone straight face he always carried. However, his slender spike spirit dropped to its knees.

"No, it's not fine!" Florian said.

"We'll also be questioning you too, Florian Lilly Cobblestone. As of right now, you could be the sergeant's accomplice," Officer Keen said. His fox grunted with a muffled growl.

Florian clenched her fist at the accusation. The attitude of Officer Keen, displayed by his fox, just fueled her tension even further.

"Little Liter." Honest and his soul trembled. "There are some things from my past I haven't told you. It happened a long time ago, and I am no longer the way I was. I changed thanks to you and Dr. Ronaldo. I promise to tell you everything later. Okay? Please calm down for now."

Florian had never seen Honest with a frown before. His slender spike spirit's head faced the ground. Its arms drooped lifelessly to its side. Honest was telling the truth.

Florian blamed herself; that was her first thought. She didn't care about his criminal background; she felt guilty that she had texted Sergeant Honest Nowell for assistance, bringing him into the situation, not knowing his criminal record. She knew Sergeant Nowell had experienced a hard life, and he was trying to change for the better. She could tell just by looking, as she could see his soul clear as day. For seven years, the sergeant had been a friend she could trust.

Blythe cried out and flailed her arms. "They protected me! They're not the bad guys!"

She pouted and fidgeted as Officer Keen and several other officers escorted her to a patrol car.

"We'll escort Blythe to her father immediately. The rest of you will stay for questioning and wait for your parents to arrive," Officer Keen said.

Florian stood up, holding back her anger, "Wait, I was in charge of bringing her home safely. I'll go with you to make sure she gets there."

"That's acceptable. We'll question you further afterward. I guess your sister will also be tagging along," Officer Keen said.

Hope and her seashell dove spirit clung tightly to Florian. She was quiet the entire time but worried all the same.

Blythe calmed down, with Hope and Florian accompanying her.

Florian looked back and saw Sergeant Honest Nowell getting placed in handcuffs. Her heart slumped. She thought of nothing but clearing their names and catching the real criminal, still at large.

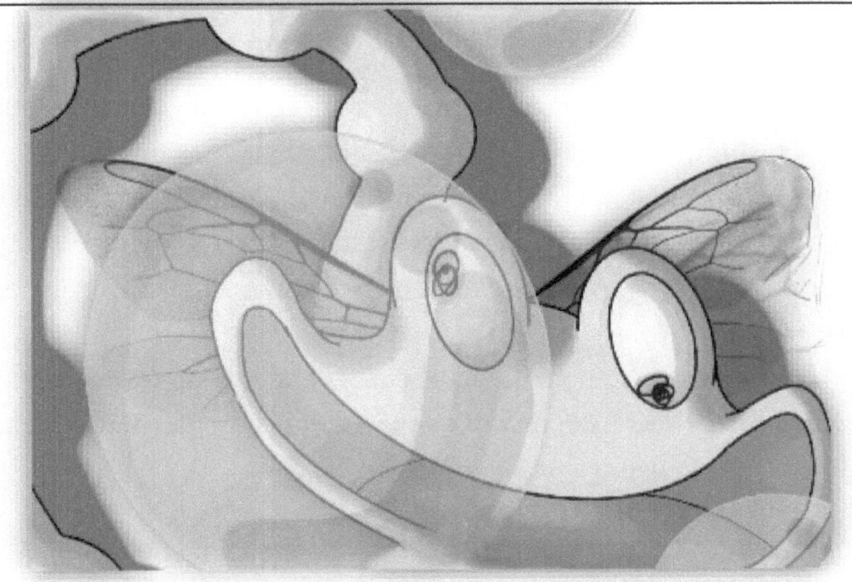

FOURTEEN
THOUGHT BUBBLE

PLINTH TERRACE
SEPTEMBER 8TH X288

The Banquet residence, 6:30 p.m. On the porch was a makeshift stage and podium. Cameras were on air, reporters silent with questions at the ready.

That was when he appeared at the center of it all. The mayor of Tarot Tori City himself, William Rite Banquet. His brimming smile outshone his perfectly pressed black suit, red shirt, and black tie.

"Good evening, my dear residents of Tarot Tori City. I am sure you are all hungry for an explanation of our current situation. Let me start with this." The sparkle in his eye turned into a sincere frown. "This afternoon, at four-thirty p.m., a ransom note was discovered in my inbox, and my beloved daughter, Blythe Banquet, was nowhere to be found."

The mayor bowed his head in silence.

The crowd murmured as camera flashes captured the moment.

"And to my amazement, while we were frantically searching for my daughter, we received countless online donations to pay for the ransom. I am grateful to you all, but I cannot accept it. It is morally wrong to negotiate with these terrorists. I swear I will use every resource at my disposal to find another way to get my daughter back."

Mayor Banquet pointed to the sky, and his stoic demeanor returned. "I swear I will make them pay for their crimes and prevent this from ever happening again!"

-POP-

The mob applauded as Mayor Banquet readied himself for questioning.

"Sir, are there any correlations between this and your reelection campaign?"

"I know the timing seems to fit perfectly. As of this moment, we don't know the purpose or what goal these individuals are trying to achieve. But I do know I will do everything in my power to protect all citizens of Tarot Tori City. Everyone's blood, sweat, and tears made this city the way it is today. I don't plan to stop offering my own."

-POP-

"May we see the ransom note?"

"I am afraid it's in the custody of the TTCPD. It's an ongoing investigation, so please remain patient."

"What about your opposition? Has she expressed anything about the situation?"

"My political rival has not made a single comment as of yet. I assume out of respect and condolence. I am not speaking ill of her."

-POP-

"Both of us candidates are unanimous in our utmost respect for each other, the city, and the previous mayor's wishes. We promise to honor his memory as we take great strides forward for Tarot Tori City. It's an honor facing such a prestigious candidate."

-POP-

"In a city as developed as ours, every citizen tends to flourish extraordinarily. This is why I love this city so much."

Florian arrived at the scene and shuddered at the large crowd. News vans, police cars, and onlookers blocked the driveway.

Blythe's soul whimpered.

"Are you all right?" Florian asked.

"I don't know what's going on. I'm not scared. Maybe a little bit," Blythe said. A single bubble came out of her soul when she said she wasn't scared.

Florian hugged Blythe and patted her on the head. "Leave it to me. I will clear things up."

Internally, Florian was still processing what to say.

Officer Keen directed the group. "Follow me."

Florian, Blythe, Hope, and Officer Keen entered the crowd.

Each person and their spirit gazed toward the stage, as if entranced by every word the mayor said.

Florian didn't let go of Hope's and Blythe's hands; she clutched them tighter.

"Blythe. If you can hear me, your father loves you, and I will bring you home. I swear my life on it," Banquet said over the speakers.

-POP-

Florian felt a chill down her spine. The entire area was engulfed in bubbles.

These were not like Blythe's dog spirit's bubbles. They took different shapes and were multicolored. They looked as if they were dancing, synchronized, bursting in a coordinated manner.

What the hell is this? Florian could no longer feel Blythe's hand.

"Dad!" Blythe ran to the front of the crowd.

"Blythe?" Banquet said over the mic as the crowd divided, revealing Blythe, Florian, Hope, and Officer Keen.

Silence ensued as the cameras focused on the group.

Florian looked up toward the stage. Mayor Banquet stood there in surprise and he smiled.

At his side was no animal or pet. It was the thing blowing the bubbles that loomed over the crowd—perched on the mayor's back like a pedestal. It had a hose-like neck, with lumps wiggling up to its head. Its gigantic distorted head had see-through wings at its nape. It was flapping and floating about aimlessly with its eyes crossed, smiling the entire time, twisting its throat, and tangling itself around the crowd. Sprouting out from its tiny body were two long wrinkly eel arms that caressed the giant bubbles coming from its huge mouth. It was monstrous, grotesque, and intimidating.

Florian couldn't think straight. The cause wasn't the stress from the events prior; it was the thing that loomed over the six-foot-three blond mayor. Just being in its presence, Florian couldn't process her world.

"Blythe!" The mayor leaped off stage to his daughter.

-POP-

A bubble popped right next to Blythe's head.

"Dad." Blythe began to cry. After all that she had gone through, Blythe finally showed her real emotions.

The mayor crouched down to his daughter; they embraced and slowly sobbed.

"I'm sorry, Dad! I'm sorry."

The press took pictures, and the onlookers applauded.

-POP-

A chain reaction of bubbles burst, clearing out most of the bubbles in the area.

"Vultures." Florian overheard Officer Keen.

Everything was happening so fast, Florian didn't have time to process what was going on.

The mayor hugged his daughter while his spirit coiled its lumpy neck around both of them. Bubbles inflated from the lumps exiting its mouth as it bobbed its head in the air. With tear-filled eyes, Blythe hugged her father unconditionally. Her bubble-tailed dog placed its paws up against the father, begging for a hug too.

The mayor glanced toward Florian with a smile. He covered his chin with one hand as if in thought. His eyes were not weeping; they were filled with excitement.

"You there, young girl. Are you the one who helped my daughter?" Mayor Banquet asked.

His soul, aimlessly floating about, reeled in its head and looked Florian directly in the eye. Its giant crossed eyes pulled together and targeted Florian dead center. It waited for a response.

Florian just froze up, analyzing what it was about to do next.

A neck lump squeezed toward its head. It inflated a bubble, like bubblegum, engulfing Florian's head. Florian's hair stood on end.

"What's your name, young hero?" Mayor Banquet asked.

Florian was grossed out and wanted to wriggle free and run away. However, that was what a younger Florian would have done.

Hope clung to Florian the entire time. Blythe clung to her father.

"Cobblestone." She could barely breathe. It was suffocating. The cameras, the press, each with their unique souls, all with their eyes fixed on Florian. She reminded herself of what Dr. Ronaldo had guided her to do when she felt anxious.

"Florian Lilly Cobblestone," Florian said, making direct eye contact with the mayor. Above the mayor, his cross-eyed spirit looked down at Florian.

Ignore everyone else. Concentrate.

"You're a mess; I can only imagine what you went through," Mayor Banquet said with a smile.

-POP-

What!? Why did his spirit's bubble pop? Was that a lie? Florian didn't let any of her confusion show on her face.

"I have so many questions," Mayor Banquet said.

"As do I," Florian said.

She could barely utter a word with the cameras flashing in her face. The countless spirit eyes scanned every movement she made. Officer Keen's spirit appeared from thin air between Florian and the mayor. Its fur color was different. It was the same color as the pavement. Its gray fur changed back to its red coat as it snarled at the mayor and the reporters.

"Hold on," Officer Keen said, adjusting his greased hair under his officer cap. "We got first dibs on questioning the kid. Get in line."

The mayor's spirit turned toward Officer Keen. It didn't inhale a single breath, yet it started to inflate another bubble.

"What a pity. Hahaha. You are. . ." The mayor looked at the officer's badge. "Officer Keen. . . Oh! The rookie who was transferred here recently."

The first bubble.

"Yeah. You know me?" Keen said as his fox spirit snarled, head low to the ground, ready to pounce.

A second bubble. It drifted over the fox spirit.

"Sure. What kind of mayor would I be if I didn't? Tell me, how are your efforts going? Any luck?"

A third bubble. This time over the head of Officer Keen.

"What do you mean?"

The spirit's eel arm reached over to the third bubble.

"You know," the mayor winked, "the dating scene."

-POP-

"How the hell do you? What?" Keen was flustered.

"Hahaha. Don't let your enthusiasm for the ladies distract you too much. Hahaha." The mayor patted the shoulder of Officer Keen.

-POP-

The chain of bubbles burst.

The cheerfulness of the mayor spread to Officer Keen. He couldn't help but let out a chuckle himself, as awkward as it was.

"Now then, Florian, was it?" Mayor Banquet turned back toward Florian and Hope, his spirit in tow.

"They protected me, Dad," Blythe said, clinging to her father.

"And your name?" Mayor Banquet addressed Hope.

Hope signed her name.

"Oh, Hope Cobblestone. I remember. I hope my letter made it to you. Hahaha. I am sad I will never get the chance to speak with you and hear your voice. We will have to settle with sign language," the mayor signed.

-POP-

A bubble above Florian and Hope popped. Florian remembered the letter from seven years ago.

He knows sign language too? I don't understand. The bubble just popped over me. Was that a lie? What lie did I fall for? Florian's internal thoughts were jumbled.

Banquet smiled and turned to the cameras.

The live feed cameras just finished setting up in front of them.

"Citizens of Tarot Tori City! These are our young heroes! Florian Lilly Cobblestone and Hope Cobblestone. These brave girls are the reason my daughter is home safe and sound.

"I look forward to thanking them properly very soon. Since this is an ongoing investigation, I will let the police take it from here. Please direct all of your questions to them from here on out." Mayor Banquet picked up his daughter and retired without answering any more questions.

When the mayor finished speaking, the chief of TTCPD stumbled up out of breath as if on cue. He tried calling out to the mayor, but the full brunt of the reporters swarmed the chief with questions.

Officer Keen escorted Florian and Hope away from the press for questioning.

"Damn it, Keen!" The chief gave him a mean look as he tried to shake off the reporters.

Keen covered his face and tilted his head, apologizing to the chief. He had lost an essential witness, Blythe Banquet.

Florian was still processing what happened. *I'm no hero; I didn't do a damn thing. The culprit is still out there.*

FIFTEEN
SCHOOL BUZZ

TAROT TORI POLICE DEPARTMENT
SEPTEMBER 8TH X288

Florian could not believe what she was writing. It had been the most eventful day of her life, yet she could not decipher any part of it in her journal. Only Mayor Banquet's spirit was lingering in her mind, unnamed. Florian was still contemplating what she should have said to the mayor. He had commanded the crowd like an orchestra. His soul had a mouth so big it could have swallowed Florian whole. Usually, she could piece events together and conclude right away the symbolism of individuals' souls. This time she was utterly stumped.

The police questioning did not go in her favor either. Sergeant Honest Nowell was still in police custody, and the lack of defining features of their assailant was not helping their case. The only thing they had to go by was that the kidnapper was male and about five foot seven inches. Even what would have been smoke-filled security footage was all lost in the fire.

When the Cobblestone parents picked up both Florian and Hope at the station, they squeezed them tight and did not let go until they all were safe at home.

☯

The following day, Florian entered her classroom, shoulders slouched. Consumed with processing her thoughts, Florian planted her face into her desk. Her classmates could almost see steam escape from her head.

Soon all of Florian's classmates crowded around her, each with their spirit in tow.

"Flori! You were on TV!" Alexander Rodriguez said, with his monkey spirit applauding.

"Yeah! What happened!?" Amalia Simmers said as her bat ogled Florian with wide-open eyes.

"I tried texting her as soon as I saw her," Samuel said, with his kangaroo spirit scratching its ear.

"Same," a boy with a horse said.

"I didn't get in contact with her either," the quiet girl in the back of the class with a snail added.

"Calm down, everyone. Flori's still rebooting from whatever happened. She's been like this since grade school. I'm sure there's a good reason why she couldn't text us back," Alexander said. His monkey waved its tail like a flag.

"The police must have confiscated her phone," Amalia said as her bat let out a big yawn.

"That must be it!" the entire class agreed.

"I was so worried when I saw Flori covered in soot," a girl with a rabbit added.

"Yeah, before the mayor's speech, there was news of a burning building," said the boy with a boar.

"Really!? Were you in a burning building? Flori?" the boy with a penguin asked.

"Florian! What did you do?" the class murmured, all worried.

"Is Hope all right?" a girl with a mongoose asked.

"The news said Florian rescued the mayor's daughter," their teacher hollered out to the class.

"Cool!"

"Flori, that's amazing!"

"That's Florian, all right!"

"When Flori feels better, let's have a party!"

The entire class was in agreement.

Florian, with her head glued to the desk, shuddered.

Amalia, Florian's trusted secretary, noticed Florian whisper something under her breath. Both Amalia and her bat spirit brought their ears closer.

One by one, the class went silent.

"What's going on?"

"Did Florian say something?"

"Shhh."

Amalia stood up. "Flori said the culprit is still on the loose."

"Wait, so does that mean they might go after the mayor's daughter again?" someone in the crowd asked.

"Even worse, they might go after Florian or Hope for revenge," another said.

"No way!?" The class started to fret.

"Don't worry! Hope goes to the same elementary school as my kid brother. I will call him up to get a group to stay with Hope after school," said the boy with the boar spirit.

"Yeah, I will text my little sister too. She can tag along," said the girl with the rabbit spirit.

"Brilliant. We will all go home in groups. If you see anything suspicious, text the group chat," Alexander said as his monkey hopped onto his shoulder.

"Don't worry about us, Flori. We've got your back," Amalia said.

Florian, still slumped on her desk, gave a thumbs up.

Her friends were very comforting, yet she did not see them as friends. They were more like thankful acquaintances in Florian's eyes. Of course, her "acquaintances" didn't see her that way.

Four upperclassmen invaded the freshman classroom. One boy had an ox spirit. Another boy had a crow spirit perched on his head. The third boy crept about with a hyena.

The girl lurking behind them had a cluster of fur for a soul. She had long blonde hair, a black headband, a down expression, and seemed out of place.

"Where's the girl that was on TV?" the boy with the ox asked.

His lackeys chuckled. The girl with the fur cluster spirit didn't.

"This is Florian's homeroom. What do you want with her?" a classmate said.

"I'm here to make the city's hero my girlfriend," the ox boy said as his ox huffed and puffed.

The hyena and crow lackey boys laughed at the sheer brilliance of their friend's plan. The blonde girl looked disappointed, as if discouraged she was in the same room as the other three.

"Wow," said a classmate.

"With her as my girlfriend, I'll be the most popular guy around. Maybe get on TV myself," the ox boy said.

"I don't think that's a very nice thing to say. At least learn Florian's name," said another classmate.

"You got a problem with that?" the two lackey boys asked. Their hyena and crow spirits mocked the others.

"Sorry, she isn't feeling well. We are going to have to ask you to leave," Alex said.

"Who are you? Her boyfriend? Well, I wasn't talking to you," the ox boy said. He high-fived his two lackeys, but the girl behind them left them hanging.

"I'm not her boyfriend. She isn't looking to date anyone for that matter," Alex said. "She isn't feeling well."

"Yeah, leave her alone."

"Get lost!"

"Posers."

The entire class was in agreement.

"Why is everybody defending this chick?" the four intruders said.

"Well, I want to see for myself if she's all that's cracked up to be," the ox boy said.

That was when even more first-year students entered the classroom.

"Is Florian all right?"

"What happened?"

"Who are you four?"

"Did someone say something about a party?"

The classroom was attracting too much attention. Even teachers were checking to see if Florian was all right under the guise of dispersing the crowd.

"Ah, bro. I think we're trapped," said the lackey with the hyena.

"What the hell is going on here?" the ox boy asked.

Even Alex's sister Sera and a few other upperclassmen showed up.

"Flori! You were a mess! You didn't look like your normal self on TV. Are you all right?" Sera asked. Her goldfish soul was now a large koi fish. Its fins were elegantly flowing in the air around the entire classroom. "What are these three idiots doing here?"

"Sera knows this freshman?" asked the lackey with the crow.

"Of course. You didn't know? Flori's special," Sera said.

"She helped me find my lost dog when I was little," the boar boy said.

"She helped me in middle school. She is so cool," the girl with the snail said.

"Is it true? I heard she beat up the national junior league boxing champ," said a classmate.

"I was there; he was an asshole and deserved it," Samuel with his kangaroo said.

"Wait, it was true?" asked another classmate.

"Yeah, everyone that went to her middle school last year knows her name," Sera said.

"Hell, most of us followed her here," Alex said.

"Even teachers tried transferring to this school once Flori applied here," Amalia said.

"Is she a superhero or something?" the ox boy asked.

"No, she's Florian Lilly Cobblestone. She's just doing what she has always been doing since grade school," Alex said. His monkey stuck its tongue out at the intruders.

Everyone from Florian's middle school told their stories of how Florian had helped them in some shape or form. Small potatoes compared to recent events. She helped teachers, classmates, and anyone else in her sight.

To Florian, she merely supported the souls in need. She thought nothing of it. Her good deeds were not going unnoticed. It caused a chain reaction of classmates assisting one another. Soon her simple, caring attitude changed an entire generation of people around her.

She was okay with it; everyone was happier and friendlier because of it. Florian could concentrate on other things too.

Like at the moment, Florian was still steaming in thought at her desk, thinking of all the events that had taken place. More importantly, she was contemplating what steps she needed to take to catch the culprit.

"Forget this. You all are weirdos!" The intruding upperclassmen ran off. The girl with the fur cluster spirit did not. She stared at Florian for a moment and sauntered off. Her fur cluster spirit gritted its teeth and glared with its deep white pupils.

"As long as we stick together, we can prevent the kidnapper from striking again." The classroom cheered and planned a buddy system to keep eyes on one another.

"Who were those upperclassmen, sis?" Alex said.

"They are nobodies, except the girl with them. She's a weird one. Her boyfriend disappeared and hasn't been to school for weeks. Rumors say she looks for him around the city every day after school. Those three idiots are close friends with her boyfriend. They sure are acting tough, but they aren't. At least they are keeping an eye on her. If the man I loved disappeared, I wouldn't know what I would do," Sera said.

"Gross," Alex said.

"What was that?" Sera asked.

Alex and his monkey spirit retreated behind Florian.

"This sounds interesting," Amalia said. "Maybe Flori can look into it when she's feeling better?"

"All right! As long as we have Flori's back, nothing can stop us!" Alex said.

Over the intercom, an announcement was made. "-orian Cobblestone, please come to the principal's office. Again, Florian Cobblestone, please come to the principal's office."

The classroom morale fell. All the souls looked at Florian. "Be careful, Flori." That was what she took from their worrisome expressions. She had an ominous feeling in her head, almost like a lump of air trying to escape her gut.

ഇ౦ణ

When Florian approached the office, the principal met her there.

"Florian Cobblestone. Someone is here to see you," the principal said, wiping his sweat.

Florian didn't see anyone she recognized until a limousine pulled up in front of the school doors.

SIXTEEN
INFLATED EGO

SOUTH TORI HIGH
SEPTEMBER 9TH X288

It was Mayor William Rite Banquet with his floating smile spirit. He was wearing completely different attire than the night before—a sparkling red suit and a checkered tie. He stepped out of the limousine with a pep in his step and an excited expression.

"Good morning, everyone. Sorry I'm late. I was taking care of some critical business in my Limo Force One. Just kidding." Banquet laughed.

-POP-

"Mayor Banquet, it's such an honor to have you here during your busy schedule." The principal continued his courtesy spiel.

The moment Banquet entered the school, his floating smile spirit looked only at Florian. It didn't drift about in any other direction. Its long hose neck stuck to the mayor's back as he walked.

Florian backed herself against the wall, staring at the spirit, knowing she had fallen into a trap. She tensed, unprepared for what to say or how to act around such a demented person.

Mayor Banquet applauded. "Yes, you have such a distinguished school. I am thrilled that you all have worked so hard to keep our citizens in top form—especially this lovely young lady who single-handedly rescued my daughter."

He addressed Florian and reached out for a handshake. "I'm so glad to have arranged this heart to heart to thank you personally. I would like you to know I am very interested in you, young hero. You wouldn't mind showing me around *your* school, do you?"

Florian studied his palm, then his self-righteous smile, and gradually reached for his hand.

-POP-

A bubble she hadn't noticed burst right as she grabbed the mayor's hand.

What? Where did that bubble come from? When was it inflated? Why did it pop? How was that a lie?!

Her panicked expression leaked through as she looked away, and her grip weakened.

"Peculiar." The mayor paused. "I take it that you are nervous. By all means, tell me if my presence becomes an ordeal."

Mayor Banquet walked a few paces down the hall and came to a halt. "Um . . . Young Cobblestone, I believe *you* are supposed to lead the way. Please excuse us, Mr. Principal." He smiled.

Florian's attention reignited as she chased the mayor, leaving the principal behind.

While classes were in session, the two roamed the school hallways.

⁊⁊

Florian escorted the mayor. "And here's our school's football field."

"Astounding!" The mayor's smile brightened as his soul hovered counterclockwise around Florian's head, analyzing her every move. Its neck slowly wrapped around her.

112

"You know, I can't thank you enough, young Cobblestone. As you may have already guessed, I didn't come out here just for a tour of the school. Tell me more about yourself, young hero."

His soul's head bobbled as it inflated a bubble right beside Florian's head.

I'm no hero. So that's why the mayor's here, to interrogate me. Wait, he called me "young hero," and a bubble inflated. Does that mean he's sarcastic? What's he saying? I need to respond.

"I'm just a normal high schooler," she said and observed him closely for his response.

"Hahaha. Surely you jest. No 'normal' high schooler could do what you did. I heard from my daughter that you even fought the culprit hand to hand. Is that right?" The spirit's mouth smiled wider.

"Yes. I did defend myself, but I wouldn't say I succeeded."

The mayor paused with a smile as his joyful eyes pierced through Florian. It was like he was anticipating, encouraging Florian to continue, but with no result.

He then responded, "I don't mean to prod, but did your junior league karate experience give you the confidence boost you needed at your most dire moment?"

Florian was speechless. She questioned how he—

-POP-

"How did I know? Hahaha, I wouldn't be the outstanding mayor that I am if I didn't." He smiled playfully. "I'm sure you're glad you had the opportunity to learn self-defense. It's key to have many extracurricular activities available to your citizens. Hahaha. Your sister, how's she holding up?"

Another bubble began to inflate.

"Just fine. She even felt comfortable going to school today."

"Tough girl. My daughter wanted to as well. I would've let her, but the police strictly said no." His pure white teeth sparkled.

-POP-

What? He just lied about his daughter. Does he not care about Blythe's safety?

"Say, do you aim to go into politics one day?" he asked.

"No, I never considered it. To tell the truth, I have no idea what I want to do."

"I see. Then you are a procrastinator? Hahaha, I'm kidding. I tend to procrastinate a lot myself. Like right now." He smiled.

Bubbles accumulated around Florian. His spirit was laughing, taunting, and reminding her of her ill preparation.

Florian did not let out a chuckle. She was getting annoyed. She understood why Blythe acted the way she did.

"Tell me, who will you vote for in the upcoming local election?"

"Oh, that's right. That's coming up, isn't it?" Florian said.

She honestly didn't care much about the election because her mind was on other things. She noticed the mayor's spirit squinting its giant eyes in suspicion.

"Ouch, you sure have a sharp tongue. It sure doesn't feel like I'm talking to an ordinary high schooler. Hahaha."

Did the mayor misunderstand my response? If I answer half-heartedly, he might interpret my words the wrong way, possibly incriminating myself. His soul is inflating another bubble! How am I supposed to defend myself? He's in complete control. I have to say something!

"I just don't know who to vote for yet," she said.

Banquet combed his suave hair. The spirit opened its mouth six feet wide and exhaled a foul yawn.

"This election, held every three years, is exclusive to Tarot Tori City. Even high schoolers are automatically registered to vote. It doesn't make a difference who you vote for, and no matter who gets your support, your vote counts. I say that with absolute certainty."

The mayor seemed to notice Florian's attention dwindling. "Hmm, so even that doesn't interest you? I'm sure there are a few who are dissatisfied with the current association or would like nothing more than to see a brand new administration. Like your veteran friend, Honest Nowell."

-POP-

Florian succumbed to another bubble. She clenched her teeth when she heard the name.

"You said you had a lot of questions. I'm right here, so ask away. The point is to make your voice heard. So speak up! Even if your opinions aren't popular ones, you will not be ignored."

How dare he say that with that wicked grin? He's mocking me. He knows that Sergeant Honest Nowell is still in police custody.

Florian twitched and turned toward the mayor.

"Finally, a reaction." He smiled. "I talked with your veteran friend; he seemed to be happy that no one other than him got hurt. It's a shame. I got the feeling he didn't like my company very much. Hahaha."

With each comment and question, he probed, testing how Florian would react. Like the way the police had questioned her.

Florian, surrounded by bubbles, glared up toward Mayor Banquet. She puffed her cheeks slightly as her shoulders broadened.

"Hey, wanna know a secret? I also spoke with the police chief; he said they found what started the fire. Some kids were playing with fireworks in the vicinity. When questioned, the kids said they found the fireworks on a park bench, just sitting there. Lighter and everything all in the same shopping bag." He paused.

"Could their horseplay have caused the fire? Maybe a stray firework entered the restaurant's kitchen window. Hmm?" He grinned at her. "I wonder who left the fireworks on that bench? Any ideas? Young hero? You're not hiding anything, are you?"

-POP-

Florian couldn't believe what he was saying. It was like he was implying she was the one who started the fire.

"Do I have your attention now?" the mayor said with a mischievous smile.

She struggled to remain calm. She couldn't stand to see the man's sparkling white teeth any longer.

"A-and here is the school auditorium," Florian said, trembling from the mayor's accusations.

The auditorium was three stories tall. Two hundred rows of velvet seats on both sides, floors carpeted the same. Elegantly engraved statues raced along the walls and columns. Rows of curtains, an arsenal of lights, surround sound speakers in every corner, indeed the whole shebang.

"Wow, such a magnificent stage. That reminds me. . ." The floating smile spirit chewed and spewed the mayor's words as if it was on cue. "I have a proposal. Why don't we hold a live award ceremony to celebrate your grand achievement? Right here, in this very auditorium."

Florian was puzzled. Just a moment ago, he was accusing her of arson, and now this.

Is this some ploy to guilt me into confessing a crime I didn't commit? Florian couldn't tell. The mayor was talking circles around her, and she couldn't keep up.

"I would like to award you a scholarship on camera for the entire city to see."

"What!?" Florian adjusted her glasses.

"In fifteen days, we will have it televised. You will have an opportunity to say a few words too. A speech! Yes! Be prepared. There will be reporters, friends, family, and enemies too." He winked with a smile.

"Enemies? What? I don't think that's a good idea?"

"On the contrary. It's a splendid idea. You can even prepare properly this time."

"What do you mean by that?"

"What you are going to say, of course. You can prepare your speech, your responses to questions the media might have, all while your friends and family cheer you on. Oh, also, including what you will use the scholarship for, the people will eat that right up."

Bubble after bubble, the swarm blurred Florian's vision.

She lowered her head. "But . . . I didn't do anything. . ."

-POP-

"Yet. . ."

-POP-

A chain of bubbles burst.

"What did you say?"

"Kidding."

"Feeling discouraged, are we? Don't forget; your school will get more attention. It may encourage more enrollment, higher funding, and even inspire your classmates to work harder to chase their dreams."

ᬇ

"Thank you so much for the tour. It was as beautiful as the day I cut the grand opening ribbon."

-POP-

"You already knew the layout of the school, didn't you?"

"Of course I did. I just wanted to see how you would handle being my tour guide. Hahaha. See you in fifteen days."

The sharp mayor hopped in his limousine with his spirit's head floating out the window like a balloon on a string. The spirit's eyes darted toward Florian as it twisted and tumbled in the air, driven away by the chauffeur.

Mayor Banquet left Florian with countless bubbles floating about, still haunting her. He was merely flaunting his psychological warfare like a toy to harass Florian.

"Why would he say that?" Florian clenched her fist. "It's like he knows. . ."

Certain doom wouldn't leave Florian's mind. Deep down, she knew this day would come. Regretfully, she had no other choice.

SEVENTEEN
FOOLISH KARMA

*S. BROOK COUNSELING & THERAPY CLINIC
SEPTEMBER 10TH X288*

Dr. Ronaldo clicked his pen shut.

"Florian called. She said she had something vital she needed to tell me. It sounded urgent," Dr. Ronaldo said.

"Eep! Dr. Ronaldo, did you see the news? I'm so worried about Florian; she might be in danger," Miss Garcia Fumblehouse said, clutching her plush turtle in front of her face. "Oh, I was so worried. Florian was on TV, covered head to toe in soot and pancakes. The mayor said Florian rescued his daughter. I couldn't believe it."

Miss Garcia Fumblehouse, now twenty-eight years old, was a regular at the clinic, and even after seven years, she remained the same.

Unbeknownst to her, she was a local celebrity with her long fluffy dress, her iconic parasol wherever she went, and her curly braided hair. She was always carrying one of her homemade plush turtles, now Sir Polyester Press Cotton the Seventh. The urban legend was if you saw the short lady with the turtle and parasol in the wild, you would have good luck for the rest of the day.

"A-and Sergeant Honest was involved too. H-have you heard anything from him?" Miss Fumblehouse said, twiddling her thumbs.

She also had a massive crush on the sergeant ever since she first met him all those years ago.

"Everything is getting straightened out as we speak, don't worry. Please leave it to me. Later today, I plan to go down to the station to clear things up," Dr. Ronaldo said.

Dr. Ronaldo was now twenty-five years old. He had not changed much on the outside. His confidently styled black hair had more strands of gray. He wore complementary glasses, a blue plaid button shirt with a green vest, and brown khaki pants.

"Oh, thank goodness. I know I can always rely on you, Dr. Ronaldo. Like when I needed time off from my new part-time coworker."

"Yeah, she ended up resigning a week into your vacation leave."

"It was the best birthday present I could've asked for; the torment she put me through for every little thing was ridiculous. Working with the library for over ten years and the single year I worked with that troublemaker was the most traumatizing thing I've ever experienced. I lost sleep, worrying about what she was going to report me for next." She hid under her plush turtle.

"I'm so happy you prevailed, as your doctor and your friend."

With strangers, Miss Fumblehouse was usually shy and had a reserved attitude that complemented how polite she was. Here she felt at home.

"When did you become so dependable? I remember when you were just a toddler running around Dr. Steinsbrook and Honest

Nowell. I babysat you so many times, and now you are counseling me through my life troubles. Oh, the sweet memories."

"It's not a problem, Miss Fumblehouse. I owe you and Dr. Steinsbrook a lot. Without you, I wouldn't have been able to take care of myself during my studies."

She says babysat but she's more like an older sister. She made sure I ate as I chipped away at my studies. We may be only three years apart, but she was the one who kept my shoes tied.

"Dr. Steinsbrook was a real slave driver when it came to your studies. I felt so bad for you."

"He wasn't that bad."

"Really?"

"Okay, maybe a little."

"Reminiscing is calming, but my heart still feels like it will burst out from my chest. Mayor Banquet is terrifying! I don't see what others see in him."

"Why do you say that? He's done so much for Tarot Tori City."

"It's the way he looked at Florian. Here. Look." Fumblehouse handed Ronaldo the current newspaper.

The front page had a blown-up photo of Florian's encounter with the mayor.

"See it?"

"It seems normal to me. Florian looks a little goofy, covered in soot, while the mayor is spotlessly clean beside her. Her face looks funny. We should frame this," Ronaldo said.

"Exactly, Florian's face. She's terrified, and the mayor is smiling like nothing's wrong. It just doesn't sit right with me." Fumblehouse shivered in her seat.

"I guess you have a point. I will ask Florian if anything is wrong. Don't worry; if she feels comfortable sharing the reason, I'm sure she'll let you know to ease your concern."

"Okay. Can we try hypnotherapy again? Even if it doesn't work, just one more time. Please."

"It's not hypnotherapy. You are talking about the white noise therapy, right?"

"Yeah, that."

The easiest way to describe noise therapy would be relaxing techniques. For example, it could help people sleep using sounds that subconsciously relaxed them, such as ocean sounds or other ambient noises. Nearly every person had a mindset that allowed them to relax after specific criteria were met, like their room's clock ticking or crickets chirping when falling asleep. It could be anything, but sound usually was the easiest to identify.

Dr. Ronaldo recommended Miss Fumblehouse search for her relaxing sounds. However, with Garcia Fumblehouse, it was another story.

"I don't know which one to choose. There are so many that help me relax, but none are perfect. I can't stop thinking my sound is out there somewhere. I tried so hard already. Please, pick one for me." She frowned.

"It has to be something you find on your own. It is supposed to be special, secret, and exclusively your own," Ronaldo said.

Otherwise, it wouldn't work. Well, there was no guarantee it would work in the first place. Miss Fumblehouse was the type to stress out about finding stress relief activities. She attended the clinic to help with her anxiety of being worried about every little thing.

"Please, it might work this time. I want the reassurance that we tried," Miss Fumblehouse said.

"Of course, as many times as you need. I'm sure we will find it this time." Dr. Ronaldo smiled peacefully.

಄ಲ

With a tap of his phone, Dr. Ronaldo synched a speaker with a relaxing sound playlist. He dimmed the lights slightly and set up conditions for the best results for mild sensory deprivation.

Miss Fumblehouse moved to the recliner, and her forehead folded together like an accordion as her face twitched.

"You don't have to force your eyes closed. Relax. Remember, you can keep your eyes open."

"Okay," Fumblehouse said.

Her face didn't change much. Dr. Ronaldo tried his hardest to contain his laughter.

"All right, here's the sound of crickets, with water flowing down a stream."

The room echoed with the breath of soft chirps as the sound of the gentle stream trickled through their memories. It was the sound of the creek before Tarot Tori City modified them into aqueducts.

"A river bank."

A few frog croaks and cicada chimes accompanied the mix. They were wistfully orchestrating the peaceful night. A hoot from a nearby owl completed the moment.

"Follow it to the shore, the beach, then the ocean."

Seagulls, wave crashes, long soft whiffs of sudsy shores fizzed through Fumblehouse's consciousness.

"What time is it?"

Nighttime. . .

"Just relax . . . and don't blink. . ."

Dr. Ronaldo made his way to the door.

"And now . . . dream. . ."

He exited the room.

∞౮౷

"I think it worked. I feel so much better." Miss Fumblehouse jumped out of her seat.

It didn't work. Dr. Ronaldo was upset with himself, wondering what he had done wrong.

Miss Fumblehouse was supposed to be relaxed or sleepy, not jumping out of her seat the way she did.

"That's fantastic. You found your soothing sounds. Since they all helped you relax, then you can listen to any of them for a good night's sleep."

"Thank you so much." She nodded with a brimming smile.

"But what do you think I should do to find the specific relaxing ambient noise that is unique to me?" she asked innocently as Dr. Ronaldo facepalmed himself.

ᲒᲘᲒᲠ

The clinic door chimed.

Miss Fumblehouse ran out of the office and hugged Florian.

"I was so worried after I saw what happened on TV." She started to cry. "How's Hope? Please tell me she's all right."

"I'm fine; we are all fine. Don't worry," Florian said.

"A-a-and Sergeant Nowell? I-is he okay too?" Miss Fumblehouse asked, holding her plush over her face. Her turtle spirit poked its head out from its shell.

"He said he just got a few scratches. Last I saw him; he had a fork and some glass stuck in his back. He was calm as always and bragged that he had gotten worse," Florian said.

"Wha!? Forks, glass, and knives stuck in his back! Does that mean he fought with someone? He might be on his deathbed. I feel faint." Miss Fumblehouse pressed her head against her plush turtle spirit.

Ronaldo's eyes went wide, and he shook his head and waved his hands. Florian gasped, realizing what she had done.

"He's still in the hospital; you can see him if you want," Florian said, winking to Dr. Ronaldo.

"N-n-no, he wouldn't want me to see him. I-I mean, he needs to recover; I'll get in the way of the nurses a-a-and—" Miss Fumblehouse tripped over her words.

"You can also call him. I'm sure he won't mind a phone call at least," Dr. Ronaldo said.

"L-look at the time. I have something to do. I'm so glad you and Hope are safe and sound. If you need to talk, I'm just a phone call away. B-bye." She left bright red and with her spirit withdrawn in its shell.

"Well, I tried," Florian said.

"You are as observant as ever," Ronaldo said.

"Oh. . . I . . . That's part of why I'm here." She had a look Ronaldo had not seen in a very long time. Like the day they first met.

"Is it that serious? I know part of what happened over the news. Tell me what's wrong."

"You said I could tell you anything, right, and it will never leave this room?"

"Of course, I stake my life on every patient."

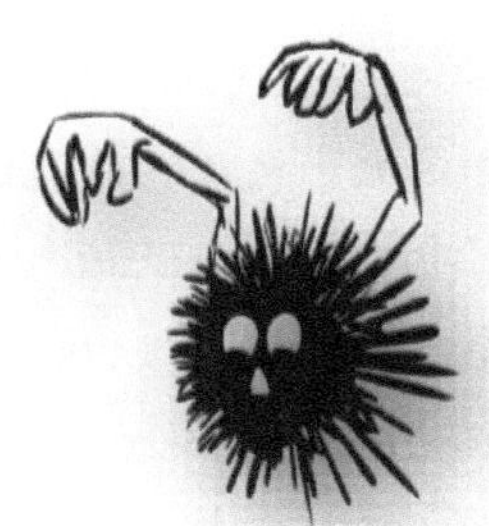

EIGHTEEN
ATTRITION

*S. BROOK COUNSELING & THERAPY CLINIC
SEPTEMBER 10TH X288*

So that's what happened. Dr. Ronaldo rubbed his forehead.

"Yes." Florian paused. "But the real reason I came to you was to tell you about something else."

Dr. Ronaldo's soul quivered its thorns. The dark urchin spirit was three feet tall, standing on its long, firm quills.

After all these years, Florian no longer feared the spirit; she cherished it. She had spoken with Dr. Ronaldo countless times, and she understood him maybe more than Ronaldo knew himself.

Without knowing of her actual struggles, Dr. Ronaldo had supported her all these years. He was one of the very few people Florian considered a true friend.

"There are a few things that don't make sense."

"I know."

"Are you sure Mayor Banquet accused you of those things? Did he say he suspected you?"

"Well, not really. The mayor heavily implied it. I could tell just by looking, and his attitude was extremely egotistical. It was suffocating."

"I understand you were nervous. Could the reason be that you were scared of him?"

"No! I'm not scared of him!"

"Then why are you so frustrated?"

She paused for a moment. "He was mocking Sergeant Nowell and me. Mayor Banquet was treating our efforts like they were utterly meaningless. I even got the feeling that he didn't even care for his daughter's safety."

Dr. Ronaldo took a deep breath. "You're overthinking it again."

Florian worried Dr. Ronaldo wasn't taking her seriously. The dark urchin's spines loosened and wiggled; it had to be on point, not sluggish. She needed him to be engaged.

"I'm not overthinking it." Florian set down her backpack and pulled out dozens of her old journals. "Here." She handed the first journal to Ronaldo. "Do you remember these?"

"These are your journals from way back. Your drawings were always so interesting. Why are there so many?"

"I never stopped."

"There's like fifty notebooks."

"Fifty-four, covering three years."

"This covers only three years? What have you been writing about?" Ronaldo opened the first binder.

It had unorganized drawings, notes, tables, and data. The other notebooks were labeled daily records, observations, and tests, each with corresponding dates.

"Sorry, it's a little messy. I may need to make a key for some of the abbreviations I used."

"What is all this?"

Florian stood up and looked Dr. Ronaldo in the eyes. Her heart wouldn't stop pounding.

"Please listen to me until the end. I've drafted many ways to tell you this. I planned on telling you sooner, but I kept pushing it back as things kept resolving themselves. But now, I fear for not only my life but my loved ones too."

Dr. Ronaldo got a serious look on his face. "All these years, I knew you weren't telling me something. . . Deep down, I thought my therapeutic practices were not helping. I felt like I didn't earn your trust. Not enough for you to be comfortable to tell me. Now, after seven years, I'll listen like I always have and forever will."

Florian mustered up her remaining courage. "I see things no one else sees. These things are manifestations of one's entire being. With this information, I can partially read thoughts and actions before they happen. I can understand individuals to a certain degree without them saying a word or even using sign language."

Dr. Ronaldo seemed like he didn't fully understand.

"I can see an individual's soul."

"Soul? Like a ghost?"

"Actually. . . I don't know what they are. All I know is each person has one, and it's connected to their mind and body."

"Are you serious?"

"Each one is unique. Many have animal features. They are like a physical representation of a person's state of mind. The actions and appearance of people's souls provide me with information that is difficult to explain. After living with them for years, I guess I'm used to them now."

"Okay . . . where do I begin? I'm not surprised you prepared all these books to help convince me this is real. Nevertheless, I still have so many questions."

"It's right in front of you. Seven years of evidence and notes of my discoveries. I broke down the mechanics to the best of my ability in these journals."

Ronaldo skimmed through a few entries. Inside were detailed encounters dating back to when Florian first met Sergeant Nowell and Dr. Ronaldo. He was calm and collected as he analyzed the strange concept put in front of him.

"So that's why Honest felt something was off about you. I should apologize to him."

"You believe me?" Florian was surprised.

"Of course I do. You had something like a sixth sense when it came to understanding others. You always had an altruistic nature that drove you to care about others before yourself. For some reason, you always went above and beyond even when it involved total strangers. Besides, the sheer amount of detail is astonishing." Dr. Ronaldo held up the drawings. "Are these what the souls look like?"

"Yes. Sergeant Honest's soul was scary at first, but as I got to know him, I learned he was grieving for someone."

"I see. I can't disclose Honest's personal information, but if you ask him, I'm sure he'll have no problem telling you. Will you tell me about Miss Fumblehouse's soul?"

"Hers is a turtle. It's like she's scared all the time. She hides from everyone. She's tough to convince once she sets her mind on something. For some reason, her soul is always in the place of the plush she carries around. It gives the turtle a plush-like appearance; there could be something significant about it."

"Impossible. Has Miss Fumblehouse told you anything about her past?"

"No. I never asked."

Dr. Ronaldo adjusted his glasses. "One day she'll tell you herself. She sees you like family."

Florian blushed slightly. She felt a huge weight disappear as she shared her secret. The dark urchin released threads that interweaved through Florian's journals, exactly what Florian wanted.

Dr. Ronaldo's voice cracked slightly. "What does mine look like?"

"I don't think telling you now is a good idea."

"Why not?"

"Just a gut feeling." Florian was a little scared that Ronaldo's soul was quivering like never before.

"I understand, maybe some other time. I'm excited. This ability of yours is truly a gift. It could change the world of psychology forever. Have you considered becoming a psychologist?" he asked. "Like how Dr. Steinsbrook took me in as his apprentice. I could teach you as my protégé."

"I-I'll think about it." Studying under someone she could trust didn't sound bad to Florian. "I do want to help others. Like the way you do. I don't know yet."

"That's good enough for me, as long as it's something you like to do. You do that," he said. "Say, what does your soul look like?"

" I. . . I don't have one."

"What do you mean you don't have one?"

Florian's voice trembled. "No matter how hard I tried, I couldn't find mine. I searched and I searched, but after all these years, it hasn't shown itself. Everyone has a soul, except me. At some points, I wondered if I was even alive." Tears rolled down her face. "I can see all of these souls at the cost of my own. Is that it? I'm jealous, all right. I'm so envious that I firmly believe I don't deserve a soul."

"That. Right there. *That* was floating in your head all this time?"

"Yeah. . ."

"I was worried why your depression persisted after all my efforts. I couldn't figure it out for seven years. I'm so glad you told me." Dr. Ronaldo started to weep as well. "Listen, you are alive, and you have a soul. I don't know why you can't see your own when you can see everyone else's, but listen here! I will work with you to find your soul, no matter what it takes! You got it!"

"Really?" Florian couldn't open her eyes from all the tears.

"Yes, like it or not, from today onward, we are partners."

NINETEEN
DONATION

TORI PLAZA
SEPTEMBER 11ᵀᴴ X288

Florian and Dr. Ronaldo drove to the heart of Tarot Tori City, the Tori Plaza. It was right beside the most efficient transportation offered, Tori Railway.

Tori Plaza was the intersection that bridged the city's business side with the city's entertainment side. On one side were an aquarium, museum, theater, indoor waterpark, and further down the Tarot Tori Stadium. On the other side were shopping districts, office buildings, government buildings, and the Tarot Tori Tower, a building owned by the mayor before Mr. Banquet. It was the most densely populated area in the city.

"Will this spot work?" Ronaldo asked.

"It's perfect," Florian said. "See that lady in the blue dress?"

"Yeah, what're you going to do?"

Florian pulled out her notebook and drew the woman's soul. She began her spirit sketch demonstration.

"It's a rough sketch, but this is close to what it looks like."

She drew at an unbelievable pace—one after another. The spirits were truly abstract and diverse.

Dr. Ronaldo was speechless. *These souls are definitely not a hallucination. It's overwhelming. It's like seeing a geyser of data just seeping from her fingertips.*

If I had a better analysis of the souls she sees, accompanied by a full-on interview of the individual in question, I could truly understand a person's entire psyche. The door to social barriers would completely shatter. Florian has had to deal with this data overload her whole life? It's no wonder she's so mature for her age.

If privacy is nonexistent in front of Florian Lilly Cobblestone, then her eyes could also be a curse. It must've been hard for her to deal with as a child. So that's how Florian knew Zachary Venmont died in the hospital seven years ago. She said recent events were what caused her to break her silence. She must be in a really desperate situation to share this burden with me now.

Page after page of souls of strangers piled up in Ronaldo's car.

"I think that's enough," Dr. Ronaldo said.

"Sorry. Finally being able to share this with someone made me get carried away."

Her smile made Ronaldo tremble. He has never seen Florian so happy.

"You've shared so much. I also want to tell you a secret of my own."

Florian was all ears.

"I've taken an interest in my mentor's old research. He was studying hypnotism during a phase of his work. I've just lightly dabbled in the concept. I thought I could use it to help Honest and Fumblehouse."

"Hypnotism? As in mind control?"

"No, the only thing my hypnotism is capable of doing is helping people relax. Like listening to calming music or counting sheep to help you sleep. Stuff like that."

"Oh, your mentor, Dr. Steinsbrook. It's the name on the sign for the medical center."

"That's him; he theorized he could go further—to possible mind control territories, but that is just ridiculous. I saw him give up on that years ago."

"Amazing. So you have an ability too?"

"I wouldn't say mine are abilities, more like parlor tricks. How about apparition vision?"

"What?"

"Apparition vision, the eyes that are capable of seeing things no one else does. At least, that's what we can call your ability in the new case file I'll make for you. I plan on giving you my full support. I'm just as excited as you are. Your eyes could also help me understand Sergeant Nowell and Miss Fumblehouse more."

"You're right. I hope to learn more about everyone too," Florian said.

"This is a big step forward for us."

"We can do this!" Florian clenched her fist with a giant grin.

"Do what?"

Florian turned to a new page in her journal and started writing as she spoke. "Here's what we know. The masked perpetrator, still at large, attempted to kidnap Blythe Banquet from me on Wednesday around five p.m. He was most likely not working alone as a ransom note and negotiations were going on simultaneously at four-thirty p.m. Since Blythe took a detour to visit my sister after school, I was with the target from three-thirty p.m. to seven p.m. I was the wrench in their plan. At the restaurant, the perpetrator's voice sounded male. He, strangely, had a gun loaded with blanks."

"Don't tell me."

"When the police questioned me, I stumbled over my own words and couldn't remember much of what happened as I was still sorting my thoughts on what the mayor said to me. I couldn't remember any identifiable physical features of the kidnapper. However, thanks to the police questioning, I now realize what information is important. Facial features, clothes, height, skin color, tattoos, anything, along with any coconspirator."

"How will we get the face of a masked kidnapper that already got away?" Dr. Ronaldo smiled as he realized where she was going.

"I don't know what his face looks like, but I saw something else. Something that only I can see. His soul, the drooling lizard spirit."

Florian drew the spirit once more. "From memory, this was what the perpetrator's soul looked like."

She showed Ronaldo the lizard with saliva flowing from its mouth. Its fins caught the saliva in a mane around its neck with a broom-like tail that swept its tracks.

Florian then pointed to the amazed Dr. Ronaldo. "You can help me stake out sections of the city by driving me around. I'll demonstrate my abilities to you and find the culprit's soul in the crowd of people. I'll then sketch his face and anyone suspicious hanging out with him. If possible, even find out where they are hiding out. After that, we can report everything to the police, clearing Sergeant Nowell's name and catching the bad guys."

Florian smiled as if nothing could hold her back.

The likelihood of finding the perpetrator is so low. I don't know how long I'll be able to help Florian with the stakeout either. However, this will definitely help with the weight on her shoulders. It feels like we're making so much progress. Thank you, Florian Lilly Cobblestone.

Ronaldo flipped through more of her journals. "They have hidden meanings behind their souls. You said the mayor had a demented spirit? Right?"

"Yes."

"He was the one that spearheaded many amazing changes that benefited Tarot Tori City," Ronaldo said.

"If you could see what I see, you would believe me."

"I don't know what to say. I've supported the mayor's every decision. The clinic wouldn't be there if it weren't for the revolutionizing opportunities he offered the city."

"He said something similar to me. I wouldn't have met you if it wasn't for this city's fortune and success," Florian said.

The two made up their minds.

ജ്ഞ

The very next day, they initiated their stakeout plan, surveying multiple congested locations throughout the city.

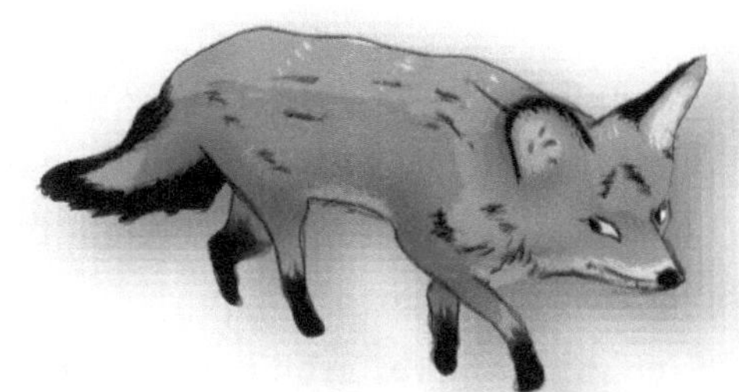

TWENTY
SITUATION

STORAGE UNIT
SEPTEMBER 14TH X288

Ten days left until Florian's televised award ceremony.
Dr. Ronaldo was rummaging through his mentor's old documents at a storage unit outside Tarot Tori City.

After a few stakeouts, Ronaldo began to lose sleep. He couldn't stop thinking about his mentor's theories and Florian's apparition vision.

"It feels like a dream. If only Dr. Steinsbrook were here. He would know exactly what to do to help Florian and Sergeant Honest."

Ronaldo remembered his mentor's last words before leaving Tarot Tori City all those years ago: "I've had enough with this city. There's nothing left for me here. The clinic's yours."

"Where is it? The old theory of Dr. Steinsbrook on hypnotism was missing a factor. I remember reading his thesis. Florian's apparition vision could be the very key my mentor was searching for." He paused.

"I can only wonder where he is now. Probably on some beach, gazing along the shoreline, holding a briefcase containing the very thesis I'm looking for."

ನುಞ

Later that day, Dr. Ronaldo arrived at the police station.

"I need to speak with the chief," Ronaldo said.

That was when Officer Keen, the one with the fox spirit, approached Dr. Ronaldo.

"Get in line. You aren't the only one that's got a bone to pick with the chief," Keen said.

"Did he put you on patrol duty again?" Ronaldo asked.

"Yep, this case with that Florian girl is not a can of worms; it's a whole damn rabbit hole filled with them. Once we find a lead, we get more questions than answers. The same day I got the case, I was removed from it. It's a complete mess right now," Keen said.

"Keen! You will keep getting dropped from investigations if you keep blabbing that mouth of yours!" the chief said.

"Yikes!" Officer Keen ran off.

"How's Sergeant Honest?" Dr. Ronaldo asked the chief.

"He's still in the hospital. He'll be under our watch until this investigation is over."

"How much longer?"

"I don't know."

"Chief, both Sergeant Honest Nowell and Florian Lilly Cobblestone are innocent. There's plenty of evidence proving it. I also have years of evidence that can vouch for them."

"I know they're innocent. But we have to comb through everything. It's undeniable that this incident happened. It wasn't some ghost pulling a prank or a veteran with PTSD and issues with the mayor. Someone or some group orchestrated this," the chief said.

"Chief, please put me on the case," Dr. Ronaldo said.

"No can do. You're literally the therapist of two of the suspects. Besides, you know how many officers are hungry for a chance at a case this big? Look, I appreciate you joining the force as a profiler. You even went out of your way to obtain a forensic psychology degree and a criminal investigation major. Hell, you are so overqualified I'm afraid the FBI will poach you from us. I just can't put you on this case."

"I've spent the past seven years assisting you any way I could. Please, don't stop me from helping you now. Now, return the favor so I can help my patients," Dr. Ronaldo said.

The chief let out a sigh. "You are not on the case, but that doesn't mean I won't share what I have with you. If you have any leads, you can bring them to me."

"Understood." Dr. Ronaldo followed the chief to his office to further discuss the investigation.

"A hooded masked man. Conveniently, we didn't see anyone matching that description on any of the security cameras in the area." He paused.

"The cameras did catch the group of girls, and Florian did occasionally turn around. Yet the cameras showed nothing in the general direction she looked. I started to believe all this was a delusion until we searched the charred restaurant."

He frowned. "There was something odd about the security footage. The problem wasn't that the footage was unsalvageable. The whole damn computer was gutted like a fish. The last time I checked, fire can't pry open a PC, remove its hard drive, and smash it to pieces.

"This perp knew every security camera in the area, started a fire, planted fireworks to throw us off, entered the restaurant, injured Sergeant Honest, and destroyed the footage amid the fire. Speaking of which, we can return Florian's phone now. The battery died as the notifications wouldn't stop. I think it was the noisiest piece of evidence we've ever brought in."

"I can return it to her," Dr. Ronaldo said.

"I'll leave it to you. As for Sergeant Honest Nowell, the assault victim, he was prosecuted for the death of his daughter nine years ago. He was ruled not guilty, as evidence showed it was most likely a boating accident. However, it's our job to keep asking questions until we find the truth. We suspected that since he's under your care, Dr. Ronaldo, Sergeant Nowell is still grieving his loss. The hypothesis is he might have had a breakdown and decided to kidnap Blythe Banquet. Did your patient state he was going to commit any criminal activity?"

"Absolutely not. Sergeant Honest Nowell is a proud veteran who served this country all his life. He's sacrificed his mind, body, and future and continues to serve every day. He deserves a new chance at life, and I'm here to help him obtain it."

ACT 3

GHOSTS

146

TWENTY-ONE
TACO-W WITH CHEESE

BURGER BOYZ
SEPTEMBER 17TH X288

Tarot Tori City was populated with many souls, each wandering like an unsuspected graveyard. Their lives ticked away as they continued to roam their unpredictable paths.

Tori Plaza seven days before Florian's televised award ceremony.

"Irina, what're you ordering?" Travis Wit Law said. He had long dreadlocks held back with a headband, a yellow short-sleeved shirt with an anchor logo, and baggy cargo pants. Both of his arms had custom-made arm cuffs that seemed more than just a fashion statement.

Irina Halt, a shaggy-haired blonde woman with a small build in a black and yellow motorcycle tracksuit, sat at their booth with her chin on the table. Her baggy eyes were glued to the glass of soda fizzing in front of her. She was too sleepy to answer.

"How about you, Sticks?" Travis turned to the gloomy kid beside Irina. A boy named Styx Caldwell, mistaken for Sticks. He wore a blue short-sleeved hoodie over his pale face and black hair that peeked past his hood a little bit.

The boy shrugged with his hands in his pockets. "A taco, I guess."

"This is Burger Boyz, and you want a taco?" Travis asked.

"Then what's with the giant taco on top of the building?" Sticks asked.

"Gaha, I guess it happened before you were born. Let me regale you with the legend. This used to be a taco joint, explaining the eight-foot work of art outside. Sadly that taco joint went out of business. Then Burger Boyz bought the building. However, they didn't want to tear down such a beautiful sculpture. After a while, they realized everyone started asking for tacos, forcing them to add them to the menu. That makes this the only Burger Boyz in the entire country that serves tacos. They're also rated as the worst tacos in the whole city. That advertisement alone draws in countless customers, daring each other to order them," Travis said.

"In my country, burgers are served vid de freshest potatoes and vodka dat is strong enough to put down a bear. Not someding chiseled out of a freezer." Irina's stomach growled.

"Irina, that sounds delicious. It makes me want to order the Big Boyz Burger. Sticks will get the Little Boyz Burger," Travis said.

"If you're paying, you can make fun of me all you want," Sticks said.

"Of course, my treat for the new recruit. When you're older, you'll have to be responsible and save up plenty of money to cover meals for your trainees."

"Really? I thought we were going to dine and dash."

"Come on, Sticks. If we did that, they wouldn't welcome us back. Do you know what's more important than money?"

"What's more important than money?"

"Spending money. That's what. What's the point of having money if you don't spend it? The more money you spend in a restaurant, the tastier the food will be the next time. Understand?"

"Don't tell me what to do. Money is the key to my girl's heart," Sticks said.

"Travis, scoot over," Juke Lucas said, out of breath. He had short spiky crimson hair, a light tan jacket, a black T-shirt, and jeans.

"Juke, I thought you were eating at your favorite restaurant?" Travis asked.

"I was, but when I got there, it was a pile of ash."

"No way? Was it *that* restaurant? Gahaha." Travis couldn't hold it in.

"Their pancakes were to die for," Juke said.

"You mean to kill for. If you die, you can't eat any more the next day. Gahaha."

"Yeah, I'll kill you if you keep laughing. I can't believe you burned down my favorite restaurant." Juke's voice curdled.

"Their pancakes were nasty, and you know it. It was the syrup that carried the flavor. Just drink the syrup strai—"

"You're digging your own grave! Travis!"

"All right, all right, jeez, don't snap here." Travis knew he'd crossed the line.

"Can I take your orders?" the waiter asked.

"Big Boyz Burger with Friez," Travis said.

"Little Boyz Burger and Ringz. He's paying for mine," Sticks said.

"Your exclusive famously bad tacos dat lure your customers in, potatoes not from last vinter, and vodka, hold de bear sedatives," Irina said.

"Pancakes," Juke said, glaring at Travis's grin.

"I'm sorry, but we don't serve pancakes," the waiter said, shivering at the tall crimson-haired man.

"What?! Everyone else's long order compared to my single-word order! And you don't serve it?!" Juke stood, clenching his fist.

"Hiiiee! Don't hurt me." The waiter cowered.

"Calm down, Juke. They're only kidding. Right? You do serve pancakes. Right?" Travis handed the waiter two hundred dollars. "Psst, take the money. I really don't want my friend to cause any trouble."

"Yes, sir! Pancakes. Coming right up." The waiter ran off.

"Gahaha. See, the more money you put in, the better the restaurant gets."

After that day, Burger Boyz added pancakes to its menu.

☙❧

"Sticks, is it all right for you to be skipping school like dis?" Irina said.

"It's all right. I'm interning with you guys, so I don't need school anymore."

"Vat about dat girlfriend of yours? Does she know vat you got yourself into?"

"All she needs to know is how much I love her and that every dime I make is for her."

"This pancake tastes strange," Juke said.

"In my country, men vere only velcomed home by deir vives if dey brought home diamonds covered in blood."

"We're not in your country, are we? But I can't deny that money covered in blood is still money," Travis said.

"Sticks, you've got to start thinking for yourself," Juke said. "If you don't, you will end up worse than just broke."

"What's worse than broke?"

"Broken," Juke said.

"I can drink to that," Travis said.

"All right, wrap it up, guys. We need to get ready for the boss's call tonight. Everyone's required to be there or else," Juke said.

"Hey, kid, isn't this your first meeting with the boss?" Travis asked.

"Yeah," Sticks said.

"I recommend only speaking when he calls on you. He tends to get scary if annoyed," Travis said.

"If only Travis behaved like that all the time," Juke added.

"Vaiter. Can I get dis to go?" Irina said for her half-eaten tacos.

"Are you really going to finish those tacos?" Travis asked.

"No, dey really are nasty. But Sophie might eat dem."

"Gahaha, wanna put money on that?"

"You're on," Irina said.

౭౦ఴ

The crew began their commute home boarding the Tori Railway, catching an east-bound train.

"Dat vas a good meal. I only regret not driving us. A good drive after a meal vould have hit the spot."

"Gahaha, we know you drink with every meal. We're not stupid enough to ride with you after a drink."

"Come on. It vill be fun." Irina lightly tipped from side to side.

"Besides, when do you get the chance to enjoy a good walk to cool off? Isn't it therapeutic? Right, Juke? Feeling any better?" Travis asked.

"Shut it, Travis! The boss put me in charge, so I order you to shut up," Juke said.

"Fine, temp leader," Travis said.

They sat on the crowded train, and the group's banter went strangely quiet. Even Irina's tipsiness sobered up.

"Irina. What's going on with you and the others?" Sticks worried.

"I don't feel like dealing vid it. I vanted to drive for a reason," she said.

"Damn, we should have driven," Travis spoke under his breath.

"What's wrong?" Sticks asked.

"Don't worry, new kid. Just keep quiet and act natural," Juke said, calm and composed.

"Can I talk now, temp leader?" Travis asked.

"Fine. Who's tailing us?"

"I have no idea?"

"FBI?"

"Nope. FBI aren't this stupid. They would be observing our hideout, not risking their cover by tailing our individual moves."

"Then who is it?"

"Whoever they are, they're good. Way better than local police. Whenever I make a sudden move, I notice a reflection in the train window. Like when I checked my phone, whoever they are, they reacted," Travis said.

"Are we just going to lead them to our hideout?" Sticks asked.

"Vant to split up?" Irina asked.

"No, they will continue to tail the easiest target: Sticks or Irina in her intoxicated state. If they're trying to capture one of us, it would be best to stick together. They won't be stupid enough to try while I'm around. Either way, if we're late, Sophie will notice," Juke said.

"Let the games begin," Travis said.

Ⴥ

"I found you, and I'm not letting you out of my sights this time."

TWENTY-TWO
PURSUING, PURSUERS, PURSUED

TORI PLAZA
SEPTEMBER 17TH X288

I can't believe it. "You actually found the culprit that attempted to kidnap Blythe. Are you sure it's him?"

"There's no question. The drooling lizard spirit's right beside him. He's in a group at the Burger Boyz across the street."

Florian Lilly Cobblestone and Dr. Ronaldo had staked out Tori Plaza every day. After school, Florian went straight to the clinic, leaving her sister guarded by her friends from school. They even hung out at the Cobblestone residence until Florian got home. It was thanks to them that Florian could concentrate on finding the culprits.

"The people around him, do you think they're working together?"

"Most likely."

Florian took out her journal, compelled to draw their spirits. She trembled with excitement. She drew all the souls on the first page, then flipped to the next to draw their faces.

The drooling lizard spirit paired with an African American man with long dreadlocks, wearing a yellow shirt and silver armbands. The lizard's long snout looked as if it was laughing.

A four-foot cheetah spirit was in a booth with a blonde-haired woman in a black and yellow motorcycle suit. The cheetah curled up next to the woman. Florian felt like she'd seen it from somewhere before but was too busy to remember.

Next to the woman was a boy that looked around Florian's age, wearing a blue hoodie. His spirit slithered in and out from his short sleeves. Observing through binoculars from across the street, she thought it appeared to be a snake spirit.

Then a tall crimson-haired man joined them. His spirit overshadowed them all. His soul was furious as it partly phased through the window. It had the arms of a gorilla, and the body, face, and legs of a black rain frog covered in fur. Dangling from its head was a glowing lure of an anglerfish.

Over her shoulder, Dr. Ronaldo studied the souls Florian drew. Without saying a word, he calculated. Ronaldo had reviewed Florian's old journals meticulously for this very moment. He hoped to break down their psyche with the few clues Florian scribbled on the page.

Florian and Dr. Ronaldo also took photos of the group with their phones.

"Their souls are acting so carefree. After causing so much trouble! How dare they?" Florian said.

The group left the restaurant and headed toward Tori Railway.

"That's it. We can report to the police now," Dr. Ronaldo said.

"No. It's not enough." Florian jumped out of Dr. Ronaldo's car, leaving her journal.

"Florian! What are you doing? Damn it!" Dr. Ronaldo chased after her.

"If we can find their hideout, it will be enough to clear Sergeant Honest's name," Florian said.

"We can't! It's too dangerous!"

"We planned for this. Message Miss Fumblehouse our location every few minutes. We can do this. I know we can. It can't be far since they're on foot."

Dr. Ronaldo hesitated. "Damn it! Fine! If they approach us, play dumb. We'll tail them to their building. That's it. One wrong move, we run. Got it?"

"That was my plan from the start."

☙❧

On the Tori Railway, Florian noticed their souls acting differently.

They were abnormally calm. The angler gorilla frog spirit refused to turn around to the others. The curled cheetah spirit was lazily licking itself while darting its eyes back and forth. The drooling lizard soul stood up straight, sniffing the air as if on the lookout.

"All we have to do is avoid their soul's line of sight, and they won't notice us," Florian said.

"What do you mean?" Ronaldo asked.

"The moment their souls turn their heads, we just have to hide. It's easy."

"Easy for you. I can't see souls."

"Leave it to me and hide," Florian said.

Their soul's line of sight, they're looking at the reflections in the car windows, trying to spot me.

I see. This is the opposite of when I was with Hope and Blythe. Now I'm tailing them. Think. What was it that put a ton of pressure on me? I was so

155

busy trying to prote— That's it! When I was in their shoes, I prioritized my vulnerable friends. The motorcycle suit woman with the cheetah was drinking, and they have a boy my age with them. Those two might be their weakest link. I know the one with the drooling lizard soul can fight and might be concealing a gun. The crimson-haired man with the angler gorilla frog reminds me of Sergeant Honest's slender spike spirit. They both have an intimidating presence that has experienced bloodshed and violence. I don't want to get anywhere near that crimson-haired man. Right now, they might be thinking the police are stalking them. I have to be careful.

The group didn't move, but their souls crept closer to the doors.

"Next stop, Tori Docks. Next stop, Tori Docks," the speakers announced.

☡∞☡

"There are so many people on board. How can we weed out our stalker?" Sticks asked.

"Follow our lead, kid. Just stay alert," Juke said.

"Our stop's next. What do we do?" Sticks asked.

"Just stick with me, kid," Juke said. "Cover my back."

The others nodded to one another.

☡∞☡

"Tori Docks, Tori Docks." The doors opened.

Countless people exited the train. The group didn't.

"This mustn't be their stop then," Florian said. "No, wait."

Florian noticed the gang's spirits exited and stood by the doors. Two on the east and two on the west exit, but the owners sat still in their seats.

156

"Are they getting off or not?" Florian's stomach turned. "They're up to something. Do I go now?"

"What's wrong?" Dr. Ronaldo asked.

"We have to leave the car."

"But they haven't left their seats yet."

"Now!" Florian gently pushed Ronaldo.

☙❧

Passengers disembarked the train, giving clear visibility to the gang.

"Doors closing. Doors closing," speakers announced.

"Now!"

The gang split back to back and exited on both sides, the east and west exits. They stared down the train seeing if anyone else jumped out at the last second to follow them.

The doors closed, and the train began moving.

"There!" Sticks yelled. He charged forward, grabbing a man in front of him. His soul coiled around his arm and sprang to his fingertips. Sticks's long reach clenched the man's neck and pushed him to the ground. The snake soul wrapped around the man's neck. "Who are you working for!?" he yelled.

"Get off him, Sticks. That's not our stalker," Juke said.

"He looked at me funny. It has to be him."

Juke picked up Sticks by the hoodie as if the two weighed nothing. Juke freed the poor man.

"He got away," Sticks said, dangling from the height.

The train left, revealing Travis and Irina on the other side.

"Anything?" Juke said.

"Nope, guess our stalker didn't leave the train in time," Travis said.

"Good. Meet us outside the east gate," Juke said.

157

৪৩

Florian panted.

Both Florian and Ronaldo had exited the train a minute before the announcement that the doors were closing. Florian's hunch was correct. Tori Docks was their stop, and they were planning an ambush. Florian had doubted herself until the last second.

"If we'd stayed, we would've lost them. If we got off when the gang did, we would be dead," Florian said.

"You were right. You predicted the gang was up to something and that this was the gang's stop. No pursuer would get off a train before their target," Dr. Ronaldo said.

"That was too close." Florian's heart pounded, terrified. They hid behind a pillar, catching their breath. "They haven't used their cell phones to call for help like I did when they tailed me. They could text, but now that they think they lost us, they should lead us to their hideout without any more issues."

"I'll text an update to Miss Fumblehouse," Dr. Ronaldo said.

"Very good."

৪৩

The gang regrouped and casually walked toward their hideout.

"Gahaha, not bad, Sticks. But if you go for the neck, how're they supposed to answer your questions?"

"I see. I'll remember that for the next time."

"Ve're still being vatched."

"We didn't lose them after all," Juke said. "They tailed us so close to the hideout, so annoying."

"So it's an organization? They might have agents all over the city to continue where the last team left off?" Travis said.

"There aren't any left like that. This city's strange, especially with that mayor in charge," Juke said.

"What do we do now?" Sticks asked.

"Ve split up and lose dem de old fashioned vay. I've sobered up. I'm ready for a fight."

"You're still drunk to me. Gahaha."

"We'll race to the hideout. If you see anyone, don't engage, lure the stalker away. Whoever's being chased, we'll cover you," Juke said.

"Right." They sprinted off in different directions.

☙ ❧

The sun began to set.

Florian and Ronaldo tailed the group for about half an hour to a series of abandoned buildings near the docks. They were old apartment complexes. One was partially submerged as if it had sunk into the river.

"I remember it flooded about four years ago. Due to rising sea levels and flooding, the residents evacuated. I thought they were demolished years ago," Dr. Ronaldo said.

"Shhh, they stopped moving," Florian said.

The two sat in cover behind the corner of a building when the gang split up, diving and vaulting through windows and alleyways.

"Damn, they're fast." Florian couldn't react in time. "Is this a trap?"

Dr. Ronaldo grabbed Florian's hand. "I'm not letting go. There's no way I'm letting you run headfirst into danger anymore. That's enough. Let the police take it from here."

Seeing the seriousness on Ronaldo's face made Florian think. She looked at his dark urchin soul that wrapped its threads around her hand. She understood.

"Their hideout must be in one of these abandoned buildings. We were so close," Florian said.

"Text Miss Fumblehouse the address of one of these buildings. She can report everything for us while we head back," Ronaldo said.

"Okay." Florian pulled out her phone. It was getting late. "That's weird. . . It's not sending. I can't get a signal," Florian said.

"Let me check mine." He called the police directly. It also had no signal.

"Weird," Ronaldo said.

Florian noticed a shadow accumulated behind him. A giant claw pierced through Dr. Ronaldo's neck.

"What's wrong?" He looked at Florian.

No. The image seared itself in Florian's mind. *Move.* Her eyes watered. *Hurry up!* She blamed herself for dragging Ronaldo along. *I'll never let someone die in front of me again!* Without hesitation, she reached forward and pulled Dr. Ronaldo toward her.

A gleam of light swiped right over Dr. Ronaldo's head.

The shadow vanished. Behind it was a woman with long black hair. A few strands covered her face. Her giant white eyes stared at Florian, and she was holding a scalpel.

"Hie hehe! What are you cute little bunnies doing here?"

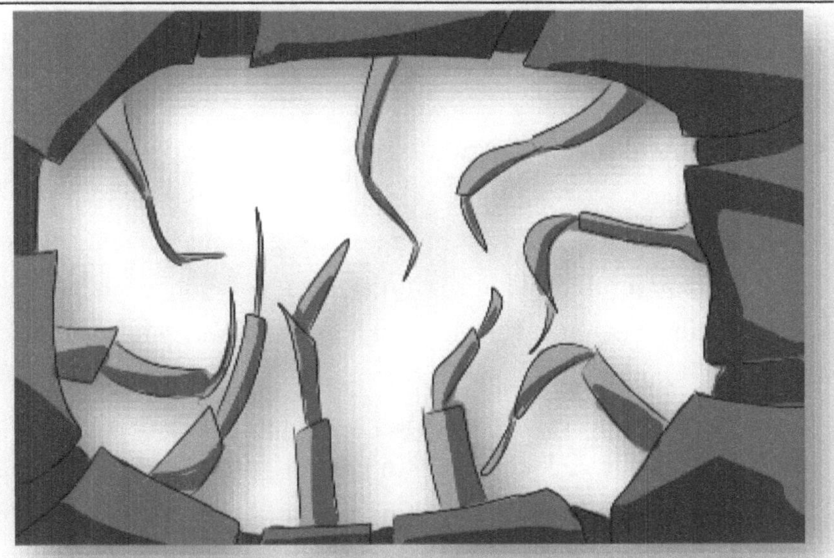

TWENTY-THREE
YUMMY BUNNIES

RUN DOWN APARTMENT
SEPTEMBER 17TH X288

An hour earlier at the hideout, a woman by the name of Sophie Squalid sleepwalked to the fridge.

"Zzz . . . so hungry."

The other members usually bought Sophie something for her midsleep snack. However, they were running a bit late.

Still in her pajamas, she sleepwalked out of the base in search of food.

"Hie hehe, meat . . . slice, chomp, chomp." She clutched a scalpel as her long black hair blew in a flurry in the wind.

She was the only person in the abandoned apartment complex.

After roaming the labyrinth of buildings, she saw two figures in front of her.

"Hie hehe, two little bunnies are wearing glasses. I must restrain myself, but they look so delicious—especially the one wearing the button shirt and vest. I mustn't. I mustn't." Sophie drooled with her eyes half-open.

"I know. I'll ask the two bunnies if they have anything to eat. Yes, a carrot or two. That's a great idea. Sophie, what a decent human being you are. I'll grab his carotid artery and ask nicely. Good girl! Hie hehe."

Sophie dove toward the two, swinging her arm toward the shoulder of Dr. Ronaldo, scalpel in hand.

"Huh? Didn't I have a scalpel in that hand? Oh well, I'll shift my hand a bit to avoid a lethal cut. That way, I can sew him back up as a reward for feeding me."

Dr. Ronaldo fell forward.

"Ara?" Sophie swung past his head hitting nothing but air.

"Did I miss? How? Aww, I wasn't even aiming for his vitals," she said.

૪૦૦૩

Florian held Ronaldo close, fidgeting, checking if he was all right.

"What happened?" Ronaldo said. He didn't have a scratch.

Florian realized her mistake. *No way. My eyes were so focused on the four we pursued that I overlooked checking if anyone was tailing us. The four didn't use their phones. How did they contact help? Was she patrolling the area? Did they know she would be here to trap us? Damn it! Dr. Ronaldo almost got stabbed. What am I doing? These guys are killers.* Florian's head was overwhelmed with dread.

The woman in purple and blue pajamas slinked toward them, head tilted, curious. Long appendages wriggled across her back in the shadows behind her, and feelers combed through her hair. "What are two little bunnies doing in a place like this?"

"Please don't hurt us," Florian begged. "We were just exploring the apartments and—"

"You're not delivery?"

What in the world is she talking about?

The woman's soul appendages kept scurrying around in the shadows.

Is this lady toying with us?

"Wait." She rubbed her eyes. "Who are you?"

Florian trembled in a cold sweat as the scornful spirit encircled them.

Dr. Ronaldo, without fear, approached the woman. His back was tall. He gave direct eye contact, didn't stutter or hesitate. His dark urchin soul was serious and reverberating in anger.

"We were looking for someone, and we wandered here. Please. Let us go. Do you want money? We'll give you everything we have," Dr. Ronaldo said. His tone was commanding yet calm.

Florian was awestruck.

"Hmmm? Are you a classmate of Sticks? Or are you that girlfriend of his?" the woman asked.

"Yes. We were worried about Sticks and followed him here," Ronaldo said.

"Really? So who are you?" Sophie yawned.

"I'm her brother. I didn't want her to go alone, so I accompanied her," Ronaldo said.

"Hmmm? That's kind of you. But—" She swung her knife again toward Ronaldo. "I don't believe you."

Dr. Ronaldo stepped back and avoided her strike. He adjusted his glasses.

"Pajamas, yawning, hallucinations, low blood sugar," Ronaldo said.

"You're a doctor? Your diagnosis is wrong. You're supposed to check if the scene is safe first. Typical, for a doctor." Sophie giggled.

"The sound of the river is quite nice, isn't it?" he asked.

"What are you talking about?" the woman said, slowly swaying back and forth maniacally.

"The sound of the crickets chirping, the water flowing, the flies buzzing. . . It's getting dark. I wonder what time it is?"

"It's time for your stitches!" She plunged forward with her scalpel.

He was right. The stream calmly flowed through the occasional frog croak. The abandoned complex was quiet. There were no cars, no hassle, no people, only nature.

"Just relax . . . and don't blink. . ." Dr. Ronaldo said, calmly stepping forward and grasping her knife, piercing his left hand.

He opened his right palm, revealing a string. It slipped from between his fingers with a ring tied to the end.

He bore the pain, grabbing the woman and pulling her in close. His left hand with the blade sticking through clasped the hand of the woman. He gently smeared his bloody hand through her hair, adjusting his watch next to her ear. The pendulum swung back and forth.

"And now . . . dream. . ." he whispered in her ear.

Florian had never seen anything like it. The long appendages in the shadows engulfed the two. The dark urchin spirit above Ronaldo cracked open, sprouting an arm made of bone. The skeleton hand grabbed one of the dark urchin's thorns, plucking it off, and pierced the woman's head. It pulled out a string, threading its needle, and began spooling it around her eyes.

"Dinner will be ready when you wake up," he said.

"Hie hehe. Mommy?" The woman collapsed in his arms. She snored soundly back to sleep. Her slim body pressed Ronaldo to the ground, crushing him.

"Help, get her off, Florian." Ronaldo squirmed.

"Are you all right?" Florian said.

"Yeah."

Florian got a closer look. The woman wasn't disturbing while asleep. When Florian lifted the slim woman, Florian noticed how top-heavy the woman was.

"Guess that does add a few pounds."

Florian was agitated that this woman had almost killed Ronaldo three times. Twice with her knife and then with her weight.

"I didn't think it would work," Ronaldo said.

"You used hypnotism, right? Wait, you're bleeding!"

"Ahh! Blood! There's a knife in my hand! Ow! Ow! It hurts!"

"I'll call nine-one-one. Where's my phone?"

"Looking for these?" Sticks Caldwell, the boy wearing the blue hoodie, said.

"How did he—"

Did he pickpocket us while we weren't looking?

"What did you do to Sophie?" Sticks said.

His snake spirit revealed itself from his sleeve, coiling around his arm. Upon closer inspection, the snake had a mouse in its mouth. No, the mouse was its head. It was a mouse wearing a snake costume like a jacket. The costume's collar protruded up like a cobra. The zipper went down its belly, and the tail shook the zipper tab like a rattlesnake.

The snake mouse spirit coiled around the two phones in the boy's hand.

"It was self-defense. I swear. Look." Ronaldo's composure disappeared, pointing to the knife in his hand. "Please call nine-one-one."

"You're not going anywhere." The boy raised his arms and charged forward.

His snake mouse slithered around his right hand. The soul flicked forward, attempting to bite Florian's face.

He threw a punch in the same path as the spirit. Florian avoided it and stepped back.

"What?" The boy paused. He raised both hands this time, and his snake coiled around only his left hand. It sprung forward, coursing a path for Florian.

The boy jabbed his right fist as a feint and then swung his left all the way through. Florian only reacted to the left fist and evaded without difficulty.

"What?! What the hell is this?"

"What do you mean?" Florian asked.

"Do you play any sports?"

"Stop playing around. Give us back our phones. I need to call an ambulance."

"If you don't play sports, how the hell are you able to move like that? I even threw in a few feints, and you avoided me completely."

"It's none of your business. Besides, you're the one trying to hit me. Why will I tell my attacker how I'm so good at dodging?"

"I'm trying to grab you. Not hit you."

"That sounds even worse. You're a creep."

"My girlfriend is a thousand times better looking than you. You did something to Sophie, and I want answers."

"Florian, just run. I'll be fine," Dr. Ronaldo said.

"No."

"Just leave me."

"The only thing in my way is this kid. If I beat him up, I can save you. If it's just this creep, I can take him."

"Really? Do you think you can take me? Try me."

"Hold your horses, kids. That's enough." The three others that Florian and Ronaldo had been tailing approached and grabbed the wounded Dr. Ronaldo.

"Vat happened to Sophie? She's sleeping on the sidewalk," Irina said.

"I saw her collapse while confronting these two," Sticks said.

"She must have fallen to the hands of hunger. Since ve vere late, she must have vent looking for us," Irina said.

"Wow, Sophie got this guy good. Right in the palm of his hand," Travis said.

"Can one of you please call nine-one-one?" Ronaldo asked.

The group laughed in unison.

"Bring them in," Juke said.

"Florian! Run!" Ronaldo said.

"Hold it." Travis pulled out his gun. "Let's talk this out like gentlemen, shall we?"

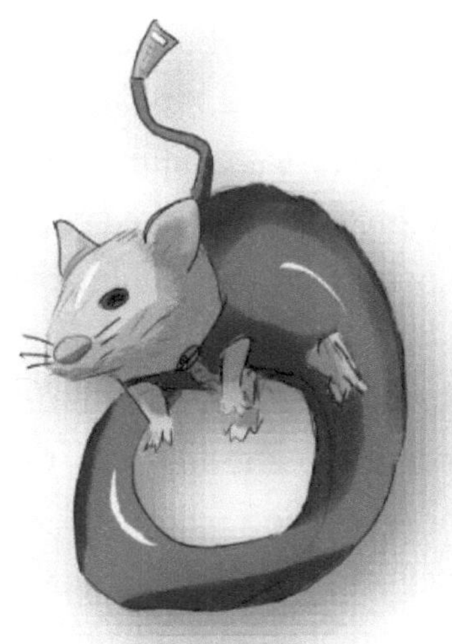

TWENTY-FOUR
STUMBLE

TORI DOCKS ABANDONED HOUSING DISTRICT
SEPTEMBER 17TH X288

It wasn't the gun that stopped Florian; it was herself. She refused to leave Ronaldo alone with these criminals. Deep down, she felt it would be the last she would see of Ronaldo if she did run.

The drooling lizard's eyes sparkled like stars through the night.

Travis pointed his gun away. "Glad you understand. This way."

The gang escorted Florian and Ronaldo to their hideout. Juke lifted Ronaldo with one hand, throwing him over his shoulder. Irina carried sleeping Sophie on her back. Sticks kept a close eye on Florian.

Blood dripped from Ronaldo's hand.

They arrived at an apartment building on the shore. The entire first floor, and half of the second, was underwater. They climbed a partially submerged stairway to the third floor.

Tall grass and overgrowth consumed the surrounding area, and moss and vines had overtaken the building. It was genuinely a relic of the previous city.

Travis opened the door to the third floor to reveal a single hallway with two rooms on the left and one on the right. They entered the first door on the left.

It was a large, well-lit room with a few chairs, a table, a few laptops, and a sofa. The table had a map of Tarot Tori City. On the wall were layouts of some buildings. In the corner of the room was a shelf holding a bunch of boxes.

They placed the sleeping Sophie on the sofa.

Florian silently absorbed as much information as possible. The more details she gathered, the better chance she had to clear Sergeant Nowell's name. She'd messed up before, but there was still hope. She listened to every word they said.

"Irina, stay on the lookout," Juke said.

Irina stared at the boys for a moment.

"The boss isn't going to like how much we screwed up. You know he doesn't like surprises. Make sure there's no one else snooping around here," Juke said.

Irina nodded and left.

They placed Florian and Ronaldo in wooden chairs in front of the sofa. Ronaldo went pale from blood loss and started getting faint. Travis wrapped Ronaldo's hand with medical tape, stopping the bleeding. The drooling lizard spat on the hand.

"Now, then. What did you do to Sophie?" Juke said as the angler gorilla frog spirit stared downward at Florian. The top of the towering beast's head phased through the ceiling. It had small squinting frog eyes, and its large frogmouth frowned in annoyance.

Florian mistook the creaking coming from the floor, thinking the gorilla's fists caused it. In reality, it was coming from Juke Lucas as he shifted his mighty strength to speak with the two intruders.

He must be the leader.

"I don't know. This Sophie person just fell asleep in the middle of the road," Florian said.

"I know you. You're the kid that was with the mayor's daughter," Travis said.

"Wait, the kid on TV?" Juke asked.

"Yeah, she's the magical girl that knows martial arts and can see through walls and stuff. She put up a good fight. Gahaha."

"So, she's the one that tripped you up." Juke glared at Travis.

"It was her tin soldier bodyguard! He came out of nowhere and started throwing tables. Did you want me to start a shootout with unarmed pedestrians?"

"You burned down my favorite restaurant!" Juke said.

"No one got hurt. I made sure of it. I followed the rules." He turned to Florian. "Kid, come on, tell me. How did you notice I was tailing you back then?"

Florian remained quiet.

"You can tell me; I'm really good at keeping secrets," Travis said.

"How the hell did you identify us, let alone tail us to our hideout?" Juke said.

Florian smirked.

"Her name's Florian Lilly Cobblestone, and the man is Dr. Ronaldo Von Nirvanas." Sticks shifted through their wallets.

"When did he?" Florian began to sweat.

"Gahaha. Nice pickpocketing, Sticks. What else do they got?"

"She goes to the same school as me. She's a freshman," Sticks said. His snake mouse spirit hissed and squeaked. Sticks clenched his fist.

"Where did this third wallet come from?" Travis said.

"The man I tackled at the railway."

"Nice one, Sticks. However, this chick's younger than you, and she gave us both such a hard time. She's like a genius or something." Travis patted Sticks's back.

Juke slammed the table. Silence overtook the room.

"Knock it off, Travis! She's not a genius; she's an idiot! She's just a kid sticking her nose where she shouldn't. It pisses me off!" The lure on his angler gorilla frog glowed bright red.

"How dare you!" Florian broke her silence. "You guys started it! You were trying to kidnap my friend! I was not going to let yo—"

"Shuuuuuut uuuuuuuuuup!" Teeth engulfed Florian, and in an instant, the jowls vanished.

Florian couldn't tell what just happened.

Juke stared directly into Florian's eyes. Up close, he glowed red, fuming like his crimson hair. His rage almost popped a vessel. The angler gorilla frog dangled its lure in front of its owner's head.

Juke paused. He lowered his voice. "You piss me off. The more I look at you, the more you speak, the more I learn about you, the more I want to throw you in the river. Maybe then you'll realize what shit you're in. I don't care how special you think you are; you're an idiot for coming out here. It's like you have no regard for your own safety."

Florian realized the lure wasn't for her; it was a manifestation of his lingering stress. It was constantly circling his head like a fly that wouldn't go away.

Dr. Ronaldo clapped his hands. "Outstanding everyone. Let's talk things out, one step at a time."

"Did you just interrupt me?!" Juke said.

"Let's talk this out, like gentlemen." Dr. Ronaldo mimicked the words Travis had used.

The angler gorilla frog opened its mouth, revealing a row of thin boney teeth spiraling a dark abyss of bowels. Ronaldo's dark urchin spiked its thorns as sharp as it could, puncturing the angler's mouth.

What's he doing?!

"You're all doing a great job. I'm a therapist, and I'll do my best to speak with you fine gentlemen."

"He's a therapist? Gahaha. We finally found Juke a therapist. Talk with him for a while, Juke. See if you can learn something."

"Can it, Travis! The boss put me in charge, so let me do my job! Don't forget you are the one that screwed up in the first place!"

"Hold up, listen, this chick is—"

"Travis! You still fucked up! You can't brush that under the rug! Right when I was put in charge, almost as if on purpose!"

"Yes. . . Excellent communication. The first step is telling each other how we feel. The next step is forgiving one another. Now repeat after me. 'I forgive you.' Go on."

"Who do you think you are?! This is between us! Stay out of it!"

Dr. Ronaldo slammed his foot. "No! This is a group therapy session. Let's all talk this out and turn over new leaves. Shall we?"

His soul, the dark urchin, was in the middle of the room, trembling its thorns violently.

TWENTY-FIVE
FUEL

HALF SUBMERGED HIDEOUT
SEPTEMBER 17TH X288

Travis sighed. "My bad, I screwed up. I didn't do it on purpose, and I don't want you to get in trouble."

"I know," Juke said, calming down. "But we can't just let these trespassers go. They'll definitely report us."

"I'm proud of the both of you," Ronaldo said, zoning in and out of consciousness.

"Juke, there might be a way to fix this."

Travis and Juke stepped outside the room. Sticks stayed to keep watch of the two hostages.

Ronaldo nudged Florian and whispered, "Florian. When they're distracted by me, get out of here and don't look back."

Florian shook her head. "Don't try anything. Just wait till help arrives."

"You have to get out of here . . . Ow."

"Wait. Something strange is going on. Their souls are aggressive, but they aren't showing hostility."

"You drew them back in the car." Ronaldo recalled the souls in detail.

"The tall man with red hair, Juke. His spirit's extremely agitated, but it isn't showing any signs of hurting us. It opened its mouth and roared several times, but all the man did was yell at us."

"He had the angler frog, right?"

"They said something earlier too. Something about following rules? I think they can't hurt us. That's why they're panicked but not murderous."

"Don't think like that. Get out as soon as you get the chance," Ronaldo said. *Florian's information is just what I needed. Anger. Aggression. Murderous intent. The shape of his soul and its actions explain so much. I know what I must do.*

Juke Lucas and Travis Wit Law reentered the room.

"There's a way to fix all of this," Juke said.

"How does joining our group sound?" Travis said.

"What?" Florian's jaw dropped.

"We can tell you both are merely civilians. In any other situation, we would have disposed of you by now. However, we have taken an interest in you." Juke squatted down to eye level with Florian. "We have a lot of questions, and I'm sure you have some as well."

"Of course, there's a lot of money in it for you. So how about it? Let's be friends and work together," Travis said as his drooling lizard spilled its mane full of saliva.

Florian and Ronaldo shuddered.

"You know too much. Joining us will spare our hideout's location from leaking and benefit us in more ways than one. It's the best option for both of our parties. If you accept, we'll let you go after proper introductions and exchanging of some information.

However, if you refuse, we'll have no choice but to kill you," Juke said with a glint in his eyes.

If we accept, we live. The answer is obvious. Ronaldo looked at Florian. Florian hesitated.

Juke folded his arms and checked his watch. "We don't have much time. So decide quickly—"

"No," Florian said.

"What was that?!" Juke said.

"I refuse—"

"You gotta be kidding me!" Travis said.

"I'll never join you!" Florian said.

Juke grabbed Ronaldo's collar and lifted Ronaldo effortlessly. "Then I guess we'll get this over with." Juke fumed.

He opened a window. Below was a two-story drop to debris and river tides. Ronaldo could barely struggle; he was faint from the blood loss. Juke dangled Ronaldo out of the window with one hand.

‼

"Tell us how you found us!" Juke yelled.

"I can't!" Florian fell to the floor, tears forming in her eyes.

"Who are you working for?" Juke yelled.

"I'm on my own! Ronaldo has nothing to do with this! Don't hurt him!" Florian said. The dark urchin soul was cracking. Florian remembered the conch crab spirit breaking the same way when Zachary Venmont died in front of her.

"Do you care what happens to this therapist?!" Juke hollered. The angler frog spirit looked Florian dead in the eyes. Its lips were frowning. The eyes were squinting with anger. Its glowing lure was no longer red but blue.

Florian smiled as tears rolled down her eyes. She wanted to test her theory.

"Kill me instead," Florian said.

"God, I hate you!" Juke threw Ronaldo back in the room.

"You aren't allowed to hurt us, are you? I wonder why?" Florian said with a teary-eyed chuckle. Their souls were giving away their bluff.

"Gahaha, this kid's hardcore. That's quality. I want her to join even more now."

"Shut up, Travis!" Juke said. He turned to Florian. "Kid. Do you have a death wish?"

Florian smirked.

"Well damn, they're going to report us. We were ordered not to hurt any resident. The therapist is already hurt, though. We can't keep them here forever, and it's only a matter of time until someone notices they're missing," Travis said.

"I know! Shut up, and let me think! Damn it! Why is it always the small jobs? I wish I could just wring that mayor's neck and get it over with." Juke crushed a chair with his bare hands.

"Take a deep breath. Hold it for three seconds, and let it out," Ronaldo said in a daze.

"What's that therapist saying?" Juke walked over to Ronaldo. "Are you making fun of me?"

"No, you're doing great. You're using your words to convey your stress. That way, we all know how you feel and can respond with words of our own." Ronaldo laughed.

"Are you really doing this right now? I dangled you out of a window, and you're laughing! What's wrong with the two of you?! Is this city full of dumbasses like you that don't know real danger when it's right in front of you!" Juke said.

Ronaldo laughed and coughed at the same time.

"Woah. Calm down. Juke!" Travis said.

Ronaldo kept laughing.

"I am calm. Do you think I'm not calm? I am the calmest guy in this room," Juke said. His soul twitched as its muscles tightened.

Ronaldo reached his wrist up to Juke's ear. "Just relax . . . and don't blink. . ." Ronaldo dangled the coin on a string in front of Juke and swung it back and forth.

"Take all that anger in a deep breath. . . Hold it. . ." His watch ticked thrice.

"Now . . . Let it out. . ."

Florian saw the dark urchin's skeleton arm emerge once again. Miasma spewed from its breaking body. It broke off another needle and threaded it through Juke's head. This time it pulled out the thread and unwound it freely across the room. The strings looked like a spiraling whirlwind of thoughts.

Florian had never seen a soul do such a thing. It terrified her.

The room went silent.

"What the hell is that? A string? Is that supposed to be a magic trick or something?" Travis laughed.

Juke stood up without saying a word.

Sticks, who was observing everything from the corner of the room, froze. Juke's eyes rolled to the back of his head. As if in a trance, Juke began whaling on Ronaldo relentlessly.

"Whoa! Stop! Juke! What has gotten into you!" Travis grabbed Juke's arm, attempting to stop Juke's barrage.

Juke just kept punching Ronaldo, shattering the floor.

The angler frog swung its gorilla fists into Ronaldo. The drooling lizard climbed the angler frog, gnawing at its antennae. Sticks and his snake mouse stayed in the corner of the room, scared stiff. The dark urchin floated above Ronaldo. Its skeleton arm just pointed toward the door. Florian stood up and ran.

Travis turned to Florian. "Where do you think you're going? Huh?"

Juke picked up Travis and chucked him out the window. Just like that, Travis vanished. He splashed into the river below.

Juke went back to beating up Ronaldo.

The coast was clear. Sticks was still distracted.

Florian took her first step but realized she was leaving Ronaldo to die. She stopped, grabbed a chair, turned around, and with all her strength, slammed it into Juke. The old wooden chair shattered to pieces, leaving only a stake in her hand. It didn't affect Juke in the slightest.

Florian took the wooden sliver and stabbed Juke in the back.

"Get off him!" Florian said.

To Juke, it was only a splinter.

"You're still here?! God, I hate you!" Juke let out a roar with his angler frog bellowing in unfiltered rage. "You can't even run away correctly!" Juke slurred.

"Calm down. Juke!" Sticks said, snapping out of it.

Florian realized Juke was no longer holding back his rage. Nothing could stop him.

Florian finally realized that her life was in danger.

TWENTY-SIX
PRIDE

S. BROOK COUNSELING & THERAPY CLINIC
SEPTEMBER 17TH X288

Thirty minutes earlier, Miss Garcia Fumblehouse waited for the next notification on her phone. She hummed her relaxing tune as she paced back and forth.

"Hmmm? They should send another text any second now."

Five minutes passed.

"Any second now." She sat staring at her phone, humming up a storm.

Five more minutes passed.

"It's not coming! No! This isn't good. Florian and Ronaldo told me that they were going to a shady part of town. They said they'll send me messages of their locations every two minutes! If they don't, call the police as something might have happened."

Fumblehouse paced frantically, tucking her head into her plush turtle.

"Something must've happened! They could be dead! Or worse? Or worse! No! This's not good! I need to do something! That's right! I need to call the police! Hurry!"

She prepared her phone. But right before calling, she paused. "What if they update me right after I call the police? I know! I'll call them and see if they pick up. It couldn't hurt."

She dialed Florian's phone number and waited.

"We're sorry, the phone you're trying to reach is either out of range or no longer in service. Please dial—"

"Something went wrong! They've been kidnapped, and they're now overseas and out of range! Wait . . . Maybe Florian didn't pay for her phone bill, and that's why it's no longer in service. Yes, that must be it. . . Or maybe the kidnappers took the phone and canceled their service plans so they can't be tracked on the phone's GPS! Oh no! What should I do?" Miss Fumblehouse panicked.

♏

"Hello, nine-one-one. What's your emergency?"

"Help! My friends disappeared, and their phones are no longer in service because they were abducted. Please, you've got to help them! Their last message told me they were near the old abandoned apartment complex at South Tori Docks!"

♏

"Officer Keen, we have missing persons in your area; please check the scene. The address is South Tori Docks, apartments eleven thirty-four through forty-three eleven. One male and one female wearing. . ." Dispatch continued with a description. "Just survey the area and radio back in."

"On my way," Keen said.

Those features sound familiar. Must be my imagination.

He arrived at the scene. The only source of light came from his patrol car.

Keen sighed. "I'm supposed to search all of this by myself?"

He radioed his arrival to dispatch. No response. He tried again. Still no response. "Oh well."

He turned off his car completely, grabbed his flashlight, and started walking. The road was deserted. Rather than turning on the flashlight, he listened. To find anything suspicious, he used all his senses like a fox hunting its prey. He smelt a faint scent of motor oil.

He noticed a light in one of the buildings near the shore. He took a closer look; it was a garage.

Inside was a shaggy-haired blonde woman, wearing a motorsports suit, working on a motorcycle. She was fiddling under the chassis, lying on her back.

Officer Keen entered the building stealthily, watching his corners. He peeked over her shoulder and said, "You do know this place is off-limits, right?"

It was Irina Halt. She froze in place.

"We got a report of missing persons in the area. Have you seen a middle-aged man and young girl, both wearing glasses?"

"I haven't seen anyone around here like dat," Irina said.

"Really? No one else? Your accent tells me you're not from around here. Explain to me why such a pretty young lady like yourself is working in a place like this?" Officer Keen took off his hat and adjusted his greased hair.

"I like vorking here. It's quiet. I can also test drive as much as I vant."

"Is that so? Do you have a permit?"

"I didn't know I needed one."

"Everyone needs a permit to drive."

"So dat's what you meant. I thought you were going to say something creepy." Irina yawned.

"You look so exhausted; a breeze could knock you over. I only flirt with women who can fight back when restrained."

"Dere it is."

"Let me see your driver's license."

"It's right here." Irina went over to her tool chest. She reached for her wallet and a tire iron.

Officer Keen heard a shout coming from a nearby building. He looked away for only a second.

Irina used that opportunity and, with all her weight, smashed the back of his head. With one hit, Keen fell to the ground, motionless. The tire iron dripped with blood.

"Damn it. How de hell did dis officer find us? Dis is bad. I'll have to tell de oders. If an officer is missing, dat's ven de audorities get serious. Dat shout from earlier can't be good eider. Someding must have happened with Juke's team."

Officer Keen stood up, face covered with blood. "This's starting to get fun. I love girls who can smash my head like a watermelon."

"How de hell did dat not kill you?" Irina said.

Officer Keen's sadism glared from his eyes. He rushed to Irina, grabbed both of her hands, and gently caressed them. "Tarot Tori City doesn't let us carry guns, but lucky for you, I bought two wedding rings just for this occasion." Keen snapped handcuffs around Irina's hands. "I'm glad they fit perfectly."

Irina pulled her cuffed hands away and swiped a kick, barely missing Officer Keen's bloody head.

"That almost hit me. If you apologize now, I'll give you a lighter sentence."

"I have noding to say to a police dog."

"Ouch, well, you're now under arrest for assaulting an officer's feelings." Keen winked.

"Do you use dat one on all the ladies dat reject you?"

"No. Only on criminals that are my type or that are suspicious like you. Don't worry. I won't pat you down. Yet." Officer Keen licked the blood running down his cheek.

Irina dashed forward, spinning a flurry of kicks at the officer. Keen blocked with his nightstick, pushed Irina off balance, and pinned her down.

"How about it? I got a big house; you'll get your very own room. I'll provide you three square meals a day. The only downside is the jail bars."

"Too bad for you. I can't sit still. You better not leave me alone; I might fly away," Irina said.

She kicked the officer off her with all her force. Officer Keen took the kick and cuffed her legs in the process.

"You see, like you, I'm not from around here. I transferred in from several towns over. I lived on the streets growing up, and taking a bullet or a blow to the head was a regular thing. Shit, I can't believe Tarot Tori is in the same country as that cesspool. This city's low crime rate dulled my senses, but no one can take away the scars on my back."

Irina couldn't move. "I didn't know dis country vas as bad as mine. If I vasn't sleep deprived, I vould have shown you vat ve do to police dogs vere I come from."

Officer Keen carried Irina to his patrol car. "You're under arrest for assaulting an officer, trespassing, interfering with an investigation, and driving without a license."

Keen tossed Irina in the back seat. He wiped the blood from his head and reported to dispatch but got nothing but static.

"Again? What the hell is going on?"

Irina didn't say a word.

Officer Keen heard glass shattering in the distance and a splash. Without thinking twice, he rushed to investigate.

He followed the noises to a grassy area near a partially submerged apartment building. The struggle was coming from the third floor.

He ran up the stairs and got his taser gun ready.

"You've jumped the shark for the last time, Keen. We're transferring you to Tarot Tori City, Keen. It'll clear your head, Keen. Who said this would be a vacation district? This is the craziest transfer yet."

He took a deep breath and opened the door.

TWENTY-SEVEN
STICKS & STONE

HALF SUBMERGED HIDEOUT
SEPTEMBER 17ᵀᴴ X288

Both Sticks Caldwell and Florian Lilly Cobblestone stood in the warpath of Juke Lucas. The angler frog's fangs clamped through Ronaldo, gnawing him as Juke mauled him with relentless punches filled with crimson anger.

"What the hell did that therapist do to Juke? If this keeps up, Juke'll kill him!" Sticks said in a cold sweat.

"We have to save Ronaldo. Help me stop him!" Florian ordered Sticks with sincerity in her eyes.

"What? Are you insane? Juke wrecked my crew with a flick of his wrist! There's no way I'm fighting him again!" His snake mouse hid under his hood.

"Fine! I'll do it myself." Florian rolled up her sleeves.

"Are you trying to get yourself killed!?"

"I don't care what happens to me! I'll get Ronaldo out of here!"

"Damn it! Fine! Don't blame me if you get hurt!"

Sticks and Cobblestone stood side by side.

"Follow my lead and get your therapist out of Juke's line of sight!" he yelled.

The snake mouse soul shot out, catching the gorilla arm in place.

Florian circled and slid behind Juke. She grabbed Ronaldo's hand, trying to pull him out of the storm of punches.

Juke's head turned to Florian. He swung his arm as if swatting a fly. His spirit's giant fist phased through Florian.

Sticks caught Juke's arm with his whole body. "What's wrong with you?! I said to follow my lead! Damn it!"

"I did," she said. *Your soul already showed me.*

Florian pulled Ronaldo's arm over her shoulder. She felt the arm was bending in the wrong direction. Ronaldo's face was bloodied and swollen. His usually clean button shirt was stained red, his vest torn, and his glasses rendered useless.

Sticks's grip tightened around Juke's arm. "Juke! It's me! Snap out of it!" Sticks was a mouse compared to the six-foot-three giant.

Florian didn't waste a moment; she faced the door and dragged Ronaldo over her shoulder. The gorilla arm of the angler frog whaled through Sticks's body and past Florian's head.

"Get down!" Florian said, and without turning around, she ducked.

Sticks shrugged. "Don't tell me what to do. You're not even facing—"

Juke's fist collided with Sticks's head, knocking him back and forth. Blow after blow, Sticks didn't let go of Juke's arm, not allowing Juke to have another arm to beat him with.

"Yooooooou idiooooooooot! I ordered you to not let them escape!" Juke bombarded Sticks with his fists.

Sticks released his grip.

Florian made it to the door and reached out for it.

"Get back here!" Juke lifted Sticks by his hood and tossed him through the door, smashing it to pieces.

Florian and Ronaldo were knocked back from the shockwave, bumping into the couch. Florian squirmed. When she situated herself, she stiffened. She hadn't noticed until now. A pile of threads lay below the sleeping woman's head.

"What's with all the noise? Is it time for my shift yet?" Sophie Squalid and her soul reemerged from her slumber with a yawn.

Florian had yet to identify the soul of the crazy woman who wielded a scalpel.

Hundreds of thin legs and hands sprouted from the back of the woman. Countless antennae and feelers brushed through the air as she yawned. She stretched her long slim arms upward, and her giant white eyes beamed through her long messy black hair.

"Hie hehe! That's weird? Why do I feel so hungry?" Sophie said, licking her lips.

The angler frog spirit stomped Ronaldo's head.

He's going to smash his head open!

"No!" Florian jumped through the frog's legs and shielded Ronaldo.

"Arah? Who're you two?" Sophie said.

Juke raised his foot over the two on the floor, about to crush them in front of Sophie.

Sophie elegantly leaped with a twirl over Juke, landing on his back. She wrapped her thin arms around Juke's neck, embracing him.

"Hie hehe. Did you forget? We were told not to hurt civilians. Why do you get to have all the fun?"

Juke, in a fit, tried to shake Sophie off.

Florian looked up at the giant angler frog getting strangled by an endless pink and black centipede. Its thick body pinched its legs all over the frog's body.

In the struggle, Sophie perched herself on Juke's back.

"Hie hehe. Are you really letting me do this? Can I really have you all to myself? I do not hear a no. Hie hehe. Finally! I get to cut someone!" Sophie drooled.

Sophie reached behind her back and pulled out a dozen scalpels. She stabbed Juke's back relentlessly. Juke didn't react to the pain; he just tried to reach Sophie, who scurried around his back and arms.

"Hie hehe. Settle down, big guy. Don't worry, I'll sew you back together later. I won't leave a single scar. Okay? Okay. Please, let me cut you up some more. Hie hehe." Sophie squealed in pleasure.

Florian had to escape. She lifted Ronaldo and made her way to the door.

"Where do you think you're going?" Sticks brushed off the rubble and blocked the doorway. "I can't let you just walk out of here. I have to put in work to make my girlfriend happy, even if she did send you here to find me."

"What're you? Who? I didn't come here for you! Move!"

"What? If Choco didn't send you here to bring me home, then how did you identify us?" Sticks dropped his shoulders. "What?"

He dropped his guard and seemed to be processing his thoughts as Florian shuffled her way closer to the door.

"Don't try to escape while I'm thinking!" Sticks reached his snake mouse soul toward Florian's head.

Florian dropped Ronaldo and dodged the jab aimed at her head.

"I don't know how you do it, but with this rematch, I'm going to break your arm," Sticks said, taking a fighting position.

I don't have time for this! No . . . If it's just him, I can handle him. He's around my age and was thrown through a door. He can't take that much damage without feeling some pain. Besides, I can tell his weakness just by looking.

The snake mouse soul wrapped around both of his arms. Florian couldn't tell which hand was going to grab her.

Sticks dove toward Florian, hands ready to apprehend her.

Which one? Florian's eyes darted back and forth.

The snake clotheslined between Sticks's arms. Florian guarded her throat with both arms, seeing through Sticks's misdirection.

Sticks grabbed her wrists and pried them from her neck, one in each hand. He squeezed and twisted them.

"It's over. It doesn't matter, even if you protect your vitals. I'll still clutch and snap whatever I touch."

Sticks lost his balance, and his vision went fuzzy. Electricity hit his brain, and he released Florian as he fell to his knees in pain.

"What happened? Why am I on the ground?" Sticks said.

Florian grabbed Ronaldo and dragged him through the broken doorway.

Sticks recollected himself.

He didn't notice her leg. She kicked him in the groin at full force. She let Sticks grab both her arms, risking them getting broken, to have a clear shot for his crotch. With his hands busy, he couldn't block, even if he did see it coming.

"What's wrong with her? No one would be stupid enough to try something like that. She had to have timed everything perfectly. She would have to know my actions before I even made them," Sticks said, watching the two leave through the hole in the door. "Get back here!" he yelled.

At that moment, Sophie was thrown through the wall, landing in the room next door. Sticks's jaw dropped.

"The stories were true. If Juke snaps, it takes the entire team to stop him. Travis was thrown out the window. That therapist was pounded into the floor. I was hurled through a door, and Sophie was tossed through a wall. What am I doing? How can I face her if I can't achieve anything?" Sticks closed his eyes and covered his head as Juke sprinted past him, gunning for Florian.

Sophie had landed in the room next door, where they kept their supplies. She hurried to her medical bag.

"You twerp!" Juke stampeded through to the hallway and caught up to Florian.

Florian was reaching for the exit when Ronaldo's unconscious body vanished from her shoulder. Juke flung him down the hallway where he crashed and rolled into the old tattered floor.

Florian couldn't move her arm. When she looked down, she saw her mangled arm dangling from her shoulder. The pain caught up to her.

She screamed in pain, collapsing to the floor. Tears, saliva, and snot spewed from her face. She was used to getting hit and bruised learning martial arts, but not like this. Her arm had been pulled out of its socket when Juke chucked Ronaldo, twisting her muscles and nerves in tandem.

The exit door opened by itself.

"Police! Hands on your head!" Officer Keen aimed his taser gun down the hallway.

"Officer Keen?" Florian panted on the floor, arm dead weight.

"You're that kid? What're you doing here?" His fox spirit groaned with a high-pitched gulp.

"Graaaaaaaaahhhh!" Juke charged toward the police officer.

The fox spirit tracked its claws and fearlessly jumped toward Juke's neck. Keen shot his taser, hitting him in the exact spot the fox landed. The jolt went through Juke's entire body.

It didn't even slow him down.

"Well, shit." Officer Keen got tackled to the floor and lifted into the air by Juke.

The angler frog hugged Keen and hopped into the ceiling. Juke rammed Keen's head through the hallway ceiling. Then he slammed Keen into the floor repeatedly. Over and over, the angler frog hopped on top of the officer's body, blocking the exit.

Florian retreated down the hallway to Ronaldo. He lay there motionless.

She looked around; the only thing she could think of was to hide in one of the other rooms. She lifted Ronaldo with her good arm.

With her first step, Sophie Squalid slumped out of that very room.

The deranged woman was wide awake, holding several syringes. She lifted her tilted head, revealing a blood-curdling smile, partially shrouded by her long manic hair. Her soul behind her, a centipede's body, peeled out from within her body. Its legs and feelers, in constant motion, wriggled behind her.

"Hie hehe! Hie hehe! Kya kya-ka!" She laughed, eyes staring through Florian. Laughing, she twirled down the hallway, waving multiple syringes in the air.

Surrounded, Florian couldn't move. She couldn't go on.

Sophie's expression was complete excitement, ready to indulge herself.

Florian closed her eyes.

Sophie ran past Florian and leaped onto Juke, who was busy crushing Officer Keen into the floor. Laughing maniacally, she stabbed Juke in the back.

"Hie hehe! Kya kya-ka!" On and on, Sophie kept stabbing.

"These people are insane," Florian said softly. It finally sunk in. Realizing what she had gotten herself into, she gave up. With the only escape route blocked by lunatics, their souls full of joy, Florian curled up in the corner of the hallway. Soulless.

"Why are they so happy?"

Juke collapsed on top of Keen. Sophie triumphantly placed her foot on Juke's sedated body.

"Hie hehe! Hie hehe."

Sophie Squalid had given up her temperance and revealed her true self. Her centipede spirit was embedded and overlapped with her physical body. Freedom to be herself, a true psychopath. "Kyakya-ka!"

"Ve're back. Oh! Sophie, you're awake." Irina entered the apartment.

"Oh! Irina. Look what I did!" Sophie presented her achievement.

"Dat's amazing, Sophie. You defeated Juke," Irina said.

"Hie hehe. That makes me the strongest! Worship me!" Sophie flipped her hair.

Another person behind Irina entered the apartment. "I bet you're hungry. I brought dinner."

"Clarissa! Thank you. I can't depend on these boys to get me anything. Thank you so much." Sophie bounced with joy, ready to indulge herself.

"What happened here? I'm gone for one day, and all hell breaks loose?" Clarissa said. She carried a bag of groceries.

"Clarissa? There's more of them?" Florian sank.

She was middle-aged and wore a white jogging jacket and sweatpants. She had brown hair and walked elegantly with confidence. Her voice was refined, and her words were motherly.

Florian didn't recognize Clarissa's face, but the soul was one she had met before.

"An octopus. . ." Florian whispered under her breath.

It was an octopus but in a different shape. It took the form of a lionfish. The tentacles sprang out and protruded sharp, mimicking quills. Fins grew from its sides, eyes glaring menacingly.

The mimic octopus spirit had hidden in her hair before. But now, with a different hairstyle, the octopus was floating in the air in its new form.

Clarissa approached Florian. When the two made eye contact, they both recognized each other. Clarissa was the mother of Florian's childhood friends, the mother of the monkey boy and koi fish girl, who had divorced.

What's she doing here? Florian thought.

"Do you know each oder?" Irina asked.

TWENTY-EIGHT
DELIRIUM

HALF SUBMERGED HIDEOUT
SEPTEMBER 17ᵀᴴ X288

Earlier, Irina Halt, locked in the patrol car, was restrained with cuffs around her arms and legs. She leaned her head against the window when Clarissa Lantern tapped the glass.

"Hey. Need a little help?" Clarissa waved.

Irina nodded helplessly.

It took her only one minute. Clarissa opened the locked police cruiser door effortlessly.

"Dank you! You're a lifesaver, Clarissa," Irina said, updating Clarissa on the situation.

"I see. So we have guests." Without trouble, Clarissa lockpicked and removed Irina's handcuffs. "It would be rude if we didn't invite them in after coming all this way."

‾

Sophie dug through the bag of food, nibbling on a piece of beef jerky.

"Sophie, I also got you some tacos." Irina handed them to Sophie with an exhausted scheming chuckle.

Sophie bit into the soggy cold tacos. "Gross! Hie hehe!" Sophie continued munching on them. Irina fist-pumped inconspicuously, winning the bet.

Clarissa stared at the pale, shivering, and injured Florian, huddled in the corner of the hallway.

"Clarissa? You haven't answered yet. Do you know that girl?" Sophie asked, mouth full.

"Nope. I've never seen her in my life," Clarissa lied without hesitation.

Clarissa Lantern, mother of Alex Rodriguez and Sera Rodriguez. Florian couldn't utter a word.

Why did she lie? Is she planning to help us somehow? She looks completely different from how I remember her. She has less makeup, but she's still beautiful. That octopus proves it's her. For just a moment, when Clarissa looked at me, her octopus reverted to its original form.

The octopus's tentacles danced as Clarissa flipped her hair, reverting into the lionfish.

"If I knew we were having guests, I would've had my hair done," Clarissa said. "All right. Get up, boys. What a mess."

Juke slowly rolled over and sat up. The angler frog's lure was no longer glowing. "Sorry, I lost control, didn't I?" Juke said with a slight slur.

"Eh? I injected you with enough tranquilizers to put down a gorilla. How are you still moving?" Sophie asked while biting into one of the sub sandwiches Clarissa had brought.

Soaking wet, Travis Wit Law combat rolled into the hallway with his gun at the ready.

"What! Everyone's here? Don't tell me it's over already. Gahaha." His drooling lizard wagged the water off its body.

"Did you go for a swim? Why can't I go for a swim?" Sophie asked.

"Juke threw me out the window. Don't mess with this man's pancakes." Travis went to get a change of clothes in their storage room.

"Travis," Juke said, stopping Travis in place. "My bad. I feel better now, so please, don't tell the boss." Juke sat on the floor, bleeding from the stab wounds, with a straight face.

"Gahaha. Why are you so serious? I would never sell out any of you guys."

"Aw, dat's so sveet," Irina said.

"Clarissa. We have to hurry," Juke said, trying to stand up.

"Juke, don't move yet; you have a lot of stab wounds, courtesy of yours truly. Let me stitch my name in you really quick," Sophie said.

"No. Patch up the therapist first. I did a number on him. I don't know what came over me. It was like I couldn't control my actions, and at the same time, I was fighting for the controls. I can't explain it." Juke looked at his hands, clenching them.

"Hie hehe, don't forget that policeman you're sitting on. So many patients in one night, all for me. This is the most fun I've had in a long time." Sophie Squalid smiled, skipping to Ronaldo.

Juke got off Officer Keen. Keen's fox spirit was lying beside him, twitching.

Irina approached Keen with a sour face. "I told you to keep an eye on me, policeman. I just can't seem to sit still in a vehicle unless I'm the one driving," Irina said semi-seductively. Irina's muscular cheetah spirit growled at the tiny fox.

Officer Keen couldn't move. "Ow, I— so many beautiful ladies. I must be in heaven. It breaks my heart to arrest angels. Ow. It hurts to laugh," Keen said, pinned in the crushed floorboards.

Irina took the taser gun and all the other weapons Officer Keen had on his person. She then blindfolded him and bound him with the same handcuffs that had bound her in the car.

"In my country, civilians arrest you," Irina said. The cheetah bit at the fox spirit.

Clarissa pointed to Florian. "What about this girl in the corner? Sticks? Is this that girlfriend you keep talking about?"

Sticks limped to the crumbled doorway, giving the silent treatment. His snake mouse soul was hiding in his sleeve.

"Trouble in paradise?" Clarissa asked.

"Hie hehe, want me to check your groin? She may have left some permanent damage. Hie hehe." Sophie cackled, making fun of him.

"Leave me alone." Sticks brushed Sophie off.

"What happened?" Clarissa asked.

"I saw everything. The girl in the corner is pretty tough; she must play 'football,' if you know what I mean. Hie hehe," Sophie said as she snipped off Ronaldo's clothes. The centipede legs and feelers fondled and groped Ronaldo's body, locating broken bones.

"She's tough, all right. I recruited her, but she declined. Can you believe it?" Travis said.

"And yet she's here, along with two other injured witnesses. In our hideout." Clarissa forced a smile.

"We really tried to fix this. These two are unbelievably stubborn," Travis said.

"You didn't try hard enough. The boss will decide what to do with them," Clarissa said.

Juke limped back into the room. Irina and Sticks dragged Officer Keen and plopped him on the couch. Travis moved Ronaldo into the room as Sophie provided medical aid.

Their apparitions cooperated with each other; it reminded Florian of her friends at school, Miss Fumblehouse, Sergeant Honest Nowell, and Dr. Ronaldo.

These criminals also had an unbreakable bond.

Clarissa turned to Florian. "Let's start things over. Shall we?" She grabbed Florian's arm, untwisted it, and popped it back into its socket. Florian grunted in pain. The octopus circled the air, hovering over Florian in its lionfish form.

Florian didn't resist because of Clarissa's reassuring presence. Florian surrendered, giving up all hope for escape. She considered accepting their recruitment just so they all could survive.

A ringing sounded in Florian's ears. It was coming from the last room down the hall.

Clarissa seemed to notice the concern. "Don't mind the noise. It's just the proximity jammer. It's completely safe, but the noise is a little unsettling."

A jammer? That's why our phones didn't get a signal. Officer Keen must have shown up thanks to Miss Fumblehouse, but he couldn't call for backup because of the signal jammer. The police should send more help after not hearing from Officer Keen for a while. Do I have to stall for time? It won't work. Ronaldo is badly injured. If the police do show up, there will be a gunfight. These six are not petty kidnappers; they're the real deal.

Florian entered the room with everyone else, quietly defeated.

The guests sat on the couch. Ronaldo sat on Florian's right, and Officer Keen, handcuffed and blindfolded, sat on her left.

Travis and Irina sat by the door, guarding it. Clarissa and Juke sat across from the couch; between them was a computer. Sticks sat at the table by the window, avoiding eye contact with Florian. Sophie was treating Ronaldo and examining Officer Keen.

"Good news, this therapist guy's stable. He's bruised everywhere, has three broken ribs, a broken right arm, a black eye, and a stab wound on his left hand. It's a good stab; who did that?" Sophie asked.

"You did." Everyone looked at Sophie.

"Eh? I wouldn't attack by standards. I don't remember. Hmmm? Anyway, I redid the sloppily done bandages on his hand, disinfected every open wound, iced his swelling, and injected him with some painkillers. He lost some blood but not enough to kill him. The police guy has two broken ribs and a concussion. I stopped the bleeding to his head too. If I inject painkillers, he may try something. So whatever. Just leave him there. The best for last, Juke! I'll start stitching you up now. Hie hehe!"

Sophie sat behind Juke and began patching him up with a cheerful look, as if proud of the injuries she'd inflicted. The angler frog sat patiently with its eyes closed and chest out.

"The LAN line's working; I guess the boss is a little late," Clarissa said, checking the computer.

Officer Keen squirmed, blindfolded. "Do you know how many laws you're breaking? All of you are in serious trouble! In a few minutes, this building will be completely surrounded. You'll be outmanned and outgunned. I'll shield this kid beside me with my body when they fill this entire building with bullets. Just you wait." His fox growled with a limp.

The gang looked at each other for a moment and broke out into laughter.

"What's so funny? Did I miss the joke? You are all going to jail! If not, die here tonight," Officer Keen said.

"The police only received a missing person case. After sending you, they won't send another officer for another good thirty minutes. When they do, we'll know," Travis said, checking one of the laptops.

"Also, de ETA for a standard-issue patrol car, or any vehicle for that matter, from any police route in dis city is roughly fifteen to twenty minutes," Irina said. Her cheetah curled up beside her.

"This building's behind four other abandoned apartments. Unless they bring the entire police force, it'll take time for them to sweep those buildings before reaching ours. Giving us even more time is a simple one out of five chance. The odds are in our favor," Juke added.

"Heh, when they find my empty patrol car, they'll find you sooner than that!" Officer Keen said.

"That would be the case if a tarp wasn't covering it. A cheap multipurpose tarp. What's so suspicious about a covered car in the dead of night beside other abandoned vehicles and buildings?" Clarissa crossed her arms with a smirk.

"What!? What's going on!? Who the hell are you guys?" Officer Keen hollered.

"Gahaha. Keep yelling, and we'll muzzle you. Didn't your mother teach you any manners?" Travis asked. His lizard panted with a smile, laughing.

"I'm sure our boss will have some questions for you. So stay quiet," Clarissa said, eyes locked on Florian.

"Well, I'm out of ideas. I guess these are the guys. Right, kid?" Officer Keen nudged Florian.

"Yeah," Florian said reluctantly.

"So it wasn't a dream?" Ronaldo said.

"Are you all right?" Florian asked.

"Wait? Is that Dr. Ronaldo's voice?" Keen said.

"You know him?" Florian said.

"At the station. The doc helps us out once in a while."

Florian hadn't known that about Ronaldo. The dark urchin spirit reappeared above Ronaldo, motionless. Florian placed her head against Ronaldo's shoulder, sighing with relief.

"When did Officer Keen get here? I feel numb." Ronaldo coughed.

"That must be the painkillers. I didn't get any," Keen said as his fox let out a howl.

"Someone gag that annoying cop," Clarissa said.

"Hey! Don't hate me. I got here and found you guys a lot sooner than your projected ETA said I would. I was kidding; come on.

Don't—" Officer Keen got muzzled. His fox let out muzzled whimpers.

The computer screen rang. A caller was coming through.

"It's the boss," Juke said.

Everyone was present and at full attention. All of their souls faced the computer screen.

Florian, Ronaldo, and Keen sat dead center of the camera feed. The screen lit up.

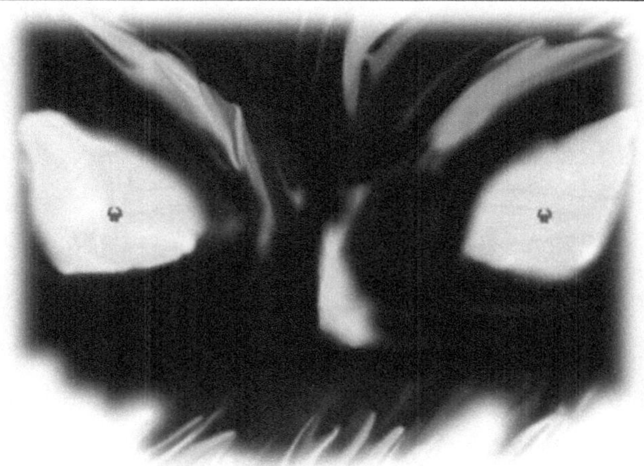

TWENTY-NINE
FADED

HALF SUBMERGED HIDEOUT
SEPTEMBER 17TH X288

A silhouette took up the computer screen. Veiled in shadow, a man leaned back in his chair with his knuckle supporting his cheek and his boot resting on his knee. He wore a tuxedo and a black fur mantle over his shoulders. His black hair darted out, flowing like a flame. His skin was as pale as his sinister eyes.

Florian squinted at the monitor, seeing part of his soul out of frame.

The footage was hazy, but the audio was clear.

The boss spoke in a deep hoarse voice. "Florian Lilly Cobblestone. When I read Miss Lantern's message before the call of a young girl finding our hideout. . . My best guess was that it was you."

Florian couldn't breathe. "It" began to seep through the laptop's screen.

"Don't be surprised; you're quite famous for saving the mayor's daughter."

"It" was fleshy, meaty, protruding, and immense. Skulls grasped one another along its decaying, pulsating, parasitic brain swell. Whatever "it" was, "it" resonated with the others in the gang. The sewn appendages of the soul stretched through the computer screen and into Florian's head. Veins of pulp, fibers, and cartilage melded with each member of the gang, spirits entwined. Florian's vision blurred; she couldn't bear to see "it" any longer.

She covered her eyes, yet the soul phased through her attempts, searing its presence directly in her mind.

"Say, Florian Lilly Cobblestone. . . Do you believe in ghosts?"

Florian puked. Everything within her oozed to the floor. She fell, throwing up, panting in a cold sweat, and fainting in her excrement.

"I'll take that as a yes," the boss said.

"What's wrong, Florian?" Ronaldo said.

The gang resuscitated Florian and cleaned up the mess.

⚭

"Pack it up; we're leaving. I know we were preparing for the big one, but luck was against us this time. Everyone! Salvage the most important tools and supplies, as much as the boat can carry. Burn everything else to the ground. Lay low outside Tarot Tori City until further orders."

"Yes, sir." The gang nodded.

"Boss. What about these three?" Juke asked.

"I know the arrangement, Mr. Lucas. If we kill them, we'll never be able to set foot in this city again. Luckily for us, we've got time on our side. Nevertheless, we can't afford them interfering with our plans in the future. Leave them to me," the boss said.

"Okay, you heard the boss. Travis, make the call on what to take with us and throw everything down to me. Sticks and Sophie, load the trailer with everything from the garage. The rest assist as best as you can," Juke said.

With stitches in his back and sedatives in his system, Juke ripped out floor panels with his bare hands. Inside the half-submerged apartment was a huge boat docked on the second floor.

Juke hopped down to the vessel and caught the boxes and tools tossed down to him. Working through the hole in the wall that Sophie had been thrown through helped speed up the process.

"Miss Halt. Distract the police with a few stunts," the boss ordered.

"Vait, you're saying—"

"Make as much noise as you can. I'll message you a rendezvous point later. Don't hold back," the boss said.

"Thank you, sir." Irina ran off in excitement. Her cheetah spirit ran beside her, slipping a bit. Sophie and Sticks followed not far behind.

Irina opened the garage, uncovering one of her favorite custom-made motorcycles. She was ready to test out her best work yet, the Fire Wheel. Her mission was to be the decoy.

Sophie and Sticks emptied the garage, loading essential equipment into a trailer hitched to a large truck. Irina started the motorcycle's engine.

Echoing back to the apartment was a boisterous roar that shook the room. The sound of the revving chariot was furious, clean, and full of pride. Flame flickers shone through the window as Irina drove off.

Carissa Lantern kept an eye on the hostages as she boxed papers and maps, setting aside what could be burned.

The computer display lit up the faces of the three guests.

The boss raised a glass. "Dr. Ronaldo Von Nirvanas. . . Is that really you?"

"What? How do you know my name?"

"It's been a long time. You've grown. You may not remember me, but I'm sure Dr. Steinsbrook mentioned me at some point. Does the name Selucius come to mind?"

"I don't know. I can't remember anyone going by the name Selucius."

"That's a pity. Have you ever heard of what happened to Dr. Steinsbrook?" Selucius asked.

"What? Do you know where he is? Tell me!"

"You don't know? I was hoping you would have some leads. I'm looking for him myself." Selucius drank from his glass.

"I don't know where he is. . . Wait. Why are you looking for him?"

"Can't say. I'm finished conversing with you, Dr. Ronaldo Von Nirvanas. It's clear you haven't done your homework. I most certainly have done mine. Among the three of you, you've disappointed me the most. For costing my team so much, I was hoping you would be able to answer at least some of my questions. I'll accept my losses and move on." He turned to the police officer. "Officer Keen, you're new and making a quick name for yourself."

"Wait, I'm not done! Answer me! What do you want with my mentor?" Ronaldo interrupted. His dark urchin aggressively quivered with anger.

Selucius continued. "Officer Keen, you've done fairly well. However, you're trespassing on private property without a warrant. As such, you were attacked by my guard dogs. No hard feelings. I look forward to more cat and mouse with this stigma over your head. When you are fully recovered, of course."

Officer Keen, blindfolded and muzzled, nodded, mumbling sarcastic groans. His fox was growling and snarling at the computer.

Florian was dazed and motionless, staring at the soul that engulfed the room.

"Now then. You truly are interesting, Florian Lilly Cobblestone. First, you impressed me by interrupting that kidnapping job. No surprise that the damn mayor rolled with it without any issues. But then you made that small job almost blow our cover. You even somehow tailed my crew to our hideout. I won't ask you how you did it, but lucky for you, we have bigger plans. You sure are a crafty one, having someone else call the police to report if you go missing. Not bad. You really did test us tonight."

Florian sat up and looked Selucius in the eyes. He had devilishly white eyes, cold and fearless.

"All of you are terrible. Why did you try to kidnap the mayor's daughter? Blythe's just a kid. If you have beef with the mayor, why not just abduct him instead?"

"Why did *you* want to track us down? You knew there would be danger and risks. Yet, you still pursued us. Why?"

"So I could stop you from kidnapping Blythe or anyone else again. All of you keep saying you don't harm civilians, yet kidnapping kids is okay in your book. What a load of shit!"

"It's called tact. Before you start preaching to me about morality, you must first realize you know nothing. Notwithstanding, you clearly have zero concern for your own safety or of those around you. That sergeant friend of yours, your classmates, or that sister of yours could've gotten hurt."

"If you lay a finger on them, I will—"

"You will what? What can you do? Nothing. Absolutely nothing because you're just a girl. A girl who doesn't value her own life, playing superhero. It doesn't matter how special you think you are. Without a firm grasp on your own life, what gives you the right to tell others what to do?"

Ronaldo put his foot down, as dazed as he was. "Florian did the right thing. Her actions are justified, whereas yours are nothing but rotten."

"Her actions were suicidal. Nothing justifies suicide. This entire situation is your doing, Florian. Whatever happens, it's your fault. If anyone dies tonight, if families get torn apart, it's all on your hands."

"That's not true," Ronaldo said. "Don't listen to him!"

"Oh, you're to blame too, Doctor. You didn't stop her. You enabled this narcissist into action. Now she's seeking danger like an impulse. Some counselor you turned out to be. One failure after another. Disappointing."

Florian and Ronaldo went silent.

Clarissa Lantern intervened. "Boss. Travis did try to recruit her. His appraisals are always worth the investment. It would be a waste to lose a golden goose."

"This girl's not the type. I can see it in her eyes," Selucius said. "If you dive into our world, you have to be prepared to risk everything. We're prepared to risk everything, every day, in fact, and we enjoy every second of it. Report us; it won't matter. We're ghosts after all, and no one can catch a ghost." He paused. "Let them go as soon as the police scanner pings any officers headed our way."

The team worked quickly, almost as if rehearsed.

Florian and Ronaldo didn't acknowledge one another. Florian sobbed, soon Ronaldo did too.

The gang members noticed the waterworks, glanced in their direction, and were awkwardly concerned.

THIRTY
OVERREACH

HALF SUBMERGED HIDEOUT
SEPTEMBER 17TH X288

The ghosts released their guests.

Officer Keen, still restrained, was supported by Florian as they hobbled to his patrol car. Dr. Ronaldo limped not far behind.

ॐ

Sophie looked around. "Where'd they go?"

"Oh, the intruders? We let them go," Sticks said.

"Eh? Aren't they new friends? I wanted to watch them heal and share scary stories," Sophie said.

"Gahaha, I didn't get to hear that kid's trick. Oh well. You didn't have to be that hard on them, Boss. They were in tears, you know," Travis said.

"Recruiting under these circumstances isn't optimal, Wit Law. Were you going to toss them in the driver's seat and just trust them with the wheel tonight of all nights?" Selucius asked.

Juke kept looking down at his hands. *What did he do to me? I feel strangely calm. Sophie's also more cheerful and well-rested. What's going on?*

Selucius, through the monitor, must have noticed the change of pace as well. He called out. "Miss Lantern. You seemed awfully kind to our guests. The entire time you were within earshot of our conversation. Have anything to say for yourself?"

"As a matter of fact, I do." Clarissa smiled with a sly look. "I can't hide anything from you, can I, Selucius?"

ထဌ

Florian removed Keen's blindfold.

"Damn it! Did they give back my keys?" Keen said.

Florian and Ronaldo shook their heads.

"Well, I guess we're walking," Keen said, holding his head.

"They have our phones and wallets, too," Ronaldo said.

"We'll find someplace with a phone and call for backup and an ambulance." Officer Keen went on ahead.

Ronaldo sat down on the side of the road. Florian stayed beside Ronaldo, worried he might collapse at any moment. They wouldn't look each other in the eye, sniffling the remaining tears they had left.

It was quiet; only the sounds of nature accompanied the night sky.

"I'm sorry," Florian said.

"No. I'm sorry. I had plenty of chances to stop you," Ronaldo said.

The sound of a motorcycle roared in the distance. It must have been Irina Halt.

"Are you feeling okay?" Ronaldo said.

"Yeah, I'm not crying anymore."

"No, you vomited back there."

"Oh, it was their boss's soul. It caught me by surprise, that's all."

"So it was his soul. What a grotesque man."

Florian disagreed. "He's right about all of it. In mere moments he understood me better than I understood myself. I can't imagine how his soul became the way it is. I'm such an idiot."

"You aren't an idiot. You're just a kid. You deserve to live. When their boss said you were "self-destructive," I couldn't help but think about your missing soul. Did you do all this because you think you don't have a soul?"

"I don't know." Florian stared up at the starry sky.

Ronaldo stared at her, silent.

"All right, the police should arrive here within ten minutes." Officer Keen hobbled back to them. "They were busy chasing someone on a motorcycle, shooting fireworks all over the city. It must have been that Irina Halt lady. She better not get caught; I'm the one that'll arrest her and all those other guys too. Just wait and see."

"Count me in. I'll help in any way I can," Ronaldo said, looking in Florian's direction.

Florian hesitated. She knew what Ronaldo was pulling, but it brought a smile to her face.

Police sirens zoomed past the trio.

"There they go! Go get them!" Keen cheered.

Florian had a bad feeling in her gut. She sat down beside Ronaldo.

After a few minutes, gunshots fired off in the distance.

"Shit! Get down!" Officer Keen pushed Ronaldo and Florian to the ground.

Florian covered her ears, but the words of Selucius echoed in her mind.

The gunfire drowned out her cries.

Ronaldo shielded Florian with his already wounded body. He held her, and even with her covering her ears, he repeated, "It's not your fault."

"It's not your fault."

"It's not your fault."

"It's not your fault."

ACT 4
RELINQUISHING SOVEREIGNTY

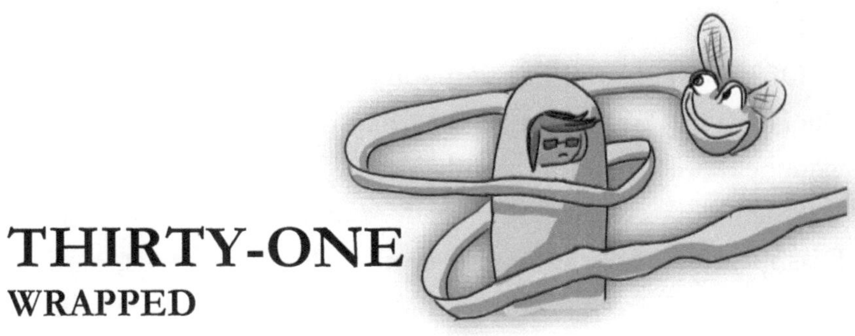

THIRTY-ONE
WRAPPED

*TORI DOCKS ABANDONED HOUSING DISTRICT
SEPTEMBER 17TH X288*

When the gunfire ceased, the serene, tranquil sounds of the night returned, easing Florian Lilly Cobblestone.

Officer Keen tried to flag down an ambulance when a fire truck sped past them, heading straight to the hideout.

"Damn it! That can't be good." Officer Keen hobbled after them. Keen's body was still injured, yet his fox spirit, full of energy, ran ahead of him.

Dr. Ronaldo turned to Florian. She stood without saying a word and walked toward the sirens, as if they were calling to her.

"Florian, I have to warn you, what we might find could be devastating. Are you sure you want to go?" Ronaldo stuck by her side.

"I'll find out eventually, be it now or tomorrow. I would rather confirm with my own eyes."

The trio went back to the hideout.

The apartment building was ablaze. Firefighters did their best to keep the fire contained, dousing the sinking building.

Dozens of police surveyed the grounds on high alert, taping off areas of interest. Medics were treating several injured officers along the sidewalk.

Florian silently gazed at the burning building, fists clenched.

Officer Keen, still restrained in his own cuffs, reported to the chief on site. He explained they had discovered the hideout and were held hostage until recently.

"Damn it, Keen! You had something to do with this? Disappearing, not answering your communications, and then reporting back from nowhere hogtied and in your underwear. I was about to fire you on the spot for screwing around while on duty." The chief sighed after seeing Dr. Ronaldo battered and bruised.

"Dr. Ronaldo too? I thought I told you you weren't on this case. Stay in the ambulance for first aid. Let me take care of a few things, and I'll go with you to the hospital for further questioning," the chief said, tipping his cap in discouragement.

Officer Keen had his cuffs removed by another officer and immediately took off to help.

"Here." A paramedic handed Florian an emergency foil blanket as she tended to Dr. Ronaldo's injuries. "Who dressed your wound? It's very well done. What kind of knot is this on this sling?" she asked, seemingly impressed that Ronaldo could walk with injuries like these.

Florian enveloped herself in the blanket, looking like a burrito wrapped in aluminum foil. She sat in the back of the ambulance, peeking from her blanket, as a few stretchers were carted off toward the burning building. She stared in their direction, awaiting their return to assess the damage she caused.

A limo pulled up, parking in front of them. Florian shrugged, tucking her head in her silver covering.

Mayor Banquet stepped out of his Limo Force One. Even at a time like this, he wore a white suit and tie. His floating smile spirit was no longer stretched out, floating, nor smiling. Its enormous eyes gazed toward the burning apartment with a frown.

Mayor Banquet approached the police chief, his smile gone. His face showed actual worry. This was the first time Florian has ever seen the mayor act that way.

The stretchers returned from the burning building carrying two injured officers. The mayor spotted them; he walked alongside the incapacitated officers, saying something. They were too far away for Florian to hear, but the spirit on his back showed genuine worry. The floating head sobbed tears of grief above the mayor, dripping shimmering droplets onto the officers.

The stretchers entered the ambulance, giving Florian a good look at the officers covered in embers. They lay motionless, bloody, burnt, with their spirits unconscious by their sides. One officer clung to his soul with his bare hand. Florian could tell just by looking that the two were fighting for dear life.

Mayor Banquet stood beside Florian and Ronaldo. They watched the paramedics attend to the injured and drive off to the hospital.

Mayor Banquet smiled and offered a handshake. "You must be Dr. Von Nirvanas. It's a pleasure to finally meet you."

"Oh, call me Dr. Ronaldo. I'm honored to meet you too. Thank you for helping the citizens of Tarot Tori City."

"Oh, I haven't done as much as you have, Doctor."

-POP-

"I just did what the people wanted. If you must thank someone, thank the very citizens of this wonderful city," the mayor said.

"You're right. I should pay it forward somehow," Ronaldo said.

Dr. Ronaldo fell for his lie. I hate this. Please. No more bubbles.

"Forgive me if I'm too upfront, but just between you and me, Doctor, I love the way the citizens think. I just can't help but poke around a little bit." Banquet smirked, looking down at the quiet person wrapped in foil beside him.

Ronaldo covered his mouth.

Florian was peeking through the blanket, watching the ambulance drive away. Bubbles began to surround her, sticking to the blanket like foam.

Without facing her, the mayor continued. "Good evening, young Cobblestone. I didn't expect to see you here."

-POP-

"Catch any bad guys this time? Or did you start this fire too?"

-POP-

"Just kidding!" Mayor Banquet smiled, unlike his spirit. The head glared at Florian, sticking its face right in hers with unbridled rage. It was red and laughing scornfully.

Florian pulled the blanket over her eyes and turned around completely.

"Oh, don't be like that. Let's have a fun chat," Banquet said.

His soul was hovering around her, eyes crossed.

Florian hunched over, covering her ears, fully enveloping herself, annoyed.

"Hmmm, you must be tired. I guess you don't want to know how many casualties there were?"

-POP-

"Casualties?" Florian muttered, shivering at the thought.

"Do I have your attention now? Well, too bad. You'll have to wait until the full report is published in the paper tomorrow, like everyone else." Banquet smiled.

Florian sunk her head entirely in the blanket.

Dr. Ronaldo stomped his foot, getting between the mayor and Florian. "Stop addressing her that way! She's been through enough tonight! So knock it off!"

The smile on the mayor's face disappeared. What replaced it was a serious, no more nonsense expression. Banquet's sharp eyes, filled with straightforward disgust, made Ronaldo shiver.

"In case I'm not making myself clear, I'm distraught by the events that transpired here tonight. More upset than the two of you combined. In reality, it all boils down to whether the individuals currently in critical condition survive or not. One thing's for sure; I despise that girl hiding behind you, Doctor. Oh, with a burning passion, I hate her so much."

"Why?! She saved your daughter, didn't she? She's a hero. Right? Those were your own words!"

"Oh, my hatred for her has nothing to do with that. I'm grateful to her for saving my one and only child." His bright smile returned for a moment and disappeared once more. "It's because we're similar."

"I'm starting to think I've misjudged you, Mr. Banquet. How's she anything like you?"

"We both think in unorthodox ways. She hates losing as much as I do. She can't stand looking at me like how I can't stand looking at her." He smiled, holding a glare filled with excited frustration.

"In fact, it's quite ironic, see. That's why I detest you, Florian Lilly Cobblestone."

Florian didn't say a word. She hid in her blanket, like a burrito, afraid that she would fall apart if she opened the wrapping in any way.

Banquet's anger receded, and his gleaming smile returned. "Now cheer up, okay. I'll see you at your award ceremony six days from now. If you thought you didn't deserve it before, well, you definitely deserve it now!" He entered his limo with a chain of cheerful waves goodbye. His spirit hung out the window as the chauffeur escorted them away.

ა◌ფ

221

"He's gone."

Florian could finally relax.

"What was that about?" Officer Keen, still in his underwear, asked.

"I don't know. He's nothing like I thought he was," Ronaldo said.

"Maybe we interrupted his beauty sleep or something? Anyway, I'm going to head to the hospital; I think my natural adrenaline's wearing off. You guys coming?" Officer Keen asked.

"Of course we are! I think the pain medicine that Sophie lady gave me is wearing off! I'm starting to hurt all over! Ow."

Florian stood up, removing the blanket. "How many casualties?" Florian said.

"What?" The chief walked over.

Florian pointed at the chief, who had a pug dog for a spirit. "I'm not leaving without knowing how many casualties there were."

The chief nodded. "As of this moment, we have three officers with minor stab wounds, four with non-life-threatening gunshot wounds, and two in critical condition with burn injuries."

Florian sighed, realizing there was more by the sad look on the pug spirit's face.

"The only casualty is an unidentified body of a woman," the chief said.

"You can't lie to me! Show me!" Florian grabbed the coat of the chief.

"I refuse to show a teenage girl a dead body," the chief said.

"Where is she? Don't you need someone to identify the body? I saw every one of their faces and heard what they called one another."

"We'll take you to the hospital. There we'll call your parents and continue questioning. You can share your information where it's safe," the chief said.

"I can help!" Florian said.

"You can help us by cooperating," the chief said.

"This isn't the first time I've seen a dead body!" she yelled. "Zachary Venmont. I witnessed him die right in front of me! I couldn't do anything. I was so annoyed with myself! I was mortified that I couldn't do anything to help him. He was a citizen of Tarot Tori City, my neighbor, and all I could do was watch him die! I refuse to just sit by any longer! Show me so I can help you identify the body!"

The chief let out a sigh. "Fine, but it won't be pretty."

The chief brought the trio to a body bag next to another ambulance. He unzipped the bag, revealing the charred remains of an unrecognizable body still with pieces of clothing, jogging pants, and a running jacket.

"We found her floating in the river. There is also a gunshot wound in her head. We suspect the culprits had a falling out. Cruel sons of bitches. So, do you recognize her?" He zipped the bag closed.

Florian nodded. Tears welled up in her eyes as she pondered her thoughts. *There's no denying it. That's the body of Alex and Sera's mom. I don't see her octopus soul anywhere. It must have died and disappeared like Zachary Venmont's conch crab soul. What should I say? If I tell them her real identity, her death will reach Alex and Sera. This entire time, Alex and Sera were guarding my sister while their mom helped me escape the gang with my life. What if they find out I played a part in their mom's death?*

Florian mustered up words. "The gang called her Clarissa Lantern; she had brown hair and. . ." Florian continued with the description but didn't tell the chief Clarissa's real identity. Florian wished to protect Clarissa the same way Clarissa had done to protect her.

Ronaldo agreed with all the information Florian gave.

Officer Keen had been blindfolded, seeing only the face of Irina Halt and the monster with crimson hair.

"All right, we'll continue this at the hospital. We also found two pairs of keys and two phones by the building. Almost like they wanted us to find them. I recognize one of them."

"You found our phones; there should be photos of a few gang members on them. And these are my keys," Ronaldo said.

"You know the drill; I've got to keep them as evidence until further notice."

"Hey, the other pair of keys are mine, but where's my phone?" Keen said.

"Keen. Hopefully, the hospital stay can fix your stupid," the chief said.

"Hey, I almost died tonight," Keen said.

They all rode with the chief to the hospital but not before stopping at Ronaldo's car.

Florian grabbed her journal, flipped past the page with her spirit sketches, ripped out the gang's profile sketches, and handed them over to Officer Keen.

THIRTY-TWO
GATHERING THOUGHTS

*TORI HOSPITAL EAST
SEPTEMBER 18TH X288*

At the hospital, six days until the unwanted award.

Florian was out like a light. While asleep, the events pieced themselves together in her mind, as did the words of discouragement and the mysterious clues.

"That's it! That's it! I figured it out. Now all I need is the evidence to prove my theory."

Her stolen motivation reignited.

Hope hugged Florian, waking her up in her hospital bed. Her parents ran to their side, embracing them both. The iguana and dog souls comforted the seashell dove and Florian.

"What were you thinking?"

"We'll never forgive ourselves if anything happens to you."

Hope snuggled her head against Florian, shivering with tears of relief. Hope gripped tightly, shaking her head, communicating that she would never let go. Her seashell dove nestled up against Florian.

Florian smiled and hugged them back in tears. "I'm sorry. I love you all so much."

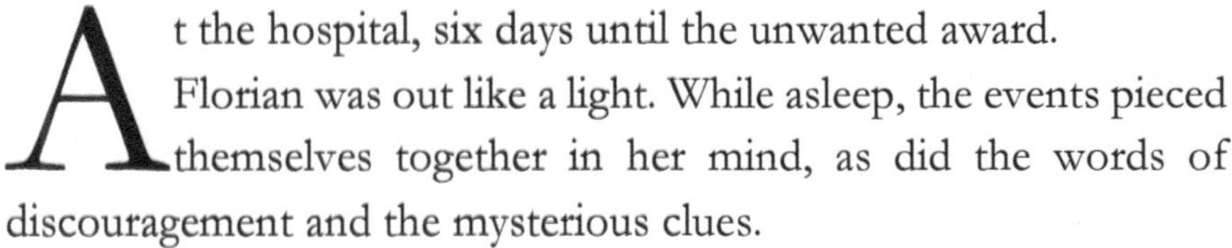

Florian tried to get up from the hospital bed. "Where's Dr. Ronaldo? There's something very important I need to tell him."

Hope and her parents stopped her.

"Where do you think you're going? After what happened, do you think we are going to just let you walk off again?" her father said.

"I have to confirm something with him. It's very important."

"We met with Dr. Ronaldo earlier. He apologized for everything, implying he was responsible for all this," her mother said.

"Of course, we disagreed with him as he didn't leave your side through the entire ordeal." Her parents were cross.

"We all know you're most likely the one that dragged him into this. You're the one that's always up to something. So we decided to ground you."

"You won't be allowed to go anywhere without one of us accompanying you."

"That's fine. I was wrong and almost got Dr. Ronaldo and myself killed. I made a huge, selfish mistake. I won't run away, and I'll accept any punishment. But this is bigger than me, bigger than all of us, and it can't be ignored. So please, come with me to consult with Dr. Ronaldo."

The Cobblestone parents sighed.

"Dr. Ronaldo said he didn't feel qualified to help you and he'll release you from his care. He insisted on not seeing you."

Florian sank a bit. "What? Is this his form of reprimanding me? Is he like this because of what that boss said? Doesn't he realize all of this doesn't make sense? That idiot."

"Don't call Dr. Ronaldo an idiot. We need to apologize to him. I'm sure he'll turn around after a few days," her mother said.

Hope signed to her sister, "Apologize to him and your friends too!" Hope's face full of tears puffed with angry scorn, then reverted as she went back to hugging Florian.

Florian signed to Hope. "I promise."

Hope nodded, pointing toward the door. There stood Alex, Sera, and Amalia. The monkey, koi fish, and bat spirits were at their side.

"I can't believe you left us out this time!" Sera said.

"Are you kidding? What could we have done to help her?" Amalia said.

"Come on, guys. We did do something! We protected Hope," Alex said.

"I'm sorry." Florian broke out into tears. She remembered what had happened to their mother.

"What's the matter? You don't need to apologize to us. We had fun hanging out with Hope," Sera said.

Florian realized they didn't know yet. "Can I borrow your phone to text your mother?" Florian asked.

"Okay? I don't know what for, but fine with me." Sera handed Florian her cell.

Florian typed and sent a heartfelt apology. "This is Florian; I'm sorry for everything. I caused so much trouble, but I will not give up. I'll get back at those that wronged you."

"Hmm? I wonder what that means?" Amalia said, looking over Florian's shoulder.

"It's nothing." Florian handed back the phone, rubbing away the tears.

The chief of police walked in with his pug spirit. "I hope I'm not interrupting; I heard you finally woke up."

"No, just the person I wanted to see. I also have a few questions of my own," Florian said.

"Whoa. You have a completely different attitude than when we questioned you a week ago. I'm impressed."

"Please, can this wait? She's lucky to be alive."

"It's fine, Mom."

Officer Keen walked in on a crutch and wearing a neck brace. "This kid here is a hero. She drove some big bad guys out of Tarot

Tori City. She got us sketches of their faces and even got us some of their names."

"Cool! It's about time you all realized how awesome Florian is!" Alex and Sera cheered.

Officer Keen grinned and tilted his head holding his greased hair back. His fox spirit sat straight with its head lifted upward.

"I arrived just in the nick of time. Doc fought hard and collapsed on the floor. I shot my taser like this. The kid protected Doc as I knocked out this big thug that was on a rampage."

I clearly remember you were the one that got knocked out by the so-called big thug.

Alex and Sera were awestruck. Their spirits' jaws dropped. "Wait till the others hear about this!"

Florian's parents were just relieved she was all right.

"Now settle down. We have a lot of questions to get through," the chief said.

Florian gave as much information as she could without mentioning her apparition vision. She told them of the remaining gang members consisting of a pickpocket, a nurse, a gunman, a man of muscle, a driver, and a boss.

"So they had a signal jammer along with blueprints of some buildings?"

"Yes, they also mentioned something about a bigger job. The attempted kidnapping was not their main objective."

"You're telling me this isn't the last we're going to see these guys?" Keen asked.

"Yeah. They're not done. We were just a hiccup in their real plans. Whatever those plans were, they haven't given up on them," Florian said.

"That confirms it, then." The chief nodded to Officer Keen.

"Confirms what?" Florian asked.

"After we talked with Dr. Ronaldo, we looked up a few of the names he brought up. With your side also lining up with his, it's safe to confirm that the gang you guys uncovered wasn't your ordinary criminal syndicate. They're notorious thieves from the underworld, wanted across the world. They're known as Ghost. The man that goes by the name Selucius is their leader, the devil himself," the chief said.

Florian clenched her teeth, engraving the name in her mind.

"Of all places, I would've never guessed they would be hiding in our city," the chief said.

Florian sat up and cleared her throat. "I have a few questions of my own; I've never done something like this before, so please, bear with me."

Officer Keen couldn't help but chuckle. "Oh, sure. Ask us anything, kid." His fox spirit nudged the chief's pug spirit slightly.

Florian took a deep breath. Her friends and family were all silently watching with their spirits locked on Florian.

"Ignoring the fact that the organization known as Ghost is in the city planning something else, their original target was Mayor William Rite Banquet. Do you have any idea why they might have targeted the mayor?"

"They were most likely trying to disrupt the election in some way," the chief said.

"Ghost stated it was a small job. Does that mean they were hired to kidnap Blythe Banquet? Possibly by Banquet's rivaling political candidate?" Florian said.

"It's possible. But we didn't find any suspicious activity when we investigated her," the chief said.

"So someone else must have hired Ghost. Does Mayor Banquet have any other enemies?" Florian asked.

"Of course he does. Outside of our jurisdiction," Keen said.

"What do you mean?"

"Mayor Banquet's one of the founders of this miraculous city. Do you know what kind of reputation a city like ours has for the rest of the country?" the chief asked.

Florian shook her head.

"A socialist regime," the chief said.

"What does that mean?" Florian said.

Keen scratched his head. "In English, it means we're the enemy. This city is so successful that it's challenging the way the rest of the country runs. The President could label us as a failed state even if we mind our own business."

"Wait a minute," Amalia said. "Tarot Tori City isn't socialist or communist."

"The previous mayors combined economic theories, established an efficient geographical foundation, and implemented decades worth of planning. We have strict rules in place that make sure individuals work and stay healthy. Capital is offered as an award for being a productive member of society. This entire city is developing because of how desirable it is to live here, with record numbers in every field."

The chief paused. "Those details don't matter. Whenever there's a threat to capitalism, labels get thrown around like wildfire. Since you grew up in this city, you were lucky to get the education to understand how this city accumulates wealth. Unfortunately, the rest of the country has no idea, and not knowing is enough to fear the next superpower."

"Superpower? We're a small city in the middle of nowhere. How's Tarot Tori City a superpower?" Amalia said.

"Mayor Banquet greenlit construction to expand the city limits a few months ago," the chief said.

"No way? You don't mean? How far?" Amalia asked.

"Three feet from the border."

Amalia and her bat went wide-eyed.

"Is this bad?" Florian said.

"Not yet. In a year, construction will be complete. What do you think Banquet will do after that?" the chief asked.

"He won't stop?" Florian guessed.

"You know him well for the short time you've known him. Anyone who doesn't want Tarot Tori City to get bigger, consuming cities or popularizing our economic ways, could be targeting Banquet and his family," the chief said.

Florian began to understand Banquet a little more. Still, she couldn't narrow down the suspects at this rate. "I see. Ghost said they were here because of a bigger job. Is there anything else in this city they might be after?"

Keen leaned back in his chair. "Who knows? This city has too much money to count, celebrities, museums, and technology exclusive to the city. Hell, they could still be targeting our political figure, Mayor Banquet."

Florian and the chief looked at one another.

"How long do you think they've been going unnoticed in the city?" Florian said.

"We have no idea. There's no way to tell," he said.

"What about other gangs in the city?"

"What other gangs? There aren't any left."

"Teenage gangs?"

"If there's any, none are causing any trouble."

"When was the last time you had reports of a gang in the city?" Florian asked.

"Maybe six years ago."

"What happened to that gang?"

"If I remember correctly, they dissolved."

"I think Ghost may have been the cause."

"What makes you think that?"

"A boy from my school joined Ghost after his teen gang confronted them. His name's Sticks. He mentioned he fought with the huge thug named Juke once before."

Sera snapped her fingers. "Wait, Sticks? He was in one of my classes. He dropped out of school, and his girlfriend Choco has been looking for him every day after school."

"All right, we'll get his parents' information from the school. Do you know his friends' names? We can question them if they encountered the huge man named Juke," the chief said.

"Of course." Sera provided their names.

Officer Keen leaned on his crutch. "You have a bright future, kid. Have you ever thought about being a police officer?"

"All I want is to put a stop to these guys once and for all and confirm that Sergeant Honest's name is cleared," Florian said.

"Dr. Ronaldo said the same thing. I'll apologize to his face when I remove the ankle bracelet, even if he doesn't forgive me," the chief said.

"You're incredible, Flori!" Sera said.

"I told you, sis! She's helped countless classmates in school, and now she's helping the police!"

"Flori would make an amazing detective!" Amalia said.

"Hmmm? Detective? Keep your cases small scale until you're older and more qualified," the chief said.

"Detective Cobblestone. That has a good ring to it," Officer Keen said.

Her parents were speechless as they witnessed their daughter find her calling.

"Detective Florian Lilly Cobblestone," her parents whispered.

THIRTY-THREE
SANCTUARY

SOUTH TORI HIGH
SEPTEMBER 19TH X288

The next day, Choco and Sticks's friends were questioned about his whereabouts.

Three boys admitted to having a brawl with a tall crimson-haired man, calling him a monster. They said he picked up a car and hurled it at them, informing them it was past their bedtime. The only one actually willing to fight back was Sticks himself, lasting no more than six seconds.

After the fight, Sticks disappeared, telling them to look after his girlfriend Choco.

Whenever Choco was approached for questioning, she fled. The police questioned her guardian, a grandmother too old to understand what was going on. They did discover the family had financial issues as her biological parents had abandoned her.

Sticks's parents were registered in the city, but they found only one bed when the police searched the address. The parents were not living in Tarot Tori City, taking advantage of the city's People Priority Policy. By falsifying their residential status and enrolling their kid at Tarot Tori City's prestigious school, they were able to take advantage of the residential flex spending to pay for their kid's entire enrollment costs.

This was against the rules; thus, the parents were cut off from the program. The only one affected by this was Sticks, as his enrollment would then be revoked.

Only the mayor would have the final say.

"If the boy named Styx will attend classes and be a model citizen, then I see no problem in addressing him as a resident and waiving the age limit for his monthly flex spending. The only question is, what does Styx want?" Banquet smiled.

-POP-

The police continued their search for Sticks's whereabouts.

ⅆⅇ

Two days before the unwanted award, Florian checked the paper. The news finally reported no deaths; the two officers in critical condition survived and were on their way to a full recovery. It had no mention of Clarissa Lantern's dead body found at the crime scene.

Does Banquet have anything to do with this?

Later that day, Florian got a message from Miss Fumblehouse that Dr. Ronaldo was out of the hospital. Florian begged her parents to let her see him.

They agreed to ask Dr. Ronaldo to reconsider his decision of releasing Florian from his counseling. Her mother accompanied her.

Upon arriving at the clinic, they found Miss Fumblehouse outside with her embroidered parasol and plush turtle soul.

"I was so worried! You have no idea!" She hugged Florian tightly and spun her around. "If only I called the police sooner."

"No, you saved us, Miss Fumblehouse. I can't thank you enough."

"I saw what happened on the news. It drove me crazy. I'm so relieved you both are all right." Miss Fumblehouse welcomed Florian and her mother into the clinic.

Sergeant Honest was waiting inside, in his military fatigues. He stood up and immediately lowered his head to Florian; his slender spike spirit bowed its tall demonic body.

"I was wrong. I'm sorry."

"What's wrong?" Florian asked.

"You went through so much trouble to clear my name. If only I communicated more. Deep down, I believed in keeping my struggles private to make others not worry about me. I was wrong. My past caused more trouble, enabling the police to suspect you as an accomplice. Please forgive my misjudgment."

The sergeant sat down and told Florian about his daughter who had passed away about nine years earlier. He had rarely gotten the chance to see her because he had been abroad in the line of duty. After losing his leg, he could finally be a father.

She was five years old when she died in a boating accident. Sergeant Honest said he could have saved her if it weren't for his prosthetic. His ex-wife accused him, but it was genuinely an accident.

Ever since the lawsuit, Honest had a stigma over his name and inside his soul.

His slender spike spirit remained on its knees, head on the floor.

Florian could tell he was sincere and was there to heal. "Please tell me more about your daughter."

"Sure thing, Little Liter."

Miss Fumblehouse broke out in tears. "All this time? I didn't know. We've known each other for so long, yet you didn't tell me!" She sobbed.

"Sorry, I thought Ronaldo told you."

"He's stricter on himself than on others. You know how he is."

"I know. Ronaldo believed I would tell you myself."

"You did, but you took too long." Her tears were like a fountain, a constant stream.

Sergeant Honest comforted Miss Fumblehouse, patting her on her back. His slender spike spirit did the same with her plush turtle soul, petting its shell.

Florian truly believed they made a wholesome pair.

THIRTY-FOUR
KALEIDOSCOPE

S. BROOK COUNSELING & THERAPY CLINIC
SEPTEMBER 22ND X288

A loud thud came from Dr. Ronaldo's office.

Sergeant Honest and Florian went to investigate.

Dr. Ronaldo opened the door to his office. He had a cast around his right arm along with a shard of glass.

"What happened? You all right?" Florian and Honest rushed to his side.

"You're here? Very good."

"What do you mean very good? You told my parents you were going to release me from your care."

Honest searched Ronaldo's office.

"Exactly. I'm not qualified enough to help you." Ronaldo slugged his way to the bathroom, ripping the mirror off the wall.

"So you're going to destroy the clinic?"

"Florian!" Honest shouted from the office.

Florian rushed over to find the office packed with mirrors, glass, scopes, cameras, and medical equipment.

"What's all this?" Honest said.

"I said I wasn't qualified yet. That was four days ago. After brainstorming, I've devised several experiments and examinations we can try." Ronaldo carried in the mirror, measuring its placement.

"Please don't destroy the clinic, Ronaldo." Miss Fumblehouse hid her face behind her plush turtle.

"He's not destroying the clinic. He's doing all this to help me." Florian noticed Ronaldo's dark urchin soul pulsating as it scuttled through the air, weaving threads throughout the office. "What can I do to help?"

"Break off the mirrors from my car," Ronaldo said.

"Wait, Ron. If you need mirrors, I can go get you some."

"Thanks, Honest. I'll need about six more small ones and two large ones."

"Will this one work?" Fumblehouse handed him a personal mirror from her purse.

"Perfect, five more small mirrors."

"Great! I-I-I'll go with you, Honest," Fumblehouse said.

Honest and Fumblehouse left for the hardware store.

"What's going on?" Mrs. Cobblestone said.

"I don't know, but I intend to find out. This is a whole new realm of study. I believe your daughter's vision is unique."

"What do you mean?" Mrs. Cobblestone said.

"Don't worry. This is a test to see if I'm qualified to continue counseling Florian or not. Nothing more." Ronaldo set up a retina eye scanner.

Florian's mother joined the others to procure the mirrors.

Dr. Ronaldo sat down in the center of the arrangement and directed how to tilt the mirrors.

"Banquet's ceremony is in two days. . . I want you to listen to what I have to say. I need you to confirm my theory," Florian said.

"Of course, but there's a more important matter that needs attending."

"What?"

"You can't face Banquet without the confidence of knowing you have a soul." Ronaldo tied a mirror to each of their foreheads.

"You mean, these mirrors are—"

"Exactly. To face Banquet's distracting floating soul, I'll find your soul right here and now. These mirrors will allow you to observe every corner of the room simultaneously. Sit here." Ronaldo turned on the retina scanner and examined Florian's eyes.

Ronaldo found nothing out of the ordinary and moved on to the subsequent optical examination.

"When I studied your journals of my soul, I felt an urge within myself rise. I feel a strange sense of confidence, like knowing who I am. If you find your soul, I know you'll come to understand yourself as well."

That explains why his soul's evolving.

"I searched all my life; I don't think finding my soul will be this simple," Florian said.

"I'm sure you have a soul. If those criminals had souls and Banquet had one, then you do too."

"I can't tell if mine needs help. Am I happy? Am I in pain? It's so easy to tell if others are happy or in pain. For me, it feels like I'm lost. I have no soul to show if I'm even alive."

The others returned with the mirrors and helped position them. Ronaldo placed a mirror between their seats and set portrait mirrors behind them.

"No, this won't work." He rearranged another mirror above their heads. "Hahaha, this angle doesn't suit you."

"Are you just playing around?"

"I'm one hundred percent serious." Ronaldo laughed and tilted the mirrors and put a glass pane over one.

Florian could see herself from almost every angle. The office turned into a house of mirrors.

After another twenty minutes of adjusting the mirrors and glass panes, the others left for the waiting area.

Florian sat in the center of the cluster of mirrors, unable to see anything but her reflection. She hadn't noticed until then how much she'd changed. She adjusted her glasses and fixed her hair, noticing her swollen shoulder clearing up.

Ronaldo sat on the other side of the mirrors in his own space of reflections. He cleaned his glasses and wiped his sweat.

"Can you hear me, okay?" The room was utterly silent except for Ronaldo's voice.

"Yes."

"All right. Now, take a deep breath and meditate."

"How can I? It's a little warm here."

"Sorry. How about this? Can you sense your hand?"

"My hand?"

"Yes, start with your index finger. What does it feel like?"

"It's warm, maybe numb."

"Numb? What else?"

"I don't know. Like a pressure of some kind."

"Good. Slowly concentrate on your whole hand from the inside."

"I can feel something in there."

"Can you describe it to me?"

"Warm, pulsating, tingly, tight, is that okay?"

"Yes. Let it go up to your arm."

"Okay."

"Sense your whole arm from the inside."

Florian took a deep breath.

"See if you can sense both of your arms then your legs at the same time."

She exhaled.

"That's your presence. What you're doing is getting yourself out of your mind. You feel it?"

"It's weird. I feel strange."

"Whenever you need to find yourself, feel your presence. Take as long as you need."

A few minutes passed.

"The next thing you can do while you're sensing yourself is to simultaneously look around."

"Look at what? My reflection?"

"Just let it come to you. Don't search for it. Just take in what you see. What do you see?"

"I see mirrors. I see your spirit."

"Very good. There's one final part. What do you hear? Sense your arms, legs, surroundings, and listen at the same time."

"I hear you. Mom, Fumblehouse, and Honest are in the other room. There's also a strange feeling around me."

"What is it? Describe it?"

"It's moving. Flowing like a stream."

"That's your soul. That's you. You're alive and right here. I have mine within me—"

"Your urchin's on the ceiling."

"Mine's on the ceiling, with me. Yours is with you right now. Do you see your soul?" Ronaldo looked between the mirrors.

Florian shook her head. "Nothing."

Ronaldo sighed. "There's one more thing I can try."

"If there's a way? Absolutely."

"Hold on. . ."

He wheeled in a custom-made contraption, a rotating door with mirrors on both sides. Between it was a see-through glass pane door.

"I have researched a method of hypnosis that allows us to trade our vision."

"Really? Is that a real thing?"

Dr. Ronaldo shifted in his chair. "Yep, it's real, and it's very dangerous. Are you sure you want to continue?" Ronaldo smiled. His dark urchin soul wriggled its tiny feelers playfully.

Florian smiled. "Yes . . . I'll try anything."

"All right. Let's start the hypnotherapy session."

Dr. Ronaldo's dark urchin spun in the air, whirlpooling its threads into a fine constellation.

"All right. Look toward the door. What do you see?"

"My reflection."

The lights went a little dim. At the press of a button, the door turned to the glass door pane. Florian could see Ronaldo.

"With this, you'll see you as I see you. And I'll see me the way you see me."

Florian felt a chill. She looked right into his eyes. The dark urchin was still in the corner of her eye, shaking its thorns and squirming.

"Don't blink. Now. Dream."

Slowly, the glass pane spun to its mirror side. Florian saw herself. The door turned again, and Florian could see Ronaldo. The wheel kept spinning from the glass pane to the mirror. Ronaldo stared into Florian's eyes, making her heart skip a beat.

"This is how you see me." Ronaldo pulled a switch.

The wheel stopped on the glass pane, and all the reflections on Florian's side turned into Ronaldo's image. She could see Ronaldo with his dark urchin from every angle.

"This is how I see you."

The turntable snapped to the mirror, showing Florian herself once again.

"You're looking at the Florian I see. A strong young hero who has the potential to do anything she sets her mind to."

Florian burst into laughter. "Is this what you meant by swapping our vision?"

"What? It's not working?"

"I get it. It's working." Florian took a deep breath. "I need to step back a little bit and see things from another perspective. Right?"

"Yeah. Like you, normal people live their lives without seeing their souls. Like you, normal people don't know if they need help, yet they still live their lives the best they can. Like you, normal people hesitate, but eventually, they move forward. Like you, normal people experience failures, and they learn from them. Like you, normal people work hard and practice to improve themselves. Like you, normal people are living and breathing. Like you, normal people search for something very dear to them. Like your search for your soul."

He paused. "You're just like everyone else; you're normal. Like everyone else."

Tears spilled as Florian smiled. The words she wanted to hear relieved the weight off her shoulders. Florian curled up in her seat, covering her tear-filled eyes.

"Thank you. Thank you. Thank you for everything." She cried. "I never had a soul to express my true self. Even with sign language, I made expressions that didn't feel like the real me. But now, I finally feel happy."

ಬಂಛ

"I guess your hypnotism worked." Florian smiled.

"What's that!?" Ronaldo jumped out of his seat.

He stared at Florian, and his gray hair turned a hint whiter, eyes wide open.

"What?"

"That thing behind you?" Ronaldo said, terrified.

"What? I don't see anything? Are you pretending to see my soul? You don't have to; I feel better now."

"No. I'm serious. It's right there behind you!" Ronaldo said, pointing directly at it.

"You can't be serious. . . I can still see your soul on the ceiling."

"It's like her journal. Calm down. They can't harm us," Ronaldo mumbled.

"Yeah. Don't panic. Whatever it looks like, it can't hurt you. Wait. What you're seeing is my soul?"

"Well. It's all around you."

"What does it look like?"

"Bramble."

"Bramble? A plant? I've never seen a soul that resembles a plant before! What else? Describe it to me!" Florian fidgeted, getting closer to Ronaldo.

"Bare vines beginning to bud, about as long as your arms. They're wrapped around your body, strangling you. Wait, they're unraveling. What's going on? They're now reaching outward. There's a brown feather sticking out of one of the petals. They're reaching toward me—"

Florian hugged Ronaldo. "A feather, the same one from my teacher a few years ago? What else?"

"They're coiling around me. Let me draw it for you." Ronaldo grabbed a pen, trembling still.

"Your hypnotism worked. But I can still see your spirit."

"What's it doing?"

"It's hugging me too, with its slack spines."

"I see. You said it was an urchin? I don't see it." Ronaldo hugged Florian back.

"I see yours plain as day. It's fascinating." Ronaldo handed the drawing to Florian.

It was a rose bush. The stalks were brambling about in a frenzy. It coiled around her arms, sprouting from her body. Still buds, the roses were growing.

Florian had finally found her soul. "So my power shared itself with you. Now you can describe my soul to me." Florian embraced the picture close. "I have a soul. All this time, I had one just like everyone else."

Ronaldo recomposed himself. "This means whoever has apparition vision can see souls except their own. However, if two people have apparition vision, then it can bypass that rule. We can describe our souls to each other. There's so much to do. How will this affect my counseling?"

"Be careful around crowds. Don't overreact either. There's so much I need to teach you. Everything's happening so fast."

"You're not alone anymore. We can work together to improve our understanding of this ability."

"Yes. I want to know more about my soul too. I want to improve myself along with my soul."

"We can both improve ourselves."

Mrs. Cobblestone, Miss Fumblehouse, and Sergeant Honest entered the office; their souls seemed concerned.

"What's with all the roughhousing? We heard Ron panicking about something."

"Whoa! That's what they look like? It's so tall." Ronaldo was startled, yet he approached Honest's slender spike spirit, analyzing its structure and posture.

"Ron? What's with you all of a sudden?" Honest asked.

"Oh, nothing. I just got carried away again."

Florian hugged her mom and Miss Fumblehouse. They spun around with joy.

"What's with the celebrating?" Honest said.

"Florian's alive!" Fumblehouse said.

"I know she's alive. She's right there," Honest said.

Florian finally had her soul. She couldn't wait for the next visit to share the apparition vision ability with her most trusted friend.

THIRTY-FIVE
FEAST

SOUTH TORI HIGH
SEPTEMBER 24TH X288

The day of the unwanted award arrived, and everyone was invited.

Mayor Banquet's committee had set up the school's auditorium days in advance. Broadcasting networks set up multiple cameras, and security was airtight.

The auditorium was off-limits for students and school staff until the day of the event.

Florian headed straight to the auditorium that morning as instructed. She saw Officer Keen standing guard, still wearing his neck brace.

"Look who's here. Detective Cobblestone. Why didn't you dress up for the occasion?" He tipped his cap.

"No one told me I needed to dress up."

"People listen to those that dress the part. Remember that."

"Any updates on your end?"

"We got nothing. Hell, we're so understaffed and underfunded, even the chief is somewhere around here guarding the mayor."

"Understood. Keep up the good work." Florian was allowed in.

"You got this," Keen whispered.

Florian, with her newfound resolve, prepared the best she could.

ಬಿಌ

Yesterday, Ronaldo and Florian discussed her plan. She'd installed a recording application on her phone.

"This is insane. I'm still too afraid to go outside! Your drawings aren't enough to prepare me for the sheer number of souls drifting about."

"I've lived with them all my life. You'll get used to it."

Ronaldo reviewed Florian's plan. "Your idea's brilliant. Let's rehearse it again. We'll practice until your thoughts are conveyed perfectly. It won't be easy, but I know you can do it."

"He'll definitely counter with something," Florian said.

"And you'll prepare a response to that and another for his next. Why? Because that's what he's doing right now. After all, it's his job to rehearse and practice speeches. I've seen him debate himself out of a corner so many times. He's a monster in the political world."

ಬಿಌ

Dr. Ronaldo's words echoed in Florian's mind.

She shivered, even after rehearsing countless times; this was Banquet's field of expertise. The school was Florian's territory; she had her classmates, teachers, family, and the police's support. Her only chance was today.

A limousine pulled up to the auditorium. Banquet and Blythe had arrived. Banquet wore a lavish white suit, and Blythe matched with a white dress. They both waved at Florian with brimming smiles.

His staff immediately confronted him. The floating smile spirit tumbled in the air, releasing bubbles filled with even smaller bubbles.

"Hey!" Blythe ran to Florian with her bubble-tailed dog soul wagging its tail.

"It feels like forever. How are you?" Florian asked.

"This is great! You're getting your reward for saving me. Thank you so much for everything," Blythe said.

"You're a friend of Hope's, and that makes you my friend too. If you need help with anything, just call me, okay," Florian said.

"I'll have you know; I won't need your help with my homework. I'm at the top of my class." Bubbles drifted off the tail of her dog.

"Whatever you say." Florian rolled her eyes.

"And here's the center of attention, Florian Lilly Cobblestone." Banquet approached them with open arms. "My daughter has a great eye for spectacle and presentation; she's in charge of the decorations staff."

Florian kept an eye on Banquet's soul, inflating tricks and lies into the air. She turned her head, not saying a word.

"I'm kidding. It's your special day after all. Please follow me. We have so much to do."

-POP-

"Why?" Florian followed, discouraged in thought. *Every time he opens his mouth, I get so irritated. His soul tells me he's never saying what he's really thinking.*

"Yes, we'll have music, make it as cheerful and elegant as possible," Banquet said, advising his staff efficiently. His soul's bubbles popped over the head of the staff members as he spoke.

-POP-

Liar.

"Oh, not at all. More balloons and confetti! We must celebrate our hero who saved my daughter and protected this city from terrifying criminals. Two officers nearly died." Banquet glanced toward Florian, as if observing her reaction.

-POP-

Florian could see his floating smile soul peek toward her.

Stop, Florian! Don't get emotional. Otherwise, he wins.

"Don't worry. Daddy sounds bossy, but he loves when other people tell him how they feel," Blythe said.

"Oh, I can't get enough of it." Banquet grinned.

Florian's family arrived and introduced themselves to the mayor. Blythe stuck to Hope like glue, allowing everyone to get along more easily.

Florian put up with the facade.

⁗⁗⁗

Sergeant Honest and Miss Fumblehouse arrived at the auditorium.

Students and faculty stared at Miss Fumblehouse.

"Whoa? Isn't that the parasol lady?"

"Awesome! She's good luck."

"Her dress is so cute."

"The urban legend in the flesh."

Miss Fumblehouse shivered. "Oh no. I feel like I'm being watched. Please don't look at me." She covered her face with her plush turtle, swiftly tiptoeing away.

"She's so adorable."

Sergeant Honest glared at Officer Keen at the entrance.

"You again," Honest said.

"Oh, the one-legged military man. How's freedom?" Keen asked.

"Great, without police breathing down my neck."

"Well, I'm keeping my eye on you. Better watch your step."

"Interesting choice of words. Want to say that again? Neck brace!"

"Was that police harassment in my ear? Or a life sentence?" Officer Keen caught a glimpse of Miss Fumblehouse. He adjusted his greased hair, stood up straight, and held the door for her. "Hello, lovely lady, I might have to arrest you for being too adorable."

Miss Fumblehouse frantically walked past him, face covered by her plush, not acknowledging his existence.

"Thanks, first responder." Honest walked through the doorway, too.

"Damn, last responder. If I weren't on the clock, I would—"
Honest and Fumblehouse found the Cobblestone family and sat with them, just missing Florian and Banquet.

Banquet explained to Florian the stage direction. "I'll walk on stage first, and when I call your name, you'll join me. I'll then hand you this portfolio, and we'll shake hands. Smile. Wave. Then, we'll walk down to the reporters below for individual interviews. If you have any questions or ideas you would like to add, please let me know." He smiled.

Florian calmly complied, waiting for her chance to confront him.

"Great." He smiled. "That reminds me. Jessica, please take Florian to the dressing room to get ready. Our hero has to make a new impression, from covered in soot to glamorous. How's that sound?"

"Understood. This way, please." The staff member, Jessica, waved.

Jessica had a blonde ponytail and wore a pink blouse with blue jeans. Her soul was that of a sting ray, swimming through the air around her.

Florian followed her, looking back occasionally at the mayor, busy directing other staff members.

The dressing room was a news broadcasting trailer outside the auditorium. It was filled to the brim with a vast wardrobe, mirrors, and makeup.

Jessica grabbed Florian's hand and wrapped a tape measure around her.

"Let's pick a dress, shall we? You're the headliner, so we should pick something daring and heroic."

"I don't care much for dresses. Can't I keep what I'm wearing?" Florian had on her favorite hoodie and jeans.

"Days like today, you should be concerned about dresses. You're only on stage or TV for a short time. The way you look conveys more words than any you can muster. Trust me. I think you would look best in this one."

Jessica presented a long black dress with a black rose-shaped bow on the blouse.

"It's beautiful," Florian said.

"And bold," Jessica said.

Florian fit into the dress. It took Jessica minutes to hem the stray parts.

When Florian put on the dress, her shoulder, still recovering, was visible. She lightly rubbed her bruise.

"Perfect. Now for a quick touch of makeup." Jessica's sting ray landed on her shoulder as she covered the bruise, pulling out a makeup kit and masterfully clearing up Florian's shoulder. She then touched up Florian's face.

"You're still young, so you don't need much. Today you'll be beside the most fortunate man in the city. With all of this, you'll be able to stand beside him on equal terms. You look marvelous, Flori," Jessica said.

She finished with the rose ribbon covering Florian's blouse.

Florian could barely recognize herself when she looked into the mirror. She wondered what her soul looked like beside her now. She was sure it would match her dress.

"Thank you."

"No. Thank you. I just wish we had more time to get to know each other. But I'm happy that I got the chance to dress you up at least once. I feel like I can now leave without any regrets," Jessica said.

"What do you mean?" Florian looked in the mirror and saw Jessica leave the dressing room.

At the last second, before the door closed, Florian saw Jessica smirk as her sting ray soul swam into her hair. Its tail morphed into suction cups, almost like an octopus tentacle.

"No way!" Florian jumped out of her seat and out the door.

The woman was nowhere to be found. She'd vanished like a ghost.

I knew it! Clarissa Lantern's alive! It didn't make sense why her entourage would kill her. The bond they shared was undeniably unbreakable. That means the dead body found at the scene was a fake or a decoy. This changes everything!

She paused in her thoughts. *Wait. Why's Clarissa Lantern here? If she's here, then the rest of Ghost is here too! Are they here to finish what they started? Everyone here might be in danger! Wait, the blueprints in their hideout! It's starting to make sense.* Florian ran off to confirm her suspicion.

"Whoa, looking good, Detective Cobblestone," Officer Keen said.

Florian caught her breath. "A blonde woman with a pink shirt and blue jeans named Jessica. Have you seen her?"

"How could I forget such a pretty face? I've only seen her once today, early this morning."

"Stop her if you find her. I think she might be up to something." Florian ran off.

"Really?" Keen radioed in. "We have a suspicious person. . ."

Florian searched around the auditorium, checking each person's spirit, one by one.

She must be around here somewhere. I can find any member of Ghost, no matter what disguise they wear!

She checked the security and the staff when students began pouring in.

I'm too late. There's no way I can do this with this many people. I won't be able to tell which soul belongs to who.

"Oh, you're done already? Brilliant. Care to join me at the catering table?" Banquet asked.

"That Jessica lady, did you see where she went?" Florian asked.

"Jessica? Oh, she told me in advance she had an urgent meeting to attend. Though she insisted she could stay to dress you. Strange, don't you think?"

"How do you know her?" Florian kept an eye on his soul.

"What? I first met her two days ago. The news station said she had been working for them for years. Is something wrong?" Banquet's smile disappeared.

"Nothing's wrong." Florian stumbled; not a single bubble came from its mouth.

"Hmmm? Have you met this Jessica woman before?" Banquet smiled.

"No, I haven't." Florian couldn't look him in the eye.

"Hmmm? Are you about to do something amazing again?" His spirit retook an interest in Florian, shoving its giant face in hers.

"Look at how worried you are. If I were you, I would get used to that feeling fast. Once you have a target on your back, it's hard to shake it off. Hahaha." Banquet handed her a plate from the catering table. "You're such a hard worker."

I have to stay on track. Banquet's right here in front of me. This is my chance.

"Mayor Banquet, I would like to speak with you alone."

THIRTY-SIX
DETECTIVE

SOUTH TORI HIGH
SEPTEMBER 24TH X288

Hmm? "Can it wait just a bit? We're due on stage in a few minutes," Banquet said.

"No. It has to be right now," Florian said.

Banquet sighed and smiled. "If it's that important, I can't help but get curious. All right, let's talk."

Florian brought the mayor backstage and opened the rear exit of the auditorium. There, only the morning breeze could interrupt them.

Florian had waited for this moment.

Banquet's soul twitched its crossed eyes back and forth while hovering circles around Florian. Not a bubble was in sight.

Finding the phone hidden in her dress, Florian tapped the record button. She took a deep breath. "Mayor Banquet. Allow me to refresh your memory."

"I'm listening."

"On Wednesday, September eighth at three p.m., you received a ransom note claiming that your daughter, Blythe Banquet, was kidnapped. However, I was with your daughter during that time. The kidnapping did not take place until four or five p.m." She paused.

"Now, why would kidnappers send a ransom note before their target was in their custody? Was it overconfidence or a mistimed event? Either way, with some help, I thwarted the attempt and even escorted Blythe home safely. You, Banquet, were surprisingly calm about the ordeal. This bothered me, so I investigated further."

Banquet was silently smiling.

"I ended up discovering the kidnapper's hideout. It turns out they were notorious international thieves known as Ghost. They weren't upset that I discovered they were the culprits; they were upset because I located their hideout. The Ghost members wanted nothing but to lie low, so much so that they only feared me telling the authorities their location."

She looked at him. "I wondered why they would risk kidnapping your daughter if they wanted to lie low. Was it out of spite for you? No. Was it for the ransom money? Unlikely. Was it for something else even more valuable? Ghost didn't even care that the attempted kidnapping ended in failure, claiming it was a small job. When I scanned their hideout, I noticed blueprints of a building I've never seen before. Whatever that building is, that's their real target."

She paused. "Yet no matter where they are in this city, I know they won't kill any civilians. Well, if you get in their way, they'll still beat the shit out of you; I learned that the hard way. That was when I realized what was most valuable to them. Security, sanctuary, or asylum."

"Hmmm? Interesting. . ." Banquet's smile didn't change; in fact, it looked bigger with the giant face floating behind him.

He says one thing, yet his soul tells me he's lying. I don't know what he's thinking. I hate this. Why isn't he saying anything?

Florian continued, "Ghost let me go, and at the end of the day, they didn't kill a single person. The only dead body found was a fake, a decoy most likely prepared for the big job they were planning. They had to leave in a hurry, leaving behind what they didn't need. Since not a single citizen of Tarot Tori City died, this reaffirmed their agreement, signaling to someone that they were honoring the terms. Meaning the deal's still on. Their eyes are set on something bigger than you or me. They're willing to jump through hoops to get it."

She gave him a stern look. "Am I right, Mayor William Rite Banquet? Only you would notice right away if big fish criminals set foot in this city. The only one capable enough to provide shelter to a group like this, for so long, would be you. As long as they lay low and didn't harm any citizens, you would let them stay in Tarot Tori City. Right under the police's noses."

"Hahaha. What a fascinating accusation." The mayor's smiling spirit turned sinister. Its neck lumps accumulated, moving up its throat and stopping at the base of the neck. It held in the air, trying to escape, in pain.

Just a little more.

Florian continued, "Based on what I pieced together, you approached Ghost first and organized your daughter's kidnapping. Why do this stunt and fool everyone?" She paused.

"To secure the election in your favor. All the publicity and attention would be on you as the victim. Resulting in your opposition looking completely suspicious, also restricting her campaigning amid the investigations. Your exceptional handling of the crisis would also secure even more votes."

"So impatient," he said under his breath.

"What did you say?"

"I said, you have quite the imagination. Tell me. How many times have you practiced this spiel of yours? It's really well planned out. Color me impressed." He cheerfully puffed out his chest and placed his hand on his chin.

Florian stomped her foot in retaliation. "What're you talking about? Aren't you going to say something to defend yourself? Are you going to confess to the police about what you've done?"

"Don't worry. I have plenty of responses; I even rehearsed them, just like you." Banquet turned to the door. "I'm just a little disappointed by how impatient you are. Don't worry; you can still make this up."

The auditorium doors opened. "Mayor Banquet, we're ready to start."

"Very good. I'm on my way."

Dumbfounded, Florian shook her head. *This was supposed to make him confess everything, and he just brushed me off?*

"We're due on stage. Don't let this second chance slip by." Mayor Banquet smiled.

THIRTY-SEVEN
BESTOW

SOUTH TORI HIGH
SEPTEMBER 24TH X288

Mayor Banquet stepped on stage with the crowd roaring. His white suit shimmered at the center of the stage. His floating smile spirit stretched its neck to the ceiling of the auditorium. The massive lump of air in the back of its throat expanded like a garden hose accumulating pressure from being pinched off. Its lips puckered as it steadily blew bubbles into the crowd.

"Ladies and gentlemen." Banquet removed the microphone from the podium and placed his hand on his chest.

"To all the citizens of Tarot Tori City, I can't thank you enough. I couldn't ask for better citizens to represent. Your generous contributions for the ransom were all compiled, and along with the survey results, the decision was unanimous. It'll be awarded to our local hero, right here and now."

-POP-

That son of a— Florian's hair stood on end as his words shocked through her body. *How dare he?*

"It's what you, the people, wanted. And it's rightfully deserved," Banquet continued.

Banquet's soul shook its goggle eyes, aimlessly darting about. The pockets of air systematically wormed their way up to its throat, reaching its mouth. The head released bubbles of different sizes, colors, and thicknesses. The entire auditorium was filled with balloon spirit bubbles. Its eel arms twisted and bent the bubbles into different shapes, animals, and objects, infecting everyone in unique ways.

"I truly feel indebted to you all. If re-elected, I'll continue to dedicate my life to implementing the previous mayor's legacy."

-POP-

Florian clenched her teeth.

"Now, presenting our young hero of Tarot Tori City, Florian Lilly Cobblestone." Banquet clapped his hands along with the audience.

His soul's smile turned to Florian. It drifted back to the stage, opening its mouth big enough to swallow the six-foot-three mayor. It exhaled the pent-up air at the back of its throat, expelling a fleshy rubber stomach lining balloon. Too heavy to move, the flesh bubble sat there, engulfing Banquet's half of the stage.

What the hell is that? What's going on? Florian was cued to go on by the staff. She cautiously approached the dome of flesh, walking on stage as directed.

Florian scanned the auditorium filled with people. The sheer number of spirit gazes made her bowels tremble. Every soul in the audience, and through the cameras, every soul in the city had their eyes on her.

In another part of town, Dr. Ronaldo was watching the live TV broadcast. Florian had no idea Ronaldo was seeing her soul, the rose bramble, slowly enveloping her. Thorns, much like the dark urchin's, grew from the foliage. Vines wrapped around her arms, covering her dress with multicolored roses. Intimidating, yet somewhat beautiful.

Florian's heart raced. The police and security were buzzing around in the background. She saw her parents, Honest, Fumblehouse, her friends, and Hope, cheering with all their might.

All I gotta do is repeat what I said before. I can do this in front of everyone! But why is his soul so excited? If I reveal everything, his entire career will be ruined. Is he insane, or is this a part of his plan? All the bubbles are already in place as if he prepared for this. Who am I kidding? I don't have proof! Everything I accused him of was just my speculation. I thought I could get him to confess in private and now look. If I make a fool out of myself, I'll never be taken seriously again. Banquet's hands may be clean, but I can tell just by looking, he's a threat equal to Ghost, that much is certain.

Florian was unable to move.

"Come on. This way, young Cobblestone." Banquet waved with a smirk.

Slowly, Florian moved toward Banquet, unknowingly already caught in his pace. She stopped when her vision blurred a bit, face inches from a wall of transparent flesh.

"What's wrong? Come forward and take your scholarship."

Florian stood in place, refusing to enter the bubble.

"It's fine; I'll come to you."

Banquet approached Florian. She took a single step back, but the bubble stayed in place. Unable to see what Florian saw, the mayor handed Florian the portfolio with his right hand. In his left was the microphone. Both were up against the wall of flesh. Banquet wasn't facing the audience; both he and his soul were staring directly at Florian, smiling brightly.

Florian reached for the portfolio.

Banquet shook his head and sighed. He pulled his right hand back and laughed. "Didn't you have something you wanted to say?"

Florian looked up at Banquet.

"Go on. . . Just like how we rehearsed moments ago." Banquet offered her the microphone.

He can't be serious? He wants me to say it?

The flesh dome inflated further to the point where it touched Florian's face.

"You were so adamant before. What's the matter?" Banquet frowned. The excitement on his face slowly disappeared as he turned toward the audience.

"She's quite shy, isn't she?" Banquet laughed.

Florian shrugged. *Why is he so annoying? He's egging me on to announce all his crimes to the city. Either my accusations were utterly wrong, or he has something up his sleeve. He wants me to choose. If I report him, I'll lose the scholarship. The microphone or the scholarship?*

Florian couldn't see her own soul, but she knew it was there. It was right behind her, just like how Ronaldo told her.

Florian raised her right hand.

She reached over toward Banquet.

-POP-

The fleshy bubble disappeared.

Florian looked at her right hand, finding nothing. *Did my soul puncture Banquet's soul?*

Banquet plopped the microphone into the very hand Florian was inspecting. Florian looked up at Banquet. His excited smile returned. Banquet whipped out a microphone for himself.

"I'll let you start, young Cobblestone." Banquet adjusted his tie and closed his eyes, full of valor.

Florian faced the audience. "I can't thank you enough for this scholarship. I'm not strong enough now, but I swear, I'll use it to apprehend any criminals that cross my sights." Florian glanced toward Banquet and handed him the microphone.

"What? Is that all?" Banquet looked bewildered.

Florian nodded in a cold sweat.

The crowd applauded as confetti and balloons showered from the ceiling. The audience cheered harder as the music elevated everyone's spirits.

Banquet handed Florian the portfolio and shook her hand. Both smiled for the cameras. Pictures flashed as they made their way down the stage. Blythe joined them for a few photo ops.

Banquet was swarmed by the majority of the press for questioning. He promoted himself and his campaign.

Florian only got the leftover press that didn't get to Banquet in time.

"Do you plan to go into law school?"

"I plan to become a detective. It's a long road ahead, and I'll have to research where to start."

"Did Mayor Banquet inspire you to become a detective?"

"No. Well, he did play some part in my decision."

A microphone pressed close to Florian. She turned to its holder.

It was a woman with long brown hair, a white button shirt, a black skirt, and piercing red eyes. She stood like an empress winking at Florian, with her spirit in her hair. Brown tentacles blending in like an accessory reached out to Florian.

The woman asked, "Do you plan on continuing your pursuit of the kidnappers in question?"

Florian looked her in the eyes. She couldn't believe it. Glaring with a smile, Florian saw through her disguise.

"It doesn't matter where you hide. I'll hunt each and every one of you down and catch you all myself. Even if I have to flip the entire world upside down."
Clarissa Lantern smiled from ear to ear. "I'm sure they heard you, loud and clear."

THIRTY-EIGHT
LEAGUES APART

SOUTH TORI HIGH
SEPTEMBER 24TH X288

Florian, still processing what had happened, waited for Banquet backstage.

After half an hour, Banquet finally finished his interviews. Florian, arms crossed in a folding chair, was dozing. He tried to sneak past her, making his way to the rear exit.

Florian stood up. "Where do you think you're going? Get back here."

"I didn't want to interrupt your nap. No hard feelings." He smiled. "Kidding."

They stared at each other intensely. His soul gently floated to his back, not a bubble in sight.

"Sir, are you ready to leave?" a staff member asked.

Mayor Banquet didn't say a word, not breaking eye contact with Florian.

The staff member backed away and shooed away the others. In seconds the backstage was cleared out.

Banquet smiled. "Well, it feels like things are winding down. I have a few more questions for you, and I'm sure you have some for me. Now that you've accepted the scholarship, no more recording. Okay? Florian Lilly Cobblestone."

Florian nearly popped a blood vessel, pulling out her phone and turning off the recording application. "Answer me! How could you use Blythe like that? She's your daughter!"

"Yes, but she's safe now. Isn't she?"

"When was it? When did you predict that I would chase down those kidnappers?" She asked.

When did he decide to trick and use me?

"Pardon? Oh, I'm just a normal human being. I'm incapable of predicting the future. All of this was merely a coincidence."

"Please, I want to know. No matter what I would have said or done, I wouldn't have won against you. Please, tell me. What did I do wrong?"

His soul landed on his back; his eyes focused on Florian. He lowered his hands and relaxed his cheerful attitude. "I realized it the moment you showed yourself at my front door after you handed me my daughter. You gave me such an unsatisfied look while you guarded your mute sister. Right there, at that moment, I could visualize you defeating me on that stage right behind us."

He seemed to have no doubt in his mind and smiled the same as always.

"From the moment we first met?" Florian said. *Wait. Defeating him?*

"The kidnapping was indeed staged. I knew from the very beginning that something could go wrong, and I could handle it. Lo and behold, when we first met in that chaotic scenario, your impression seemed abnormally confident. I began to suspect you had some form of evidence that could ruin my reelection. I soon gave in to my curiosity and checked into your background, finding something remarkable. Ambition."

He paused. "Junior league karate tournament winner. Prized junior high role model helping others. Compassionate older sister learning sign language. And now, let's add aspiring detective to the list. It dawned on me that I wasn't dealing with an ordinary high school girl. I had a gut feeling that Florian Lilly Cobblestone would spell my doom if I didn't play seriously. In fact, you intrigued me so much, I anticipated the worst, confirming my suspicions with my first move, forcing—sorry, offering you into a corner."

"The scholarship," Florian said.

"Correct. It was even made up of the donations going toward paying the ransom. It makes it even more heartwarming, doesn't it? Understand? That was the exact moment I could see the events transpire, the big picture, if you will. I won."

"You're insane."

"Not in the slightest. I knew all the risks. You were the one who went above and beyond and chased away those sketchy criminals. Your stunt did scare me. I thought Ghost ran off because they killed someone, you or an officer. When you were wrapped like a burrito, refusing to look at me, I had a hunch there was a casualty. I later confirmed there was a dead body, one of their own. I was devastated. But it was only a moment ago you came to me, telling me the body was fake. Your information made it all click, and I finally understood their message. All that remained was handing you your award."

"Do you think this is some sort of game? What's wrong with you?!"

"This is most certainly a game. All the pieces on the board are after something. I bet even you were searching for something. So why can't I play too and help all the players win? Well, help all the players I deem worthy." His soul panted, laughing without a single bubble in sight.

"You trusted people you've never even met with your daughter's safety? Me, a complete stranger and notorious criminals, seriously?"

"I trust Mr. Selucius as a worthy enemy. My daughter trusts you as you saved her life. So I decided to believe in you too. I would be foolish not to trust someone risking her life to save my daughter. After all, they didn't kill you. Did they?" Mayor Banquet walked toward the exit.

Florian followed him. "When I'm older, I'll make you pay for all this. I'll put a stop to your lies once and for all."

"Lies? Hahaha. Oh, I look forward to it. I really enjoy a good debate. It's the only chance I get to truly be myself. Though it's a pity we couldn't debate on stage today. I admit it would've been too good to be true. A freshman high school girl who could not only chase away infamous criminals but also debate against me as an equal. It's my fault for expecting that much from a child. I don't regret overestimating you. You're definitely a wild card that sees the 'world' in a unique way."

They exited the building and made their way to his limousine.

"Some mayor you are. Do you even know how many people were caught up in this mess? I'll never, ever cast a vote for you."

"You got it wrong. I became the mayor because I love Tarot Tori City and its people. I want to improve this city and prove our legacy is capable of making a difference. I'm willing to walk alone to Satan's door and conspire a staged kidnapping to show Satan that I do not fear them and that I know they're in my city." He grinned. "That's my way of saying, I got my eyes on you. Of course, if Satan wants to play in my room with my toys, they must know I don't like to share. Oh, how Mr. Selucius smiled, happily bothered. I only wish we had more time to play." Banquet paused for a second and looked away as if hiding his face. His soul carried a deflated frown.

Florian was caught off guard, thinking he was shedding a tear.

Banquet turned around with a steady scowl. "Florian Lilly Cobblestone . . . I pulled a lot of legs to make this work out for the both of us. If you waste that scholarship of yours, next time, I'll pull your leg for real."

Florian gritted her teeth in silence.

Without saying another word, the mayor walked toward his Limo Force One, leaving Florian in the middle of the parking lot.

She couldn't wrap her head around this, accepting the results. She wanted nothing to do with him.

Florian turned around. Behind the dumpster of the auditorium, she noticed a dark-haired boy and a blonde girl with a headband. Their souls were intertwined.

Florian's face turned bright red, looking away. Their spirits were a snake and a cluster of fur.

Wait. She got a closer look.

It was Sticks with his snake mouse and his girlfriend Choco with her fur cluster spirit. Their eyes met Florian's. Both were frozen. Sticks pulled his hood over his head and took off running, reentering the auditorium.

"Hey! Get back here!" Florian ran after him, lifting her skirt to run.

Choco blocked the doorway to the auditorium; her fur cluster revealed its white eyes and teeth. "Leave my boyfriend alone!"

Florian slipped past Choco with a slide and a step and chased Sticks into the auditorium and through the crowds of people exiting the building.

Sergeant Honest and Miss Fumblehouse were in Sitcks's path.

"Honest, stop him!" Florian shouted.

"Roger, Little Liter." Honest blocked Sticks's escape, protecting Miss Fumblehouse.

Fumblehouse's eyes spun as she crouched to the floor. She shielded Hope and Blythe with her tiny body.

Sticks changed direction, running through the aisles of seats.

Officer Keen joined the chase, radioing help. "We have a suspicious person inside the auditorium. . ."

Choco followed Florian, trying to stop her from apprehending her boyfriend.

"Stupid dress!" Florian said, trying to keep up with the pursuit.

THIRTY-NINE
DECLARATION

SOUTH TORI HIGH
SEPTEMBER 24TH X288

Mayor Banquet was about to enter his limousine when his phone rang.

"Hello."

"Only the haunted know when their life is in danger."

Banquet's smile contorted his face, overwhelming his features with pleasure. Wrinkles folded over his eyes, pinching them into beady slivers.

Finally. . . An opponent worth crushing!

He let out a chuckle. "I was having so much fun; I was afraid you were going to leave without saying goodbye. A little birdy just told me the body found at the crime scene was a decoy. So I guess you did keep your end of the bargain. Right, 'the devil himself,' Mr. Selucius?"

"You should be careful with what you say. Otherwise, you'll be the one who winds up caught," Selucius said.

"Is that a declaration? I sure hope so. After all . . . I'm your biggest fan." Banquet couldn't contain himself.

"So that's it. Your compulsion is just too great. How pathetic. At your core, you are nothing more than an egotist."

"Really? That's how you see me? How cruel. I hope young Cobblestone doesn't share the same opinion." Banquet looked over to Florian chasing a young boy wearing a hoodie into the auditorium.

Look at her go. Always busy.

"I now realize why this city is called Tarot Tori City. Not only is it your territory, but the people themselves are special. With advanced education and opportunities, a lot of unique people come out of the woodwork. They're either right side up or upside down. For instance, you are the wheel of fortune, flipping back and forth like a roulette wheel full of bluster. The girl in her own world, with her therapist, the magician, who are both right side up. On the live stream, she seemed even more confident from when I last saw her. It looks like I couldn't steal her spirit after all. I guess Dr. Ronaldo Von Nirvanas isn't as incompetent as I made him out to be," Selucius said.

"Please, underestimate me as much as you want. Just don't underestimate my city, Mr. Selucius."

"Neither should you, Mr. Banquet. We're citizens of Tarot Tori City too."

Mayor Banquet was approached again by the press. "Mayor Banquet! What're your views of the dead body found at the crime scene? Is it true it's a decoy?"

What's this? That's not public knowledge yet. Not even the police realized the body was a decoy. Unless. . .

"You wanted to play. Then let's play." Selucius hung up.

A woman with long brown hair, piercing red eyes, a white button shirt, and a black skirt was the one who'd asked the provocative question. She appeared to be an independent reporter mixed in with the official ones.

The official reporters grew silent. None of them expected a muckraker.

Is this Clarissa Lantern? This woman? Is she questioning me about her own dead body found at a crime scene? Banquet tried his hardest to contain his laughter. *This is just so much fun.* He grinned.

"The police department hasn't made that public yet. But yes, a dead body was found at the crime scene. Before making it public, they wanted first to identify the dead body and notify the next of kin. As you said, if the body's a decoy, I can speculate it's an already deceased body from the morgue. You'll have to ask the police for further information."

-POP-

Clarissa Lantern had a smile from ear to ear.

"The people must know. Who were the ones targeting your daughter to ruin your reelection campaign?"

Hahaha, it was your organization. But I can't say that. Who should I blame this on? Hmmm? "My best guess is the hundred-billion-dollar company Fossil Burn Industrial. They probably see our city as a threat since we're the only city in the world that no longer needs to rely on fossil fuels."

-POP-

The reporters gasped, inhaling the bubble's released particles.

"Are you implying that we are under attack?" Clarissa said, instigating further.

It's a shame, really. I was saving this for my victory speech, but . . .

"Absolutely right! But not by Fossil Burn Industrial, but by nature itself. Honestly, part of me wishes to let this matter die without making any more waves. However, recent events have uncovered a prevalent problem that can no longer be ignored. As seen in the footage of the burning half-submerged hideout, our city is not sinking, the sea levels are rising. The reason for not demolishing those buildings were to show the physical proof to the world that even our city is affected by the decisions made by the rest of the world.

"Every citizen, the previous mayors, and all of us here today dedicated our lives to making this city what it is today. Tarot Tori City's a miracle, and I would love to share the methods to accomplish its status. I want the entire nation to experience what we have achieved and make it so we can preserve our investments and sacrifices."

"Does that mean you plan to-" The other reporters began to blast questions, drowning out Clarissa Lantern's. "I'm not done yet! Move! Out of the way!"

"I'll most certainly make many enemies along the way. So please, I ask you," Mayor Banquet pointed to Clarissa Lantern, the press, and the cameras, "work with me to make the next great leap forward for humankind."

-POP-

⚇⚉

Clarissa Lantern stomped away. "He straight up gave us a job offer while we were trying to ruin his image. The nerve of him. He turned our sting operation into an incrimination of Fossil Burn Industrial. Now the FBI will do his dirty work for him by suppressing the movements of Fossil Burn Industrial with an investigation." She decimated a water bottle with her foot, stomping repeatedly.

"Fossil Burn vould have been his enemy eventually. He drew de first punch. He's dangerous." Irina Halt prepped her motorcycle.

"Using underhanded tactics like this, he's treating politics like an absolute joke." Clarissa put on a helmet. "Damn Conquistador of Politics. We still have so much work to do for the big one. I hope Florian doesn't tell my kids. The text she sent me was so sweet. Florian really thought I was dead, didn't she? She's such an innocent girl. I could have taught her so much." Clarissa cheered up, thinking about Florian.

"Ve got to help Sticks." Irina revved the motorcycle.

"Oh, Florian's chasing him. How do I look?" Clarissa posed.

"No one vill be able to tell vho you are vith de disguise and de helmet on."

"A woman's gotta represent. It's called femme fatale. When Florian saw me at the hideout, I was dressed in rags, and my hair was a mess."

"I'm flooring de pedal." Irina pressed the gas.

"You'll never understand."

The two rode the motorcycle over a low car. Irina pulled the front wheel up, ramping them up the vehicle into the air. They smashed through the glass auditorium window, disrupting the commotion inside.

೮೮೮

The two landed on the stage, startling everyone.

Even though they were wearing helmets, Florian saw the octopus in its lionfish form.

"Clarissa Lantern."

Next to the vehicle was a giant scarred cheetah with steam emitting from its body.

"Irina Halt."

Sticks waltzed over the rows of chairs, vaulting over to the bike.

"Yes! My boyfriend is getting away. But who the hell are those two ladies?" Choco's eyes pulsated, trying to escape her head. Her mixed feelings turned into rage.

"You're not getting away!" Florian yelled.

"Let's do this again sometime," Clarissa said.

They picked up Sticks and drove out the rear exit doors of the auditorium, leaving everyone in the dust.

The roar of the engine grew to silence as the distance widened.

Florian, Hope, Sergeant Honest, Miss Fumblehouse, Officer Keen, and Choco all lined up outside the doorway, gazing at the afternoon sky.

Florian raised her fist. "Just you wait. We'll catch you all!"

FORTY
BEGINNING

TAROT TORI POLICE DEPARTMENT
OCTOBER 1ST X288

A few days later, Officer Keen was at the police station reviewing his report.

"That's funny. In the end . . . Florian got the ransom money. I suspected she was the kidnapper's accomplice, but I guess she was the mastermind."

He laughed, stuck with his neck brace.

When the police reviewed Florian's and Ronaldo's phones, the photos of Ghost had been mysteriously deleted. After many attempts, they couldn't recover them. All they had were the pictures Florian had drawn.

Keen analyzed the journal page Florian had given to the police, burning the hand-drawn faces of the gang members into his memory.

With intense inspection, Keen noticed some indications of more sketches. Indentions and creases were left over from the previous page of the journal.

He placed another sheet of paper over the journal page. He rubbed forensic charcoal over it.

He discovered a few of Florian's spirit sketches. They were overlapped with some animal drawings from prior pages.

"What a weird girl. . . She's a good artist."

The police radio sounded. "A motorcyclist with an extra passenger is currently speeding southbound on route eleven thirty-four. Requesting back up."

"I bet that's them. I've got to get better quickly. Those Ghost guys are still out there. I can't chase them down like this."

❧

Florian was lecturing Dr. Ronaldo. "Don't you get it? A person's soul shows how an individual is feeling and what they went through. Each one is a manifestation of their true self. Their unique characteristics change their souls too."

"Isn't that reading too much into it?" Ronaldo asked.

"What do you mean? These are people's souls we're talking about. No two are alike, and you should never underestimate them."

"I have a lot to learn. I hope I can use apparition vision to help my patients."

"I'll be with you every step of the way."

"Thank you, Florian."

Dr. Ronaldo's soul, the dark urchin, grew. Its exoskeleton sprouted arms and legs, emanating his new way of thinking.

Through Ronaldo's vision, Florian's rose bramble soul began to blossom. Red roses with thorns accumulated, surrounding Florian with determination.

"Next is finding the building Ghost is targeting. I drew the blueprint from memory. It's not accurate but close." Florian showed Ronaldo.

"What a strange layout. I've never seen a building like this before. Though, when we figure it out, we'll know where Ghost will strike next."

"I'll stop by after school. Try going outside; you won't get used to apparition vision if you don't."

"You can count on me." Ronaldo looked through Florian's journals once again. "Mayor Banquet won the election with a landslide victory."

"I don't want to talk about him, but because of him, I now know what I must do." Florian left and soon received a text from Sergeant Honest.

"Let me know if you're interested in some basic combat training. That way, the next time you chase down some bad guys, you can take them down, no matter how big they are," he wrote.

Florian texted him back. "Miss Fumblehouse will help me plan my college majors and career path this Saturday. How about Sunday?"

☙ℭ

The next day, Florian escorted Hope to school.

"Have a good day," Florian signed.

Hope hugged Florian, signing "I love you" with a bright, loving smile. Her seashell dove spirit pressed up against Florian.

"I love you too." Florian hugged Hope tightly.

☙ℰ☙

Florian, now a celebrity in high school, confronted her friends from grade school. They were as supportive as ever and were the first to take action when Florian asked.

"If I'm going to be a detective, I'll need more experience. So, I decided to start an after-school club to assist others. Will you guys help me?"

"Of course! Then maybe some of that luck will rub off on us," Alex said. His monkey spirit grinned.

"I want in. Are we stopping some bad guys?" Sera asked, tuning her guitar. Her koi fish swam through the air around her, just like her mother's mimic octopus.

"Will you be investigating more crimes with this club?" Amalia said, her bat spirit stretching its wings.

"Well, I doubt big crimes will be happening every day. If I practice with some small-scale problems, it might help me with the bigger ones," Florian said.

"What kind of club is this again?" Amalia asked.

"It'll be the Support, Investigate, Kindness, Encourage, Understand, Progress Club. The Psych Up Club!" Florian said.

"That spells sike up, not psych up," Sera said.

"We'll start this club for anyone in the school. We'll help with any problem, no matter how small," Florian said.

"Any problem? Even if it's just homework problems?" Alex asked.

"Even homework problems. . . Then once we're ready, we'll unveil it to the entire city! Making it a private investigation organization," Florian said.

"I'm in! I need help with my homework!" Alex said.

"I don't mind tutoring," Amalia said.

"I want to catch bad guys!" Sera said.

"Small-scale cases, the first step to becoming a real detective," Florian said.

Choco entered their classroom. "Is Florian Lilly Cobblestone here?" she asked.

"Is this our first case? We haven't even established the club yet," Alex said.

Choco made eye contact and calmly walked toward Florian. Her fur cluster soul shuffled behind her; its large white eyes peered through its fuzz, clacking its square teeth together.

Choco raised her hand, and a moment after, the giant hamster raised its paw.

Delayed movement? She's hesitating. . .

Choco smacked Florian's face as hard as she could. "Return my boyfriend to me!"

Everyone's jaws dropped. "Whaaaaaaaaat!?"

The entire class had misunderstood the meaning behind Choco's words.

Florian stood up from her desk.

The fur cluster hamster began to pant as its hair curled.

I thought letting her slap me would calm her down. This might get ugly. "Do you have any pets? You know, it takes a lot of responsibility to care for one."

BOOK 1

END

ABOUT THE AUTHOR

"No one's born for a single purpose; they're born for the infinite possibilities of the future."

Eliot D Esparza is a rising author born in North Carolina. He's half Filipino and half Hispanic.
He writes with his whole spirit using his accumulated knowledge from his life. He has a Bachelor of Arts in Liberal Studies from the University of North Carolina Greensboro. He studied and explored multiple career paths, from Education to Anthropology.

He worked in AmeriCorps ACCESS with the Center for New North Carolinians and AmeriCorps National with Forsyth Habitat for Humanity, supporting the community.

He is the son of a librarian- volunteering since he could walk in the public library.

He is an amateur astronomer- participating in numerous public observations, engrossing himself in science at a very young age.

He enjoys playing tabletop games, TCGs, and video games.

He loves analyzing thought-provoking stories across all mediums and strives for the most entertaining science fiction possible.

S. Brook Counseling
& Therapy Clinic